RAISING EIGHT ON 80

Nettie Balzer
Raising Eight on 80

njbalzer@sasktel.net

Printed and bound in Canada

Cover Design by Christopher Tyreman

ISBN 978-0-9880661-1-3

ABOUT THE AUTHOR

Nettie Balzer is a mother, grandmother and great-grandmother. Writing has always been a passion for her, whether it was creating stories or preparing devotionals for Women's groups. She spent eleven years working as a church secretary and nearly five years as a Women's Ministry Director. In 1992 she became the 'keeper' of her mother's life story and diaries written in her mother's hand. Helena, her mother, wrote in German, using old German script letters combined with English letters, which is how she wrote to her children.

In 1998 Nettie translated those stories and diaries. She hoped one day to bring these stories to life for her grandchildren and in 2012 published her first book, "Helena – A Peek Into the Past". **"Raising Eight on 80"** is a sequel to the first book.

Born in 1898, Helena lived to be 102 years, having lived in three centuries.

TABLE OF CONTENTS

INTRODUCTION

"**R**aising Eight on 80" is a sequel to my first book, "Helena – a Peek into the Past." The 'Helena' stories contain the first 41 years of Helena Banman Friesen's life up to the year 1939. Readers contacted me and said, "There must be more to the story; it ends too soon". There were indeed many more stories to write and thus "Raising Eight on 80" came into being. Each story contains background and conversation created around actual events and memories of the Friesen Family.

This book picks up where the first one ends; in 1939 when World War 2 began. The war, along with continuing drought conditions across the prairies, brought hardship to many people. Those who lived through those years will be able to relate to many of the stories. Those who are younger may get a glimpse of life then, as compared to now.

Since this book contains local history which affected our family as well as others, I'd like to thank the many people who gave me permission to include their family names in the stories.

'Raising Eight on 80' ends in 1959-60 and concludes with an epilogue on Helena, who lived to be 102 years old.

I'm very grateful to my remaining siblings, Jacob(Jake), Tena, Christine and Daniel who contributed their memories as I wrote.

Special thanks to my brother Daniel who suggested the title of the book and to my daughters, Verdeen, Karen and Carmen who edited and proof-read my documents. Thanks also to Christopher Tyreman for the excellent cover design.

Nettie Balzer

FOREWARD

By Verdeen (Balzer) Bueckert

My earliest memory of Grandma Helena is scrawled in phonetic English on a yellowed scrap of notepaper. Apparently, as a 3 year old I had thrown a tantrum after spilling water on the floor. I "ktit de and skriemed" (kicked and screamed), until she "taut it was a littel to mushs" (thought it was a little too much) and threatened to get the strap. I looked her in the eye and said, "You can't spank me. That would be embarrassing."

Fortunately for me, my impertinence sent her into a fit of giggles, and by the time her shoulders stopped shaking (which is how she always laughed – and she laughed often), the spanking was no longer required.

This little scrap of history is evidence of two things:

1. Grandma Helena chronicled everything, despite no more than a grade 2 education, and none of it in English. She was the ultimate historian. She saved letters and documents. In her diary, she tracked visitors, buns, chickens and sermon texts. She likely had no idea this would someday become part of a book about her life.
2. Family was central. In my somewhat nomadic upbringing, Grandma's house was the one constant. It always smelled of smoked sausage and homemade bread, because she cooked and baked every Saturday, hoping for Sunday company. We'd drive 3 hours from Swift Current to arrive in time for church and a lunch of fried chicken, pluma moos and farmer sausage. We'd stay for late afternoon faspa (buns, jam, coffee and cookies) and drive home. Prairie sunsets faded and the moon followed us until we woke up at home, too drowsy to move to our beds and too cold to stay in the car.

The yearly Banman reunions continued in Osler until Grandma sold her house at age 87. Grandma's aging siblings, step family and offspring came together every August to feast on food and fellowship. The Mennonite food was rich and abundant – but it was the music that fed the soul. Dozens of us crowded into the living room and blended our voices in rich four-part harmonies with Aunt Gen's high descant trailing melodically above, accompanied by Aunt Chris or mom on the old dark upright piano.

Our family was rich; rich in music, love, laughter and learning. Aunt Helen (Lena) sent us books from Texas for Christmas and birthdays. Uncle Dan gave me my first Dr. Seuss, McElligot's Pool. I still have a copy. I blew my first bubblegum bubble for Aunt Anne. I eavesdropped on heated debates on theology and politics between Julius, Ray and Lorne – then watched them set aside their vigorous disagreements and sing together. Uncle Julius took an interest in my writing and English awards and encouraged me just as he had encouraged my mother Nettie. Aunt Tena laughed at the ridiculous original dramas we cousins recorded on the old cassette player. I learned to enjoy seaweed from the rice crackers sent every Christmas by Jake and Junko from Japan. Much later, Uncle Jake mediated the adoption of our son, Nathanael Jacob.

My coolest clothes were hand-me-downs from my cousins, daughters of Aunt Chris and Aunt Tena. We had lots of good times together, we cousins, in the well-appointed upstairs playroom filled with antique dolls and homemade furniture, and later on, wandering through Osler as teenagers on lazy Sunday afternoons.

When I moved to Saskatoon after high school, Aunt Anne called periodically and grilled me on the contents of my fridge. "Do you have any vegetables? Do you have any bread? Do you have any meat?" After a thorough inventory (of my 2 carrots and half cup of oatmeal) she would show up with a bag of groceries. The Friesens looked after each other.

Our last celebration of Grandma's birthday was in 1998 when she turned 100. The next time we came together was for her funeral. She was 102. I happened to be in the right place at the right time, when her old dresser and piano needed a new steward. These are daily reminders of a family heritage I could never deserve.

These days, Grandma's picture watches me from a prominent shelf behind my computer monitor. Her eyes twinkle, and she looks like she is ready to burst into a fit of giggles. I feel like I know her better now. It has been a real treat to work with mom on this book. Mostly I probed for more detailed descriptions out of my own curiosity, and edited out my least favourite (and mom's favourite) verb tense.

Not everyone lives such richly storied lives. I hope you enjoy getting to know Helena and her family, and feel warmly welcomed. Fresh coffee is percolating; homemade buns and jam are waiting. There's always room for one more at the Friesen table.

Helena and Jacob strolling down 21 St. in Saskatoon

RUMOURS OF WAR

CHAPTER 1

Helena and Jacob Friesen pulled off the sandy Blumenheim village road with the horse and buggy, and headed home. For Helena it was a relief to sit back on the buggy seat and listen to the reassuring familiarity of clip-clopping hooves on the country road. She glanced at her husband who was deep in thought. She knew he was troubled and likely mulling over the visit at his parents' home.

Conversation between the men of the joined Friesen and Janzen family often became loud and argumentative. Everyone, it seemed, had their opinion and voiced it. Jacob's blind father David, a very large man, sat and listened, drumming his fingers on the arm rests of his chair and humming in the few quiet gaps in the conversation.

It was 1939 and the world was in trouble. There was war and unrest in many places. It seemed to be the main topic of conversation wherever they went: after church services on Sundays, in visits with neighbours and family, and at the general store where the men smoked, played checkers and discussed local and world events.

Now it was quiet. The sky was blue, with a few fluffy white clouds. In the buggy, two year old Danny sat on the floor at their feet playing with the dangling ends of the horse's reins, pretending to help Jacob drive. Eleven year old Julius, eight year old Tena, and six year old Christine sat in the short box at the back with their feet hanging over the edge. Julius pointed out a large hawk circling over a rabbit in the nearby field as they passed by. They watched the rabbit zig-zag around the field avoiding capture.

Except for the uncomfortable shaking of the wheels as they rolled over ruts and the ever-present flying grasshoppers, it was a pleasant drive home. Finally they pulled on to their long driveway and then into the yard.

"HO!" Jacob called, as he pulled on the reins and brought the horse to a halt half way between the house and barn. Helena carefully climbed off the buggy, then lifted little Daniel down. Julius jumped off and helped Christine as Tena lowered herself off the edge and dropped to the ground. The girls wandered toward the garden while the others turned toward the house.

"Julius!" Jacob called, as he drove the buggy to the side of the barn, "Help me unhitch Topsy and put her out to pasture."

Julius turned back to undo the harness on one side of the horse. His dad freed her from the other side of the buggy. After pulling the collar off her neck, he handed the reins to Julius while he returned the harnesses to their hooks in the barn.

Julius followed his father to the gate, leading Topsy. Jacob slipped the halter off of her head and slapped her rump. She walked eagerly toward the water trough where she drank deeply. She was thirsty after pulling the buggy the six miles from Blumenheim.

Sixteen-year-old Jake, a tall lanky young man, walked out of the barn toward his dad. He and his sisters, eighteen-year-old Lena and fourteen-year-old Annie, had just finished the chores.

"Dad," he asked, "The girls and I want to go to Osler to see friends this evening. May we go?"

Above: Jake feeding calves
Below: Jake with Babe & colt

Jacob hesitated a moment. "Are the chores all done?"

"Yes," answered Jake. "We've just finished. The cows are milked and the pigs have been fed. I fed the calves and cleaned the gutters and the girls are washing up the cream separator and milk pails."

Jacob held up his hand toward the sky, measuring the handbreadth distance between the sun and the western horizon. He didn't need a clock to tell him approximately what time it was.
After squinting up at the sky, he said, "It's already seven o'clock. Where will you go and what do you plan to do?"

"We're going to meet cousins Abe, Jake and Dave and then get together with other friends in town to play music and sing. Lena is bringing the guitar and I'm bringing the violin."

Jake learned to play the violin after ordering it from the Eatons catalogue for $4.00. After a few lessons with his school teacher, Mr. Miller, he caught on quickly and played well.

"All right, but don't be out too late," Jacob relented. He turned toward the house, and joined Helena in the living room where she was preparing Danny for bed.

The teens soon came down the stairs carrying their instruments.

"Remember – don't be late!" their father reminded them. He went to the window and watched them walk down the lane, then turned to sit down in his favourite arm chair to read the newspaper. It was not good news.

Since 1937 there had been various wars around the globe. Japan was at war with China. In 1938 Germany's Hitler began an all out attack on the Jewish people. Hitler also made a pact with Stalin to take over the country of Italy. It seemed there was no stopping him, and more countries were becoming involved in what looked like another World War.

"I can't believe this is happening. How can the German people be part of such a terrible thing as destroying another race?" he commented to Helena as she led Danny to the kitchen. "I just hope Canada does not become more involved. I don't want to see our young men sent out to war."

"Oh, I hope that won't happen," Helena said. She shuddered at the thought of young Jake being sent as a soldier. She reached for a box of cornflakes, set it on the table, put Danny in the high chair and called Tena and Christine to come in from the garden.

Julius walked into the house, shoved his slingshot into a back pocket, washed his hands and poured a bowl of cereal and milk. Beside his bowl was his notebook and pencil. Julius often wrote poems and stories.

"Dad," he called to Jacob in the living room, "Are you done reading the news paper? I want to read it, too."

Jacob brought the paper to the kitchen. He was pleased his children loved to read.

Tena and Christine emptied cornflakes into their bowls and added milk. Helena pulled the waxed paper from the box, spread it out, wiped it clean and folded it. All waxed paper from packages was saved to wrap sandwiches for school lunches.

Once the children were in bed, Helena's responsibilities were finally done. She was very tired. It had been a long day, but Jacob couldn't relax. He walked to a west window to see if his older children were on their way home. There was no sign of them.

"I wonder where they are," he murmured as he climbed into bed. Every few minutes, it seemed, he raised himself on an elbow to look at the clock. Nine o'clock... nine-thirty...ten o'clock...

Lantern: Osler,Sask. Museum

"What's wrong?" Helena finally asked. "Could you please lie still? I really need to sleep."

"I haven't heard the children come home. I'm going to town to find them," he said.

Helena sighed, "They'll be home soon."

"They should have been here by now," he answered.

Settled comfortably, Helena drowsily asked, "Do you remember before we were married, when I worked for your uncle and aunt? We went on a buggy ride and you were upset that your uncle insisted you bring me home early. You said when we had children they would be able to stay out as long as they wanted."

"Hmph," Jacob grunted. He gave her a disgusted look, climbed out of bed, and lit the lantern.

"Jacob, I prayed for the children. I'm leaving them in God's hands and getting some sleep!"

She sighed again as she heard him leave the house. She snuggled back down in bed and pictured the music jam session interrupted by a worried Jacob. She smiled at the irony and fell asleep.

Annie with guitar & a friend with Jake's violin. Photo taken at the Friesen farm. (the girls are sitting on edge of the cattle trough)

THE LAST ONE

CHAPTER 2

After years of drought across the country it was a relief when the clouds began to darken and a gentle rain fell for several days. In the Low German language such a rain was called a zudda rae-yen. The family could plant the oat crops and garden in soft moist soil, but would it remain that way through the summer?

So many hard years of drought, so many dust storms that blew into every crack and so many grasshoppers – they hoped it was finally over. Young Jake and his dad kept busy cultivating the fields and seeding the crops.

Helena was anxious to get the garden in and hoped Jacob would soon take time from the fields to plough the garden. A few days later, Jacob sharpened the blade on the single bottomed plough to make sure it would cut into the garden soil properly.

Jake and Julius led Babe and Topsy to the plough and hitched them to it. After attaching a single harrow section behind the plough to smooth out the rough, turned-over soil, Jacob climbed up and sat on the small metal seat.

"Giddy-up!" he commanded. The two horses began pulling, their leather collars creaking on their heaving shoulders as they plodded on. The harnesses stretched taut as the plough blade dug deeply into the ground but these two horses were up to the challenge and moved together as one. The harrow dragged behind and smoothed over the ridges of freshly turned earth.

Once the long garden plot was ploughed, Jacob hitched the horses to several harrow sections which smoothed out the ground even more and brought small stones to the surface so they could be picked up.

Jacob pulled a row marker across the potato field in both directions creating lines to space the potato rows. The garden was ready to be planted.

Lena, Annie, and their mother Helena wore gunny sack aprons, the large pockets full of small potatoes and cut-up pieces of larger ones.

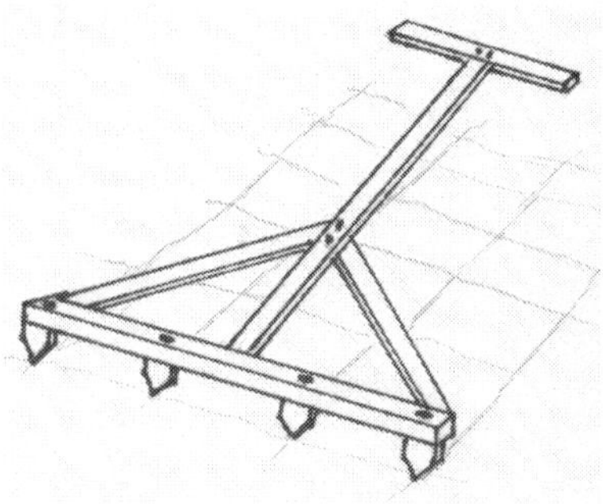

Row marker: Drawing by Nettie Balzer

They dropped potatoes into the planters Jacob had made, pushed them down into the soil at each mark where two lines met and pulled back to let the spring loaded planter open up in the ground and drop the potato.

Potato planter built by Jacob W. Friesen. (Still in use)

Julius was often called on to bring another pail of potatoes to fill the aprons. Tena and Christine ran through the soft cool soil with their bare feet and kept Danny out of trouble. At nearly two years of age, he was quick to get in the way and needed to be watched.

The potato field was big and the children complained that it stretched almost all the way to the highway! It seemed never ending when they had to weed or pick off potato bugs, but the family was not the only one to benefit from the huge patch; other folk whose potatoes did not last until the next spring often received potatoes from the Friesens.

After the potatoes, Helena planned where to put the rows of other vegetables and how to arrange her flower garden. It was more difficult this spring with a baby due in two months. Finally the planting was done and she hoped for more rain and an abundant harvest.

But as spring turned to summer, the dust and Russian thistle piled up along the fences again. The drought was not over. It remained hot and dry.

On a warm morning in late July, Helena walked to the barn. Jacob looked up as she approached him.

"It's time," she said, and turned to walk out of the barn. Jacob rose from his milking stool and handed his pail to Jake who had just emptied his.

"Time for what?" asked Julius.

"Just finish the milking," Jacob responded. "After breakfast, you boys clean the barn, then hitch the horses up to the mower and go out to the hay field." The boys glanced at each other and went back to milking.

"Annie, when you finish milking Blossom, go and help with breakfast." He turned and walked toward the house to call the doctor in Warman. Lena was away working for another farm family.

Annie finished and got up to empty her pail into the strainer. She hurried to the house, changed out of her barn clothes and washed her hands and face. She found her mother standing in the summer kitchen, stirring porridge.

"Get the little ones up and dressed, Annie. Give them breakfast and then take them to the Heins' farm," Helena told her. "Here, take the porridge to the house."

Annie knew the baby was coming, so she hurried upstairs to wake Tena and Christine and then into her parents' bedroom to wake Danny. She dressed him, washed his face, brought him to the table and filled the children's bowls. Helena walked into the house and to the bedroom. Jacob was on the phone with the doctor as they ate.

As Jake and Julius came in for breakfast, Annie gathered the youngest three and put Danny in the carriage. "Come on, we're going to the Heins' place," she told the girls. They followed her down the long driveway and across the highway to the neighbours.

"I wonder if we'll have a boy or a girl," Tena mused. Annie looked at her sternly and said, "What makes you think there is going to be a baby?" Children were not to speak of such things. Tena fell silent.

Christine looked up at Annie and asked, "Will there be a baby in the doctor's satchel?"

"Of course not!" exclaimed her big sister.

The neighbours answered the door; the children were welcomed in and were soon busy playing.

At the Friesen home, Helena spread the new baby clothes and blankets she had made into the cradle in their bedroom. Then she lay down in her bed hoping the baby would wait until the doctor arrived. Soon she heard the crunch of gravel on the yard and the doctor's voice as he walked into the house.

It wasn't long before the tiny baby girl cried. Helena had not been looking forward to having another baby, but as this little one was placed in her arms, she was again filled with overwhelming love; how precious each child was. It was July 29th, 1939. Jacob and Helena decided to call her Agenetha, but soon everyone was calling her Nettie. This was Helena's eleventh child. Three had died in infancy, leaving a family of eight children.

A BABY SHOWER

CHAPTER 3

Baby Nettie was two weeks old when a neighbour called on the telephone. A group of ladies from the Osler church and community wanted to come to the Friesen home the next Saturday afternoon for a baby shower.

Helena had never had a shower for any of her other babies and felt a bit embarrassed that others wanted to bring her gifts, but agreed for the ladies to come.

Saturday morning was a feverishly busy time for Annie, and for Lena who had come home for the weekend. They made buns and a cake and worked hard at cleaning the house. Eight-year old Tena dusted furniture and little six-year old Christine wiped down the rungs of the chairs. Annie and Lena cleaned the floors and made beds, as Helena still needed to rest. Aunt Margaret would be coming soon to help with the work when Lena went back to her job. Aunt Anna Friesen helped the first week.

The afternoon guests arrived and were invited to the living room. The room was full of women and there was lots of visiting and laughter. Helena brought the baby from the cradle in the bedroom and she was passed from one woman to another. Helena enjoyed their company and was overwhelmed with all the gifts piled near her chair.

Lena and Annie stood near the door to the kitchen, listening and visiting with the ladies. Tena stood with her big sisters so she wouldn't miss anything. Danny stood behind his mother's chair.

Helena began opening the gifts, receiving new cloth diapers, baby blankets, undershirts and nightgowns. There was a mauve crib quilt cover with yellow borders and an appliquéd rabbit on the front of it.

As Helena opened the gifts, Christine stood next to her asking, "Is there something for me?" Her mother and the other ladies chuckled as Helena told her, "No, this is only for the baby."

Christine thought it wouldn't hurt to keep asking and did so again and again, receiving the same answer, "No, I told you this is only for a baby. There is nothing here that would fit you."

As Helena held up another nightgown for the baby, she commented, "Oh, this one is much bigger and will fit the baby a year or two from now. Thank you." As she bent down to pick up another gift, Christine grabbed the larger nightgown and hurried to her parents' bedroom where she squeezed into it overtop of her dress. She came out proudly and stood before her mother.

"See, Mama? There IS something for me!" This brought a chorus of laughter from the ladies, including Helena. Still laughing, Helena took the nightgown off of Christine and put it with the baby clothes.

"Christine, go to the kitchen and ask Lena to give you a piece of cake." She reached behind the chair and led Danny out, gently pushing him toward his big sisters. Lena came forward and took his hand. Disappointed in not getting any of the new things, Christine turned toward the kitchen where her older sisters gave her, Tena, and Danny each a piece of cake. Then the ladies were served their lunch.

It was a wonderful day. Helena was thankful for all the new things and very tired. It was good to get to bed and rest.

She drifted off into a deep sleep, and hearing the baby cry, automatically reached out for the cradle to rock it, hoping the baby would go back to sleep. Suddenly, there was a loud crash. She woke with a start. Jacob sat up and asked, "What was that?"

As they looked beside the bed, Helena realized that in her sleepy state she had rocked the night table with the coal oil lamp instead of the cradle, causing the lamp to fall off and break the glass chimney.

Helena's lamp (now at Nettie's home)

She reached for her shoes under the bed, shook them to remove any glass and got up, stepping carefully. Putting the lamp back on the table, she went to the kitchen for the broom and dust pan. Danny stirred in his crib and Jacob leaned over to cover him.

Helena swept up the glass, and then went back to bed where she nursed her baby, finally getting her back to sleep and into the cradle. Helena sank back into bed, breathing an exhausted prayer of thanks that the lamp had not fallen into the cradle. She pulled the covers over herself and slept restfully until morning.

I'M NEVER GOING BACK!

CHAPTER 4

"**S**it still!" Annie told Christine for the fourth time, "I can't get your hair combed properly if you keep moving! And stop talking – you talked almost all through supper last night!"

Helena lifted the stove lid and slid in a few pieces of wood. Glancing over at her excited six year old, she smiled and said, "She's just happy about going to school."

Christine smiled broadly and wiggled again, "I'm going to see my friends and read books!" Rolling her eyes, Annie combed the last bit of hair and fastened a clip to hold it in place. "All right – now you can wiggle all you want!"

"You'll love school, Christine," her mother said. "There is so much to learn and you'll have lots of friends."

"I think it's like an adventure – and when you can read you'll love the library," Tena said. "There are lots of fun stories!" The small school library had opened up a whole new world for Tena.

It was the first day of school. Jake strode ahead of his siblings, carrying a syrup pail with his lunch inside. He was going to pick up correspondence courses for grade nine, and then would soon help another farmer with harvesting. He would be back in school for the winter.

Annie walked quickly, holding Christine's hand and turned around from time to time to check on her other siblings. "Julius, come on! We're going to be late! Tena – what are you doing? Don't just stand there, move!"

"I'm getting a grasshopper out of my shoe," Tena said as she shook her shoe upside down. "I'm coming!" She ran, caught up with Annie and took Christine's other hand. They hurried through the neighbour's caragana hedge and across their yard to the road to Osler.

Soon they heard voices on the school yard. Just as they walked through the gate, the bell rang and everyone ran for the doors. A new school year was about to begin.

At home Jacob sat at the table with another cup of coffee, while Lena cleared and washed up. She would soon be leaving for a job some distance away from Osler. It was only for a few months, but it would help the family financially. She planned to take correspondence courses as well.

"Lena, I'm glad you're taking high school courses while you work at your job. I hope the people give you time to study so you can finish," her father said.

"I hope I can finish too," replied Lena. "It's been good to be home for a while though and I've enjoyed holding the baby."

"At our School Board meetings we've been discussing how to get high school here in Osler. One or two of us will be going to Regina soon, to check out the possibilities," Jacob said.

"That will be so good for the rest of the children!" Lena exclaimed.

"If we get high school in Osler, the children won't have to travel far away to get their education," Helena added.

Back at the school house, the teacher called everyone to order and told them where to sit. Annie found her desk and discovered Christine close by her side.

"Go sit down with the grade ones!" she whispered urgently. Christine shook her head and tightly wrapped her little arms around the iron bar between the desk table and chair. "Go!" Annie whispered, as she tried to pry Christine's arms from the desk.

"Christine Friesen," the teacher called, "come sit down at your desk." Christine tightened her grip on the iron bar and shook her head. The whole classroom watched expectantly. Annie turned red with embarrassment, while Jake shook his head in disgust. Julius sat quietly with an amused look on his face. Tena felt badly for her sister.

Finally the teacher walked down between the desks, pulled Christine's arms from the bar, picked her up, and carried her to the assigned seat.

"Class," the teacher said, "please stand at attention while we sing 'God Save the King', and 'O Canada'." Everyone stood at attention, faced the flag, and sang. The teacher bowed his head and said, "Let's pray," and the children joined in saying the Lord's Prayer.

"Our Father who art in Heaven,
Hallow'ed be Thy Name.
Thy Kingdom come, Thy Will be done
On earth as it is in heaven.
Give us this day our daily bread
And forgive us our trespasses
As we forgive those who trespass against us.
And lead us not into temptation
But deliver us from evil

(Note: Canada was a British Colony and flew the Union Jack Flag)
Drawing by Nettie Balzer

For Thine is the Kingdom,
And the Power, and the Glory,
Forever and ever, Amen."

"Class be seated," the teacher said. The older students were given their work for the day, while the teacher handed out the grade one and two readers and wrote some spelling words on the black board for grade three.

Osler School class 1939. Christine – first row, second child from front, underneath the blackboard. Osler Historical Museum photo

At the supper table that evening Helena asked, "So how was school today? Did you all enjoy it?"

"I'm never going back! I don't like school!" Christine emphatically announced.

Jacob grinned and chuckled as he said, "I'm afraid you don't have a choice – I'm the attendance officer."

"Mom, it was so embarrassing!" Annie complained. "She wouldn't sit down with the other grade ones and she hung on to my desk! The teacher had to come down the aisle, pull her off of my desk and carry her to her seat!"

Anne – seated last and Tena seated at the front in second row from the right. Osler Historical Museum photo.

Looking down at Christine, Helena promised with a smile, "Oh, but it will be so much better tomorrow."

Tomorrow came, but Christine had not changed her mind and it took some persuasion before she could be convinced to try again.

A few months later Jacob took the train to Regina and met with the Saskatchewan Department of Education, where he brought forward Osler's request for a high school. The request was considered favourably and soon things were in motion to bring in grades eleven and twelve.

Jacob had taken night classes back in1932, studying English as well as other subjects. He became concerned that higher education should be available for all of his children and the surrounding area. Now his dream could soon be a reality!

ANXIOUS DAYS

CHAPTER 5

The School and Church Christmas concerts in the town of Osler were well attended. Helena and Jacob's children enjoyed their roles in the plays and music.

School holidays were a mixture of farm chores, skating on ponds and sledding with friends at the ravine near the Peter Peters' farm. After outdoor winter fun they returned home to warm their insides with Helena's hot chocolate, while thawing numb feet near the open oven door. Crokinole tournaments by lamp light were enjoyed, while munching on peanuts from their Christmas treat bags. The singing of carols accompanied by guitars and violin was always a highlight for the family.

Now the Christmas season of 1939 was over and it was 'back to school' in early January of 1940. Several of the children had colds during the month of December and as the older children recovered, Helena noticed six-month old Nettie becoming restless and feverish. Soon she wasn't eating much and a severe cough got a hold of her chest.

One evening Helena moved her crib near the warm stove in the living room. After placing a chair at either side of the crib and draping a bed sheet over them and the crib, she placed a pot of boiling water beside one of the chairs to steam little Nettie and try to ease her coughing. Helena mixed flour, dry mustard and hot water, spread it on a soft cloth and placed it on the baby's tiny chest. After a few minutes, she removed it and covered the baby with a warm blanket. It was late and Helena longed for sleep.

"Is she getting any better?" Jacob asked, raising himself as Helena sat wearily on the edge of their bed.

"I don't think so," sighed Helena.

"If she doesn't get better by tomorrow afternoon, I'll see if I can get the doctor from Warman," Jacob said.

After an hour Helena warmed up the mustard plaster poultice and placed it on Nettie's little chest again, waiting just a few moments before removing it. She didn't want the poultice to burn the delicate baby skin. Finally, little Nettie fell asleep and Helena carefully placed her back in the cradle close to the bed, covering her with a blanket warmed near the stove. Then she dropped into bed, wrapping a warm wool quilt around herself.

She was up many times during the night and was finally fast asleep when the 5:30 a.m. alarm went off. Jacob started fires in both stoves, and called upstairs to wake the children. Lena was home again, and came downstairs to start breakfast.

That morning, after the children left for school, Helena sat near the kitchen stove where she fed her baby and nodded off to sleep herself, several times. While Lena cleaned up the table and dishes, she glanced at her tired mother and at the pale little face of her baby sister.

As the infant was put back into the crib near the warmth of the stove in the living room, she began to cry and cough again.

"Here, mom," Lena said. "Let me carry her while you rest." Picking the baby up in her arms, she held her upright against her shoulder so the coughing wouldn't be so bad. She walked the floor while her mother rested.

By afternoon the baby was much worse. The coughing, crying, and choking sound made everyone worry. Her fever was back and much worse.

"I'll call the doctor," Jacob said, walking to the phone mounted on the wall in the kitchen. He cranked the handle at the side to ring the operator and asked for the town of Warman. After speaking with the doctor, Jacob returned to the living room where Helena sat near the pot-bellied stove rocking little Nettie.

"He's coming on the next train. It's too bitterly cold for him to come by car," Jacob said. "I'll get him with the caboose(*a closed-in sleigh with a small stove).*"

As the evening wore on, the older children and their parents became more and more concerned. As Jake walked over to his little sister he saw how pale her face was and that her eyes didn't seem to be focussing. Just then his dad moved his hand near the baby's eyes and there was no response.

"Lena," Helena said, "please put Danny to bed. And Tena and Christine – you should get ready as well." The girls reluctantly got ready for bed, but were soon back in the living room curled up at one end of the couch in a blanket, while Danny went to sleep in his crib in the bedroom. The girls were sleepy, but worried about their sister.

When the evening train arrived, Jacob was there to meet the doctor and they quickly climbed into the caboose and covered up with blankets.

"Giddyup!" Jacob called to his horses as he snapped the reins. They started off at a trot, eager to get back home into a warmer place. The doctor questioned Jacob about the baby and how long she had been sick. It didn't take long to get to the farm and Jacob quickly tied the horses to the fence post, then followed the doctor into the house.

After removing his coat and warming his hands, the doctor said, "Well, where is your little one?"

"In the living room," replied Jacob as he led the way.

Helena sat near the stove holding her baby. Little Nettie wasn't coughing as much but she wasn't responding either. She seemed to be sleeping, but her breath came in quick gasps, and her eyes were half open.

Helena looked up as the doctor walked in. He bent over to look at the tiny white-faced child but didn't bother to un-wrap the baby blanket to examine her. Shaking his head he looked up at Helena, and then at Jacob, and said, "She is beyond earthly help. I'm sorry. She will be gone by morning."

At the doctor's words, Helena clutched her baby close, and a soft wail of anguish poured out of her. "Oba Nay! (Oh No!) Not again – not again! It's just like our other babies," she sobbed. "Six months – that's all they had too."

Jacob's eyes filled with tears as he walked the doctor to the door and out to the sleigh. He urged the reluctant team of horses back to the road to drop the doctor off at Osler.

As the others stood nearby crying, Jake turned and fled into his parents' bedroom where he knelt beside the bed and cried out softly, "Please, God, please don't let this baby die! I can't stand to see my mother cry!"

Coming out of the bedroom, he walked over to the crib where his mother had just laid Nettie down. He didn't really expect anything, but looked closely at her face and thought she had a little more colour in her cheeks. Her eyes seemed to have more of a spark to them. It was too much to expect and believe though, so he picked up a coal oil lamp and slowly walked upstairs to bed. The others followed and some of the children noticed a determined and stubborn look on their mother's face. After a while, they heard their father return.

As they shivered under thick, woollen quilts in the cold upstairs rooms, they prayed for their little sister. Down in the living room, Jacob put more coal on the fire so the stove pipes going through to the upstairs would generate a little heat for the children in their beds.

Helena coaxed a little boiled, cooled water into the baby's mouth. Sponging her hot face and changing her diaper gave Helena something to do. She was determined! She would fight to keep this one. Constant, whispered prayers were lifted to heaven as she worked. Jacob finally went to bed. Morning milking time would soon arrive.

As morning dawned, Jacob woke, lit the lamp and hurried to the living room where he found Helena bundled in a thick quilt, fast asleep in the chair. Peeking from the folds of the quilt was a bright-eyed baby girl who smiled at her daddy as he looked down on her. Jacob's face broke into a grin of relief and joy. He set the lamp on a table and opened the stove door as quietly as he could to add more coal to the fire. Helena did not wake up. Going to the stairwell, he softly called up to the children, "Get up, it's milking time!"

Jake hurried down the stairs, pulling up his suspenders. His siblings followed and hurried to the stove in the living room to get warm. They stopped when they saw Helena with baby Nettie. Their faces registered relief and delight as the baby looked at them and smiled.

Helena stirred in the chair and looked up at her family. Gazing down at Nettie she smiled and said, "Her fever left her shortly after you all went to bed. She has eaten several times since then so I think she will be fine! God has answered our prayers!"

Jake's heart was filled with gratitude. As the children pulled coveralls over their warm jackets, he called over his shoulder, "I'll beat you all to the barn!"

They rushed out the door, pulling on their fur lined caps, pushing and laughing as they ran into the dark bitter cold to see who would get to the cows first.

FROZEN WELLS

CHAPTER 6

The winter continued to be very cold. Inside the cattle barn, the warm breath of the animals coated and insulated the walls and windows with several inches of thick frost. Although this kept the barn warmer, the concrete floors were cold and the animals needed lots of straw to sleep and stand on.

In the midst of all the work of keeping the animals warm, fed and watered, the windmill pump stopped working. The windmill was crucial for pumping water from the well, both to fill the trough for cooling milk and to fill the cistern (underground tank) in the lean-to for watering the cattle. There had been little or no wind for several days so the windmill wheel had hardly turned. When that happened water would rise and freeze around the pump rod. Now it was suddenly windy and a gust of wind restarted the windmill wheel, producing enough power to break the pump rod above the water line.

The pumping apparatus was attached to wooden rods, which were one inch by one inch square and in 6 -7 foot lengths. They were held together with metal couplings and put down inside a six inch diameter metal casing.

The broken rod needed to be pulled up and repaired. Jacob sighed with impatience at this inconvenience and walked to the house to warm up.

"I'm tired of using a block and tackle to pull up the entire casing with the broken pump rod, fixing it, and then putting it all back together," he said while sitting near the open oven door sipping his coffee. "It happens too often in winter. There has to be a better way." It took time to fix and working outside in minus 30 degrees was difficult.

Glancing at the table where Jake sat doing homework he said, "Jake, you can bundle up warm and come help me in the shop."

"Have some faspa before you go out again," Helena said as she rose to put buns, butter and gooseberry jam on the table. "I'll boil some kettles of water for you. You'll need it to pour down the pipe." Helena had been through this before and knew what needed to be done.

After finishing their faspa, they went out to the shop across from the horse stalls in the barn. Jacob lit several lanterns so they would have more light in the dark little room.

Underneath the rough work bench, Jacob had a treasure trove of metal. He rifled through the different lengths of pipes and found just what he wanted. It had to be long enough to drop and slide over the pumping rod, small enough in diameter to fit inside the six inch casing, yet big enough to fit around the one inch square rod. Next he pushed aside several small sheets of metal until he found some pieces of spring-steel.

Now Jacob was ready to start on the pipe. He drilled a single hole on each side of the top of the pipe and fastened a strong wire to each side to form a handle. To this he would be able to fasten a length of cable with which to lower and raise the pipe into position. He laid it aside and reached for the spring-steel pieces. Fastening the pieces tightly in a vice, he reached for his gloves and turned to Jake.

"Give me the blow torch and those big pliers, Jake," he requested. Jake handed him the torch and laid the pliers on the work table. He watched as his dad lit the torch and held it to the steel until the pieces were red hot. Jacob turned off the torch, handed it back to his son and reached for the pliers to remove the steel from the vice. Gripping the pieces firmly with the pliers, he held them over the side of the anvil while he hammered the softened metal ends down over the edge until they were bent to his satisfaction. He plunged both pieces into a pail of snow to cool them.

Jacob picked up the long pipe and attached the bent spring-steel inside the bottom end of the pipe. Young Jake began to see that the steel pieces would serve as 'teeth' to grip the pump rod and pull it up. Jacob picked up the pipe and carried it to the pump house.

"There," Jacob said. "Jake, go get those kettles of boiling water from the kitchen." Jake hurried to the house where Annie handed them to him. He hurried back to the windmill pump house where Jacob was hanging up both lanterns so they could see what they were doing. The pump house had only one tiny window and it was getting dark outside.

Jacob poured both kettles of water down the casing, melting the ice. He then raised the extractor pipe he had made, lowering it over the rod inside the casing. Once the ice melted, there was room for the pipe to slide well past the broken rod end.

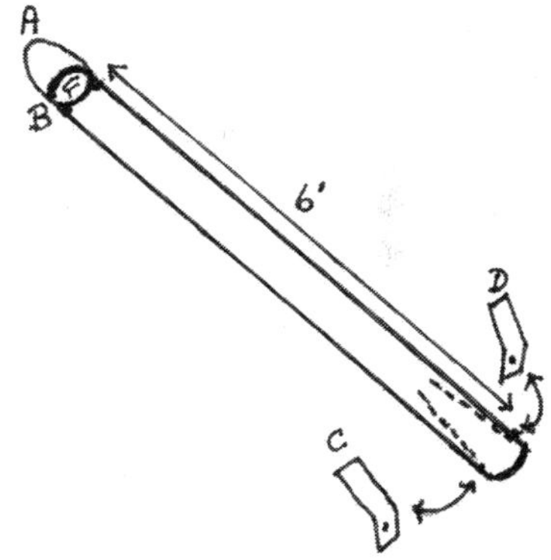

***A**: Bail wire to lower& raise extractor*
***B**: Holes drilled for bail wire.*
C&D**: Spring steel strips riveted to inside bottom of pipe.* ***Drawing by Jake Friesen

Since he couldn't see how far down the break was, he lowered the pipe until he felt the weight slacken. Holding

it straight, and raising it a bit, he let it drop until he heard a slight clank of metal against metal. He pulled up on the extractor chain until he felt it hold and knew the device would work!
Fastening a cable and pulley to the wire handle, he began to pull up the extractor pipe. It held to the rod! Soon, with both of them pulling, they had the broken wooden rod out. Jacob quickly repaired it and put it back in the casing. He left his extractor pipe leaning against the wall for the next possible break.

There was a slight wind, so Jacob slowly released the pump lever and they watched the windmill begin to turn. The pump moved safely up and down. Jake looked at his father with new appreciation. His dad was an inventive genius!

"Well – let's get warmed up again," said Jacob. "I think supper is almost ready and then it's milking time." They returned to the house and stood close to the hot kitchen stove warming their hands and feet until they could warm their insides with hot summa borscht and sliced ham with buns.

SPRINGING OUT OF A COLD WINTER

CHAPTER 7

The family was tired of digging for firewood from under snow drifts and the coal bin was nearly empty. They needed to go Osler for coal. The boys hitched the horses to the big sleigh and drove to town.

When the first heavy snowfalls came, the wagon box was removed from the wheels used in the summer and placed on runners for the winters, turning it into a horse-drawn sleigh.
***Photo 1**: Babe & Ruby hitched to sleigh, with colt.*
***Photo 2**: Jake, Anne & Julius catching a ride to school with neighbours. This wagon is a 'Bennett Wagon'. Wagons with rubber tires were named after Richard Bennett, Prime Minister of Canada from 1930 to 1935.*

Like so many other houses in the area, the walls of the Friesen home were filled with wood shavings for insulation, which settled over time. There was no other source of heat besides the cook-stove in the kitchen and the pot-bellied stove in the living room. Constant burning of wood and coal caused a build up of soot in the stove pipes.

There were a few times through the winter when Helena watched anxiously as the build up of soot caught fire in the pipes. The stove pipes then became red-hot and there was nothing to do but watch the walls where the pipes passed through to the chimney, water buckets at the ready. The walls were mostly covered in wall-paper so fire was always a concern, but there was asbestos behind the stoves. Asbestos would not burn.

"I'll be so relieved when spring comes and we can clean all of the stove pipes and the chimney!" she sighed after another close call.

Jacob agreed, "We'll do that as soon as it warms up."

February and March were still quite cold and newspapers and the letters from family members were welcome escapes. Helena was pleased to receive letters from her sisters, Agnes and Susanna, announcing the arrivals of their new babies. Agnes had a daughter named Mary and Susanna had a son named Alvin. That made eight little cousins born within a year and a half of each other. And that was just on the Banman side of the family; there were more of the same age on the Friesen side.

It was a great relief for them all when temperatures climbed and the snow melted. It did cause more difficulty for the horses as they made their way to town. The tracks made by the sleighs during the winter had become hard-packed. Now as the snow around them melted, the tracks stood higher, causing the sleigh to slide off of the tracks and tilt dangerously.

Soon there was water everywhere; a problem for the cattle let out of the barn for the first few times in early spring. Their hooves sank deeply into the mud behind the barn but once they were in the pasture, there was solid ground already turning green in places. The cattle munched contentedly on new green plants.

The family eagerly listened for the bird songs and the children each hoped to be the first to hear a meadow-lark. It wasn't long before the familiar trill was heard from the yellow breasted bird with the black v-neck. The family's interpretation of the song was "Fritz Franz kielkje zup (Fritz Franz noodle soup)"

Along with the meadow larks came robins and other birds, singing early in the morning and winging their way from tree to budding tree.

"I wonder if the pussy willows are out," Annie said one morning. "Let's go to the Puddle after school to find out."

The Puddle was the name given to a small pond in the neighbours' field right next to the Friesen farm. This was a favourite place to enjoy nature. They loved to listen to the many song birds as they built their nests, see the mallard ducks on the water and hear the frogs croaking.

Soon the Puddle would be full of melted snow water and the children would haul barrels of water from it on the horse-drawn stone boat. Once it dried up in the summer, the family hauled water from neighbours John Driedgers who lived a few miles away. The water was used for bathing and washing clothes, since their own well-water was only fit for cattle and watering the garden.

Sidestepping the lingering snow banks, Annie and Julius, with Tena and Christine following, made their way to the pond. It was nearly full and the bushes and trees around it were showing green.

"Look," Julius said, "The pussy willows are out!" He sank into the wet snow bank under the willow bushes, reached for the nearest soft pussy branches and broke some off, handing them to Annie. She held them to her face, feeling the softness of the seed buds.

"Maybe we'll be the first to bring some to school," Annie said.

"Let me feel them!" Christine said and reached for them. Annie held them out to Tena and Christine. Julius broke off a few more branches for his younger sisters.

On the way home, Annie spied purple crocuses poking out of the grass close to a snow bank. "Look at this! The crocuses are out!" She reached down and picked one.

At supper that evening, the children talked about all the signs of spring they had seen that day. Helena enjoyed their descriptions and Jacob listened while he ate. He knew Julius would soon write about it and Annie might draw or paint pictures of the spring scenery. She was very artistic.

"When more of the snow banks are melted, there will be more crocuses," Lena said, "and buttercups and bluebells will show up in the grass and weeds."

"When will the wild strawberries be ripe?" Tena asked.

Helena smiled, "It will be a while before the strawberries are ready."

On the first really warm day, the dirty job of cleaning the stove pipes arrived. First they put newspapers on the floor around the stoves and removed the sections of pipe.

Then they took them outside, away from the house. The soot inside each section was loosened by standing the pipe upright and banging on the sides. News-papers and old rags were pushed through them with old broom handles until the pipes were clean. After putting the pipe sections back together and re-connecting them to the stoves and chimney, the girls helped their mother wash soot off of walls, floors, and stoves.

Spring planting was soon upon them and the fields and gardens were ploughed and planted. Next came yard raking and the usual bonfire with potatoes baking under the burning pile of dried grass. The children sat on benches in the veranda and peeled the sooty parts off of their potatoes, added salt, and enjoyed them.

"Look at those clouds," Helena said at supper one evening. It had been a hot day and now the heavens were about to shower them with refreshing rain.

It was a short heavy cloud burst and when the sun came back out, everything glistened. The air was fresh and clean. The birds sang their praises and the yard was covered with puddles.

Tena and Christine ran through the puddles in their bare feet, splashing in the water. It was great fun. The dog felt their delight and joined them, barking and running circles around them. Looking down at their legs and feet, the girls realized how dirty they were.

"Let's run through the wet pig-weed!" Tena said.

"We can clean our feet in the wet grass," Christine added. So the girls ran back and forth through the tall weeds.

"Girls," Helena called. "It's time to come inside and get ready for bed."

They ran to the house where their mama had placed an old enamel pan full of water on the bottom step. After running back through the muddy puddles and pig-weed, they now had mud and green leaves on their feet.

"Sit down girls, your feet are a mess," Helena said as she bent down to wash them. The girls enjoyed the gentle way mama washed and then dried their feet on a towel. It was a lot of work making white bed sheets out of flour sacks and no child of hers was supposed to go to bed with dirty feet!

Flour was sold in cotton bags; some material was white and some printed.

The lettering on the bags needed to be removed with bleach in order to use the cloth for making sheets, pillow cases and tea towels. Helena worked hard to keep her whites white!

Photo of flour sacks taken at Osler, Sask. Historical Museum.

THE AERODROME

CHAPTER 8

Back in September of 1939 Germany invaded Poland and that same month Prime Minister William Lyon Mackenzie King requested that Canada join with Britain and other countries in the war against Hitler's army. He had announced that he needed to increase the number of men in the armed forces. Jacob hoped the fact that they were Mennonites and opposed to going to war would keep Jake and other young local boys from being recruited.

Now, a year later, Jacob Friesen sat at the table by lamp light reading a news-paper and pondering the world situation. Canada had, indeed, become increasingly involved in World War II and needed relief air fields to train more pilots.

Canada was a big open country and soon these small airports sprang up across the prairies. In Saskatchewan several aerodromes were built. As Saskatoon already had an airport, it became a training school for young pilots. It was called the Saskatoon No. 4 relief airfield; however it was not large enough to handle all the air traffic they expected. The government needed more land.

A mile east of Osler, a three-quarter section of flat grassy land was chosen as another site, and it was to be known as Saskatoon No. 2. It was situated east of the Friesen farm yard and cow pasture and included land Jacob Friesen farmed. He rented 160 acres from Abram Driedger. One day Abram drove on to the Friesen yard to speak with Jacob.

"I'm sure you have already heard that the government wants to build an airport east of your place. They want 80 acres of the land you're using as part of the airport property."

"I've heard about that and I have seen the surveyors out there, but it's hard to lose my haying land," Jacob said.

"I know, but I don't really have a choice." Abram answered. Jacob understood, but it was disappointing.

As soon as the ground thawed in spring, work on the runways began under the direction of Perseski's Construction Company of Saskatoon. Soon bulldozers of every size appeared on the land. Some were small and some were ponderous earth movers and graders. The children watched with excitement. Jacob watched as they moved across what used to be his hayfields.

The Friesen family got used to hearing the early morning rumbling sounds of the big machines, as they cleared ground for landing strips. Back and forth they went, with dust rising into the air along with clunking noises as they ran into large rocks under the top soil.

Local men and boys, along with the Friesens, were hired at 40 cents per day to mark rocky spots with willow branches so the stones could be removed after the graders passed and the dust settled. Farmers of the area chuckled at the difficulties faced by the men trying to smooth out the runways. They knew very well that land east of Osler was rocky, but that apparently hadn't been noticed by the surveyors. Construction workers had not counted on removing so many stones.

The local workers followed the graders, picking up rocks that were not too big to handle, then carried them to stone boats pulled by horses. The rocks were piled on the northwest corner of the air field and soon became known as 'Perseski's Piles'. A lot of hard work went into smoothing the runways for landing planes.

By mid summer, construction of the hangar and barracks began, and Jacob was given the opportunity to work for the company.

At home, Helena, with Lena's help, rushed back and forth between the table and hot stove, serving a big breakfast to several strange men at their table. The construction workers took their meals at the Friesen home and Jacob engaged them in conversation while they ate.

In her high chair next to her father, one year old Nettie looked fearfully at them. Who were they? And what were they doing in her house? The strange men would be there for meals for a long time.

When the men left to work at the airfield, Jacob sat a while with his coffee cup while Helena and their children finished their breakfast.

"What will we do now that we only have 80 acres?" Helena asked.

"Well," Jacob sighed, "for now I'm working on the buildings at the airport and I've got the contract to build the fence around the whole area. The government has also given permission to continue haying on the fields around the runways. That will give us some hay for the winter, but other farmers also want to do that."

"When the airport is finished we'll still have our dairy cows," Helena said.

"But not enough land to grow the crops and the hay we need to feed them," he finished for her. "When I'm done the fencing contract, I'll have to get another job," Jacob said as he rose, put down his cup and headed for the door.

"What are the names of the men who eat here?" one of the children asked as they cleared the table.

"The really big man is nicknamed 'Tiny' and the foreman's name is Ivan Nickolyavich Drabotie. I don't know the other men's names," Lena answered while filling a dish pan with hot water.

The foreman's name sounded funny and foreign to the children, and they soon nicknamed him "Nick go bode dee" – which when translated from the Low German meant, "Nick, go take a bath". This brought private giggles and smiles to their faces whenever they saw the man, but they never mentioned it in his presence.

"Nick, go bode dee", however, was often heard through the years as water was poured into the round metal bathtub and the Friesen children were reminded to have their Saturday night baths.

BUILDING FENCES

CHAPTER 9

On June 21, 1940, the Canadian government passed the 'National Resources Mobilization Act'. This would affect every adult citizen in Canada. It included a Registration process to identify people and resources that could be used during the war.

Interviews were held in cities across Canada, often in school buildings. Posters everywhere informed people of the registration and it was in all the news papers. Anyone who had reached the age of 16 years had to register by the month of August. Jacob, Lena and Jake all registered. Each one received a small wallet with a card which was shown to authorities if required.

As the Aerodrome runways and buildings began to take shape, Jacob started on the airport fence and hired several young relatives to work for him. It was a big job to pull all the old posts out of the ground and then build a good strong fence all around the perimeter of the airport property.

After several days of wrestling old posts out of the ground, the young men complained about the hard work. Jacob stopped to sit on a stone pile for a drink of cold coffee and a smoke. As he reached for his tobacco and paper, one of the young men offered him one of his own cigarettes.

"Here, have one of mine," the man offered.

"Oh no, I only smoke Ogden's Fine Cut tobacco!" Jacob replied.

"Bet you couldn't tell the difference," the young man said.

"Yes I could." Jacob leaned back against a large rock and relaxed with his smoke, deep in thought.

"Well, boys, I'm sure there has to be an easier way to pull out these old posts," he said finally. "I'll try to come up with an idea. It's nearly time for supper and chores, so let's go back to the farm and eat. Then you can go home."

Ogden's tobacco can. Photo taken at Hague, Sask. Museum

They climbed on the wagon and rode back to the Friesen farm for their meal. The men went to a wash basin standing outside the summer kitchen and washed, while Jacob went to the barn to check on some things before milking time. As the young men sat down to eat, one of them had an idea.

"Hey, Jake, where does your dad keep his tobacco?"

"On that shelf on the wall," Jake said, pointing to the shelf.

Chuckling, the young man quickly took down the tobacco, removed some of Jacob's brand and replaced it with his own. As Jacob walked by the kitchen window, the young man quickly returned to his place at the table.

After a hearty meal of potatoes, carrots and fried eggs, Jacob leaned back and took down his tobacco from the shelf. Pulling out a thin cigarette paper from its little package, he picked up a pinch of tobacco and rolled it. Licking one side of the paper to seal it, he struck a match and sat back to enjoy the smoke.

He was in a reflective mood and didn't notice the smirks on the young men's faces. He finished and looked up to find them grinning and laughing at him.
"Do you know what you just smoked?" one of the men asked him. "That was my brand of tobacco! I switched it and you didn't even notice!"

Jacob grinned sheepishly while the laughter increased. The joke was on him, but he could take a joke!

"Time to do chores," he said and grinned as he pushed back his chair and looked at his children. The other young men rose and left for their homes. They would be back the next day.

That night Jacob lay awake a long while, thinking of ways to pull those posts out. He came up with a plan. When the alarm clock rang, he woke, quickly got out of bed and dressed. After assigning the children to the milking, he hurried into his blacksmith shop and found two discarded wheels from old machinery, some iron bars and a small piece of strap-iron about three feet long.

Jacob searched behind the shop for a long sturdy timber. He found a log that was twelve feet long and pulled it out of the scrap lumber pile. Using an iron bar, he fastened the wheels to each other so they would roll together and then placed the 12 foot log over the wheel fulcrum, about three feet from one end of the post. He secured it to the rod between the wheels.

He then heated the strap-iron with his blow torch until it was red hot, bent it up at one end and cut a V in the upturned end. After it cooled he fastened the iron strip to the end of the post with strong bolts and attached a light logging chain at the V. And then it was time for breakfast.

"What were you making in the shop so early this morning?" Helena asked at breakfast. Jacob took a spoonful of cornflakes before answering. After a short pause he said, "The boys have been complaining about how hard it is to get those old fence posts out of the ground so I came up with a way that should make it easier."
"How?" asked Jake.

"You'll see," his father answered as he took the last sip of coffee and rose from the table. Jake followed him outside.

Taking hold of the long end of the 12 foot log, Jacob rolled the device to an old fence post on the yard. "Lift the long end of the pole, Jake," his father told him. When he did this, the short end moved toward ground level.

Jacob wound the logging chain around the old fence post and together they pushed down on the long end of the log. The old post easily rose out of the ground. Jacob grinned at the delighted look on his son's face.

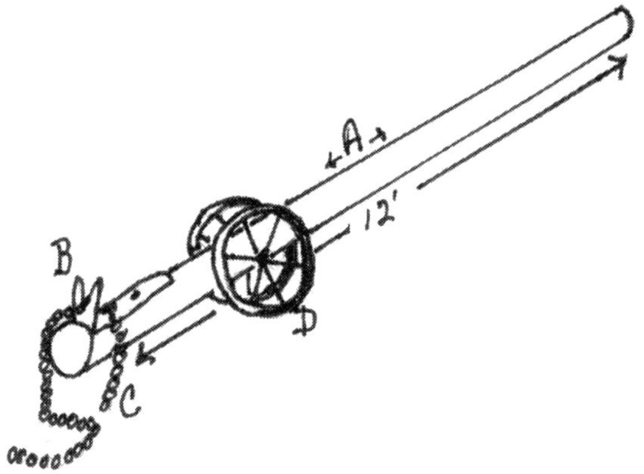

A; *Straight sturdy timber to work as lever over wheel fulcrum to raise & lower stubborn post.*
B; *Stap iron heat-bent with `V` to hold chain.*
C;*Light logging chain to wrap around base of post to be extracted.*
D: *Wheels from discarded machinery for easy transport along fence line.* ***(Drawing by Jake Friesen)***

"It works!" Jake exclaimed. They took the post extractor across the field to the airport property and soon the other young workers arrived. They were in awe of

Jacob's ingenuity and there was no more complaining about the extractions as the men took turns sliding old posts out of the ground and digging holes for new ones.

Jacob was fussy about every detail of the fence. It had to be perfectly straight and the shiny barbed wire evenly spaced. As the strong straight fence went up between the airport and the Friesen farm, Jacob built a wooden stairway over it so the boarders didn't have to climb through the wires every day.

One day one of the young labourers managed to find out how much Jacob was being paid and then complained that all the workers should be paid more. Even though the workers were very young and inexperienced, soft hearted Jacob agreed to raise their pay. That gave him less to take home for himself and his family. He became known in the area as the Minister of De-Fence – a term his son Jake did not appreciate.

WILLOW WHISTLES

CHAPTER 10

When the airport runways were smoothed out the year before, Jacob was one of the farmers given a contract to seed crested wheat grass on the runways to keep the dust down. They would be allowed to harvest the hay in the summer. Young Jake spent many hours on the metal seat of the four horse seeder drill that spring.

Now summer was nearly over again and the haying, swathing and garden harvest kept them all busy.

On a warm and beautiful fall evening, after a full day of work, Julius and Jake threw fast pitches to each other in the lane between the farm and the neighbour's field. It was a relief to have finished the harvesting and have a bit more free time.

"Boys, come back to the yard and let's play ball!" Lena called as she and Annie appeared with a baseball bat. They walked out to the yard on the east side of the old summer blacksmith shop and set gunny sacks out for bases. Tena and Christine sat down in the grass to watch.

Soon their father walked out of the house and joined them in the game. He grabbed the bat and walked to home plate.

“Let’s play ball!” he said as he faced Julius who was pitching.

Jake crouched down behind his dad and signaled to Julius. A nicely aimed pitch flew toward Jacob who swung hard, sending the ball out past the bases. Lena ran for the ball as her dad sprinted toward first. Annie waited at second base to catch the ball and tagged Jacob out.

Helena looked up from time to time to watch her family bat and run the bases while she picked the last gooseberries in the garden. Danny and Nettie played with kittens nearby.

"Come on, Tena and Chris," Julius called. "Don't you want to play too?" The girls left their grassy spot and took their turns at bat.

After a while they were tired of the game. Jake reached down, picked a long blade of quack grass, put it between his thumbs and blew through it, making a sharp, shrill whistling sound.

Jacob paused to listen, and said, "If you can find some thick green willow branches about a foot long, I'll show you how to make a willow whistle." The boys went to the willow bushes, found the branches and brought them to their father.

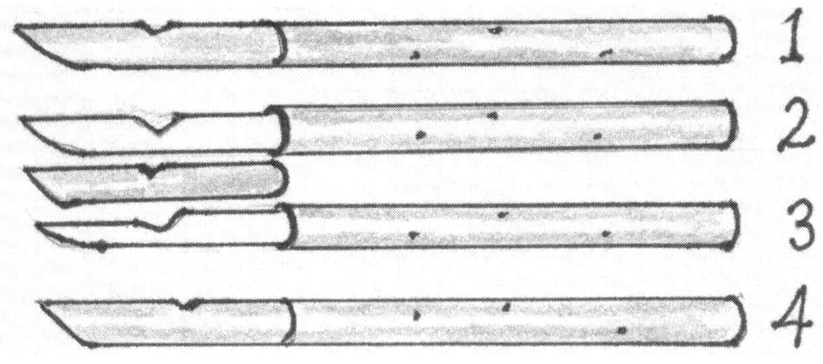

Drawing by Nettie Balzer

On the veranda, Jacob showed them how to use their jack knives to cut the top at an angle.

1. He cut a small wedge into the bark and wood beneath it, about three inches below the angled tip.

2. About two inches below the wedge, he cut all around the branch, just through the green bark, then, tapping it gently with the knife handle while turning the branch, he loosened the bark and carefully pulled it off.

3. He cut the wedge in the green wood deeper until about halfway through the branch.

4. Shaving off a flat plane from the notch to the top, he then replaced the bark and blew the whistle. A shrill sound filled the air around them.

There were smiles of delight on the children's faces. Tena and Christine both reached for the whistle.

"Here – let me try!" they said.

"I'm going to make my own," Jake commented.

"So am I," Julius said.

"Good idea," their father said and added, "If you want to use them again, put them in water so they won't dry out." He handed his whistle to the girls to try.

The boys made several whistles as Tena and Christine took turns blowing on the one their papa made. Lena and Annie tried the whistles their brothers handed to them but soon joined their mother in the house to get away from the constant shrill sound.

Tena, Christine, Danny & Nettie on the old veranda. Helena in the background, hanging her wash on the washline.

Jacob leaned his chair back against the house wall in the veranda and relaxed. The western sky displayed a brilliant orange and red sunset, and the few clouds reflected pinks and purples as the sun lowered in the sky.

The neighbour's caragana hedge and Osler's town elevators became black silhouettes against the changing colors in the west. Sunrises and sunsets were his favourite times of day. It was like God was painting a peaceful picture just for him.

THE OLD BARN

CHAPTER 11

Just across from the house and south of the big water trough stood an old run-down barn, sometimes known as the horse barn or bull barn. It was a square clapboard building with a high peaked roof and a lean-to on the south side,

which was sometimes used for chickens. Just inside and to the right of the barn door were the family's outhouse and a ladder to the loft.

Old Barn in background. Nettie & Danny with kittens in foreground

Beyond the ladder was the pen which housed their enormous pure-bred Holstein bull, an animal even Jacob treated with great respect. He had a long heavy stick with a hook at the end in case the animal became dangerous. The hook on the stick was slipped into the ring in the bull's nose before the gate to the stall was opened, so the bull could be led out and in again.

One day Julius went to get the cows for milking and forgot the bull was in the pasture.

He didn't have the dog with him. Suddenly he heard a roar and turned to see the bull with head lowered, ready to charge. Julius' legs became 'wings' as he ran toward the barbed wire fence, clearing it with about an inch to spare. The bull skidded to a stop a few feet away.

The children heeded their father's warning about the bull and preferred playing in the barn when the animal was out to pasture. If he was in his pen, they took care not to disturb him when climbing the loft ladder.

There were times during the depression of the thirties that 'rail-riders' slept in the loft of the old barn, always being warned by Jacob that they were not to smoke in the barn and to be aware of the bull. These men hopped freight trains from town to town and walked out to the local farms to work for food. With the Friesen farm being close to Osler, these men often appeared on the yard asking to work for something to eat.

The barn loft was filled with birds, too many of them - mostly pigeons, sparrows and barn swallows. Their droppings soiled the straw and hay that was kept in the loft for the bull. Jake and Julius often climbed to the loft to kill them with sling shots. Some days the boys brought the best of the freshly killed pigeons to their mother to clean and fry up for supper. It wasn't like chicken, but it was fresh meat.

One day Julius again climbed to the loft to shoot birds. Ten-year-old Tena saw him and followed. There was an opening from the loft onto the roof of the small lean-to. Julius climbed through and sat down to peel the bark off a forked branch with his jackknife.

"What are you doing?" asked Tena, who suddenly appeared at the opening and climbed onto the roof to join him.

"I'm making a new sling-shot," he said as he glanced up.

After he had peeled the branch, Julius carefully measured and cut the forked branches to the right length. Fishing into his pocket, he pulled out a length of rubber from an old tire inner tube and cut it just the right width and length.

He pulled out a small piece of soft leather from the tongue of an old shoe and cut a slit at both sides. Threading the rubber band through the slits, Julius positioned the leather exactly in the middle and then tied the ends of the rubber to each forked tip of the branch. From his other pocket he pulled out several little stones and tried them out. Putting a stone in the center of the band he pulled back on the rubber, aimed at the corner of the barn roof, let go of the band and sent the stone flying. After a few tries, he hit his target.

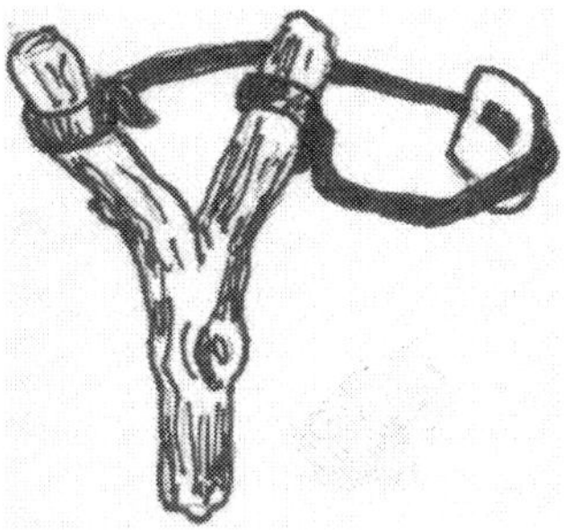

"Tena," eight year old Christine called from the ground below, "what are you doing up there?"

"Come on up, Chris," Tena answered.

"I'm scared," Christine said.

"It's not scary," Tena said, "I'll meet you in the loft." Her younger sister climbed the ladder carefully, keeping a wary eye on the bull. Both girls settled onto the cleanest hay they could find and watched Julius take aim at the birds. This provoked loud cooing and flapping of wings. The girls covered their heads to avoid the wings and loose flying feathers. The swallows swooped angrily over Julius. When a bird fell from a stone, most of the flock flew around the loft in fear and then out through a window.

With many birds out of the loft, Julius raided the nests and removed the eggs and skinny baby birds. He broke off the mud nests the swallows had built. A few birds were fun to have around, but too many were a nuisance for the farm.

He climbed back out onto the roof of the lean-to, walked down to the edge and jumped down with his bag of birds and eggs. His new sling shot worked well and he was proud of his accomplishment. Still, he felt badly about destroying so many birds. He loved to watch them flying about the farm and enjoyed listening to the early morning and evening bird songs. He just wished they would stay out of the barn loft. He thought of a plan. He would build bird houses and put them up in as many trees and on as many fence posts as he could!

The girls had followed him out of the loft and sat down on the lean-to roof for a while.

"Christine," Tena said, "let's jump off the roof like Julius did!" She proceeded toward the edge.

"No!" Christine exclaimed. "Don't jump, Tena! You'll get hurt!"

Tena laughed and jumped into the soft grass. Looking up she called, "See? It's easy and it's not high – just jump."

Christine gingerly inched towards the edge. The roof seemed so high and the ground so very far away.

"I'm too scared!"

"Just jump!" Tena urged.

"I can't!" Chris said as her chin quivered. "Help me down!"

"I can't lift you down – go back to the loft and come down the ladder." Tena walked back into the barn. Christine appeared above her and looked down from the steep loft ladder to the dirt floor of the barn.

"I'm too scared! I'll fall!" she said. The bull rumbled menacingly in his stall.

Nothing could encourage Christine to budge. Tena ran to the house for help, interrupting a visit with guests in the living room.

"Dad, I can't get Chris down from the barn roof," she said. "Can you help her?"

"The *barn* roof?" Jacob asked in surprise, "What is she doing up there?" He got up quickly and strode toward the barn. There he saw Christine standing on the lean-to roof, sobbing loudly.

"How did you get up there?" Jacob asked, reaching up for her. "Jump into my arms. I'll catch you." Christine carefully stepped closer to the edge of the roof, bent down and allowed herself to fall safely into her father's arms.

"Now," he said, "How did you get up there?"

Christine wiped her tears with her arm and answered, "Tena told me to come up to the loft and jump off of the roof like *she* did."

Sternly he turned to Tena and scolded, "What were you thinking? You could have broken your legs. How could you tell your sister to jump off too? Now go play somewhere else, and don't get into any more trouble!" With that he put Christine down and turned toward the house and their waiting visitors.

"It was just the lean-to roof!" Tena muttered as her father strode away. Her face was downcast as she stalked toward the big trees in the garden where the rope swing hung from a large branch. She was soon pumping hard and swinging high and fast. Christine dried her tears and went to find her sister.

As she walked toward the swing, Tena gave her a furious look, "You told on me! You got me into trouble!"

"But you told me to jump!" Christine said, as she stomped toward a caragana bush and sat down in a pout. She pulled seed pods off the branches above her and angrily flung them around.

After a while both girls were bored with their anger. They were still best sister-friends and there were better places to play.

“Let’s go to the cow barn loft and see if we can find the kittens.” Tena suggested.

“The mama cat had them hidden yesterday. Maybe we’ll find them today,” Christine added.

They ran off toward the cattle barn and climbed up the ladder for the search. After listening closely, they heard the faint mewing and found the cat with her babies. She hissed at them so they settled on the straw to watch the squirming balls of fur.

The girls giggled and smiled at each other. This was so much more fun than fighting!

FODA GOES "HOME"

CHAPTER 12

In late November the weather turned colder. Crops had been harvested and there were oat sheaves and hay stacks to feed the animals through the winter. The cellar bins were filled with potatoes, turnips, beets and carrots. The shelves displayed canned peas, beans, pickles and fruit. Food ration coupons were available for things they could not grow.

On December 15th, 1941, a windy snowy day, the telephone rang in the Friesen house.

"Hello?" Helena said after picking up the receiver.

"This is Anna, is Jacob there?" his sister asked, "Foda (father) died this morning." Jacob's father had been ill for some time.

"He's in the barn. I'll get him." Helena laid down the receiver, quickly put on her coat, and hurried to the barn.

"Jacob," she called as she entered the barn, "your sister Anna is on the phone. Foda passed away this morning."

Jacob sighed. He had been expecting this. He leaned the pitch fork against the barn wall and followed Helena. As they walked to the house, he looked at the heavy snow coming down and listened to the wind howl. He hurried in and picked up the phone. "Hello?"

"Do you think you can come home to Blumenheim today?" Anna asked.

"We'll come, but I'll pick the children up from school first. This will be the last time they'll see their grandfather," he answered. "Will you call the rest of the family?"

"Yes, I have already called the nearest brothers and sisters," she said.

He changed his clothes and hurried back to the barn to hitch the horses up to the caboose. He started a fire in the small stove inside the sleigh. Soon he was on his way to Osler. As the wind whipped up snow across the trail, Jacob strained to see through the frozen glass and finally opened the window a bit in spite of the cold wind.

The children were working quietly at their desks while the teacher gave the fourth graders their lessons. They all turned at the sound of the school door opening. Their teacher glanced up and came to the back of the room to see what Jacob wanted.

"The Friesen children may be dismissed," the teacher announced after a few minutes. Surprised, the children hurried to put their books away, went to the cloakroom to put on their coats and boots and followed their father out to the caboose.

"What's wrong?" Annie asked her quiet father.

"Your Grandpa Friesen died this morning and we're going to Blumenheim to see him. We may not be able to travel tomorrow, since the storm is getting much worse."

The children sat quietly thinking of their big, blind grandpa. It was hard to imagine what it would be like with him not being at grandma and grandpa's house anymore.

When they arrived back at their farm, Helena was ready with Danny and Nettie. They crowded into the caboose and Jacob snapped the reins. With a "Giddy-up" they were off to Blumenheim.

Other sleighs and a few cars already stood near grandma and grandpa's house when they arrived. Jacob unhitched his horses and led them to the barn. After walking through the gahnk (*the room between the attached house and the barn*) the family removed their boots and coats and met their solemn aunts, uncles and cousins

"It looks like everyone is here," Anna said as she led the way to the big room. There, grandpa's body lay on the lid of the schlope benk, a sheet covering him up to his chin. Grandma sat quietly beside him. (*a schope benk was a wooden "hide-a-bed" with a drawer that pulled out to make a bed.)*

The original Kjist still in use at the home of (Paul)Anne Janzen's children.

Jacob led Danny, and Helena walked in carrying Nettie. The other children and the Friesen and Janzen cousins followed their parents into the crowded room. After standing for a bit and gazing at her father-in-law, Helena moved to the side of the room, where grandma's bright red kjist (*trunk*) with shiny black and gold trim stood. She seated Nettie on top of the trunk, and turned to join the family around the body.

Nettie's interest moved from the crowd to the kjist. It was shiny and red – her favourite colour! She sat contentedly kicking her little feet against the side of the trunk, while running her hands over the four shiny gold domes on the lid just above the big key in the lock. She was too young to understand why everyone was so sad, and of course did not comprehend that her big grandpa had taken his last breath that morning.

The relatives gathered in another room to plan the funeral, while some of the Aunts prepared faspa. After sitting through the discussion and faspa, Jacob glanced at Helena and nodded his head. He got up from his chair and put on his coat. It was time to get the horses hitched to the sleigh and go home for chores. In the barn, Jacob walked to where his father's horses stood. He stroked the handsome animals, remembering how much his father loved them even though he could not see them. His father was known in the area for the beautiful horses he kept. As Jacob stood next to them, he felt the grief of losing his father deeply. Another sudden change had come into their lives.

The door creaked and Julius called, "Dad? Is it time to go home?"

As one of the horses nudged Jacob's shoulder he replied, "Yes son. Let's go home."

I JUST COULDN'T LEAVE HER

CHAPTER 13

The drafty old house was hard to heat as the cold intensified. Except for a few milder days, the cold continued all through Christmas, making travel to concerts and church difficult. At home the family played board games, as close to the stoves as possible. They still enjoyed their decorated tree and the gifts they received, along with the traditional Christmas meal of roast goose with bubbat dressing (*a steamed or baked biscuit-like dough filled with prunes, raisins and currants)*.

Nettie in high chair near Christmas tree.

Holidays were over too soon and it was time to go back to school. The children trudged through snow drifts on milder days and were driven by horse and sleigh in colder weather.

The usual flu and cold germs made their rounds among the school children and the Friesen family. At home, two year old Nettie came down with another chest cold.

"This time we're not waiting so long," Jacob said one evening. "I want to take her to Warman to see Dr. Wilkin tomorrow." Helena agreed.

The next morning they bundled up in the sleigh, where Jacob had a fire going in the little stove. It was fairly warm inside the caboose as they made their way to Warman and to the doctor's office. Dr. Wilkin took his stethoscope and listened carefully to Nettie's chest.

Straightening up he said, "It sounds like she has the beginnings of pneumonia. Because of how sick she has been several times since she was born, her lungs are not strong. I want you to take her to City Hospital in Saskatoon on the first train tomorrow morning."

It was hard to think of leaving her at a hospital, but Helena was relieved to know her little girl would be cared for in a warm place, by people who knew what to do.

She was up almost all night with a very sick little girl. Next morning, Jacob and the children finished the chores and at breakfast it was decided that Annie would stay home with Danny and Jake would take the other children to school in the cutter.

"Make sure you go home right after school to get the chores done," their father told them.

Arriving at the railway station, Jacob dropped his wife and child off so they could sit near the stove in the waiting room while he went to the town livery stable to shelter his horses. After returning to the station, he purchased their tickets.
Soon the train whistle and chug-chugging noise of the steam engine signalled the arrival of the train.

After squealing brakes brought the train to a stop, the conductor got off. Parcels and mail for the post office and boxes of food for the store were unloaded. Finally the conductor called, "All aboard!"

Jacob and Helena left the warmth of the station house and boarded the train. As they travelled, people often turned to look at the little one who coughed so hard. Jacob looked out of the window as they passed the town of Warman. Soon they would be in the city and on their way to the hospital.

Osler CN Railway station. Note Livery stable in background
Photo courtesy of Osler, Sask. Historical Museum

As they walked down the train steps in Saskatoon, Helena handed Nettie to Jacob to carry, tucking the blanket over the child's face. They walked into the station, where the high ceilings made the busy noises of the station echo, and then continued through to the street doors.

Out on the street Jacob found a waiting taxi and opened the doors to the cab. Helena got into the back while Jacob sat in front with his daughter. It wasn't long until they were at the hospital and Nettie was in the care of the nurses and a doctor.

They were allowed to stay with her for the afternoon and then had to leave to catch the train for home. Nettie clung to her mama. It was frightening to be in such a big strange place. Finally a nurse distracted her long enough for them to leave.

They rode home in silence, wrapped in their own thoughts. As they walked into the door of the house Danny saw them and ran to his mother. She hugged him tightly for a while.

The older children asked about their little sister, but Helena could only tell them she was relieved the child would get proper nursing care. That night, after praying for her children, Helena slept soundly for the first time in what seemed a long time.

They were busy all week, clearing snow from paths between the house and barn and doing the regular chores with the cattle, horses, pigs and chickens. In the house, the children did their homework by lamp light in the evenings.

When Saturday came, Jacob announced at breakfast that he was going to Saskatoon to pick up a few things.

"Are you going to see Nettie?" Julius asked.

"Probably," his dad answered. "Jake, you can take me to the station. Pick me up when the train returns."

Jacob took the train to the city, looked after a few errands and made his way to City Hospital. Arriving at the hospital, he went to the children's ward and asked about his little girl.

"She's doing fairly well, but she is still very sick," he was told.

"May I see her?" he asked.

"Yes, but make sure she doesn't see you. She may cry, and that will increase her coughing," the nurse cautioned.

Jacob quietly walked to the ward and peeked through the doorway. At the end of the room he saw little Nettie standing in a crib, watching the other children. He moved a bit closer, trying to hide behind a curtain. It was too late. She had seen him and started to cry, "Papa, Papa!"

He couldn't stand it and made his way to her, picked her up and held her close. She clung to his neck and stopped crying. When it was time for him to go he tried to pull her arms from his neck, but she immediately began to cry and cough again.

A nurse walked toward him saying, "That's what we were afraid of. It will be harder for her when you leave now."

Jacob gazed at the little girl and made up his mind. "I'll take her home with me," he said.

"But you can't! The doctor has not discharged her!" the nurse reminded him. "She's still very sick!"

"It's all right. My wife will look after her and we have a good doctor in Warman. Where are her clothes?"

The nurse brought the clothes and said, "But you have no blankets."

"I'll wrap her in my coat," he said, as he began to take off Nettie's hospital gown. He dressed her in own clothes, warm coat, hat and mittens, then unbuttoned his own coat and wrapped it around her.

The young nurse watched in frustration, as the father walked away carrying the sick child. Parents could be such a problem sometimes!

Hailing a taxi, Jacob carried his daughter to the cab and asked to be taken to the station. It was almost time for him to catch the train.

On the way home, Jacob pondered Helena's reaction. He looked down at the sleeping child and sighed. He hoped he had not done the wrong thing.

Jake was there to pick them up and was surprised to see his little sister. "Is she better?" he asked.

"No, but she'll get better," Jacob answered.

Arriving at home, Jacob carried the little girl in his coat and entered the kitchen. Helena was at the stove and turned to greet him. She was about to ask how the Nettie was, when Jacob unwrapped his coat. She gasped in dismay!

"Why have you brought her home? Is she well?" she asked. But when she reached for her child Helena knew she was not well at all.

"What have you done?!" she exclaimed angrily, "How am I supposed to get her well in this cold house? She was warm in the hospital and she had nurses and doctors to care for her!"

Jacob looked down sheepishly and said. "When she saw me she cried and then wouldn't let go of me. I just couldn't leave her there!"

In a few weeks, Nettie was well and happy, playing with her brother again, but their mother looked forward to warmer spring and summer days. Illnesses did not seem as severe when the children could get out into the warm sunshine.

VBS AT GRANDMA'S VILLAGE

CHAPTER 14

Work on the Aerodrome continued in the spring and summer, keeping the family busy as the temperatures climbed. As July's heat intensified the younger children were bored and listless. Helena was thankful for a phone call from her sister-in-law.

"Helena," Anna said, "there will be children's Bible school at the Renfrew School near Blumenheim next week. Would Tena and Christine want to come? They can stay with us here at Grandma's house for those days."

"That would be a good idea. We're so busy with the gardening, haying and airport work. It would be good for them to have something to do. Thank you!" Helena answered.

On the following Sunday afternoon, Jacob and Helena took the girls to grandma's house. After a visit and faspa, they returned home with Danny and Nettie.

Tena and Christine ran into grandma's garden to play hide and seek among the plum trees for the rest of the afternoon. The soft black garden dirt felt good under their bare feet. They wished the plums were ripe enough to eat.

"Come in for supper," Aunt Justina called. The girls ran to the house and through the back door into the gahnk. On their way to the kitchen, they admired grandma's big mangle. It was made up of a series of highly polished wooden rollers on an equally polished bed. It was used to 'iron' sheets, tea towels, pillow slips, and more. Sheets were smoothed out, folded once, and sent through the rollers by turning a crank at the side of the mangle. The sheets were folded again and sent through again, until they could be put away neatly.

Mangle: drawing by Nettie Balzer

The girls continued on through the kitchen door, washed their hands and sat down at one end of the long table. They enjoyed bowls of hot cooked rice with milk, sugar and cinnamon. On the table stood a bowl of boiled eggs which they peeled and ate with salt.

"Girls, you can help dry dishes," Aunt Annie told them, as she filled a big dish pan with hot water from the kettle on the stove.

After helping with the dishes, the girls chatted with grandma and watched her knit while she sat in her favourite chair near the red corner china cabinet.

At bedtime the schlope-benk was opened up and bedding arranged for the girls. Christine and Tena recited their bedtime prayers with Aunt Justina and settled in for night.

"Do you think grandma looks sad?" Christine whispered.

"Why?" asked Tena.

"Because grandpa went to heaven," Christine replied.

"I don't know," Tena answered, as she rolled over to her other side.

"Well, I think she's lonely because grandpa is gone," Christine said. She looked around the room at the dark doors and woodwork. The curtains were drawn closed and even though it was not yet dark outside, she felt closed in and suddenly lonely for home.

"Are you scared, Tena?" she asked.

"No," Tena replied, "go to sleep. Tomorrow we're going to Bible school."

Next morning, they awoke to the noises of breakfast preparation in the kitchen. They were soon washed, dressed and seated at the long table. Aunt Justina poured dry cereal into each of their bowls and added milk.

Tena began to eat and enjoyed the food. Christine stared at her bowl and hung her head. After a while her grandma and aunts noticed.

"Why aren't you eating, Christine?" asked grandma.

Christine nudged Tena and pointed to her bowl. In it was a large green worm. Tena looked up at her aunts and said, "I think there's something in her bowl." Aunt Justina came to investigate.

"Oh my! No wonder you don't want to eat!" she said as she poured the cereal and milk into the slop pail. She brought the bowl back to the table, picked up the cereal box and poured more cereal into the bowl, adding milk. Christine was still afraid to eat it because it came from the same box, but finally at Tena's urging, she tried it.

"All right, girls," Aunt Justina said, "I'll take you to the school house for Bible School." They walked down the sandy street to the east end of the village and then turned north to the Renfrew School building. As they neared the school house, they saw some of their Friesen cousins running around the yard.

"Here you are," their aunt said, as she gently pushed them toward the door. She turned and walked briskly back toward the village road. Tena walked into the school house with the other children. *(Note: the Renfrew School house is now located on The Hague(Sask.) Museum grounds)*

"Come *on*!" Tena urged, as she looked back at her sister. Christine hesitated.

"Well, stay outside then. I'm going in!" Tena said.

Christine heard the children inside having fun as they sang and listened to stories. Finally, since Tena didn't come to get her, she turned toward the road and slowly walked back to grandma's house and to the garden, where her grandma picked currants and her aunts pulled weeds.

"What are you doing here?" asked grandma, "Why aren't you at the school house?"

"I was too shy," Christine answered.

Aunt Justina looked disgusted as she dropped her hoe and took Christine's hand. "We've got a lot of work to do here and you will have fun if you stay at the school, so we're going back!" She led her niece back and made sure she walked all the way *into* the school house. Christine enjoyed the next few days as she played with cousins and got to know the other children and the teachers.

OBA KJINGJA, OBA KJINGJA!

CHAPTER 15

Shipping cream or milk required a barn and equipment that passed inspection. Every year a milk inspector would arrive to make sure all the dairy farms around Osler were up to standards. He tested the percentage of butter fat in the milk.

Milk and cream separator at Rosthern (Sask.) Museum

Jacob never knew just when the inspector would arrive. He made sure the inside barn walls were white-washed each summer and the manure gutters cleaned everyday. The pails, cream separator and milk cans were washed and scalded with boiling water after use.

One particular inspector had Jake and Julius' attention, because he showed an interest in them and their lives. As he arrived one day, he saw the boys pushing each other around and punching each other playfully, pretending to box.

"Hey, boys!" the man said as he got out of his car, "Do you ever listen to the Joe Louis boxing matches on the radio?"

"We sure do," replied Julius as they walked toward the inspector, "They call him the Brown Bomber."

"Would you like a few lessons in boxing?" the inspector asked.

"Sure, but we don't have boxing gloves," Jake answered.

"I just happen to have several pairs of them in my car! Give me a hand in the barn and cooling house with the inspection, and I'll give you a few lessons on the right way to box," they were told.

They followed the man around the barn, as he asked questions and made notes in his book. Jacob joined the discussion. When the inspector brought out his milk testing equipment, the boys were intrigued with the machine with its circular array of little glass bottles that spun on a turntable.

"Well, that about does it for the inspection. Jacob, I've promised your boys a few boxing lessons. Is that all right?" the man asked.

"Certainly," Jacob replied, and then stood at the sidelines to watch. They were taught how to stand, how to move, how to avoid punches and how to deliver them. Since the boys enjoyed this so much, their father thought it would be a good idea to buy them their own boxing gloves.

After the inspector left, Julius asked, "Dad, may we get some boxing gloves?"

Boxing Gloves:
drawing by Nettie Balzer

"Let's look in the Eatons catalogue to see how much they cost," his dad answered. As they sat at faspa later that afternoon, the boys found the gloves in the catalogue. Jacob hesitated at the cost. One pair cost $2.75.

"That's a lot of money," he said, as he considered the idea. "Two pair would cost $5.50 plus tax."

"I've got a little money left," Jake said.

"So do I." Julius added.

"All right, you boys pool your money and I'll add what is needed," their dad offered.

They ordered two pair and in about a week the order came. The gloves were tried out as the boys pranced about, swinging their gloved fists at each other and laughing.

But, the Friesen children didn't always get along.

It was one of those days. Early one morning, Helena heard an argument erupt from an upstairs bedroom. Lena and Annie's voices rose in anger and continued as they noisily ran down the wooden stairs to the kitchen.

"Girls! Stop this!" Helena said, trying to calm them down.

"She started it!" Annie said as she grabbed her barn jacket.

"Well, leave my stuff alone!" Lena hissed.

"I would – if you would clean it up!" retorted Annie.

Lena turned furiously as Helena stepped in to keep them from coming to blows. "Girls, please – it's 5:30 in the morning and you'll wake the younger children!"

The girls rolled their eyes at their mother, glared at each other and flounced out the door and on to the barn.

In the barn, Jacob saw his daughters grab their pails and slam down milk stools beside the cows, making the animals sidestep nervously. They milked in sulking silence. He stood for a moment looking from one to the other, then thought better of asking what was wrong and went to feed the horses.

Throughout the day there seemed to be no peace between them and they made sure they weeded the garden at different spots, far away from each other.

Helena had her hands full with the younger children. She sent Tena and Christine to gather eggs. The girls brought them to the house where they carefully wiped them with a damp cloth and then took them to the cooling house to store. She let Nettie and Danny play in the living room.

As the afternoon wore on, Lena, with Annie following at a distance, went into the house for a cool drink and a snack.

"Where are the kitchen chairs?" demanded Lena as she entered the kitchen just ahead of Annie.

"In the living room," Helena said, "Danny and Nettie are playing train with them. They've been visiting their imaginary friends, the 'Miyagash'."

"What a mess!" Annie exclaimed, as she looked into the living room and saw the lined up chairs, along with dolls and other toys littered around the room. Danny was the driver of the train at the front and Nettie rode in a back chair holding her doll.

"They were just having fun," offered Tena as she walked in to look.

"Well then, maybe you want to clean it up," Lena retorted as she tossed her head in disgust.

Helena sighed in frustration.

At supper Jake teased Julius, "Hey, Shorty, pass the carrots."

"Don't call me that!" Julius snapped. Soon complaints, insults and accusations flew back and forth. Jake continued teasing, while Julius sat gripping his knife in one hand and his fork in another, seething in anger.

"Boys! Leave the table!" Jacob ordered. As the boys rose Julius threw down his knife and fork and flew at his bigger brother. They were soon on the floor wrestling.

Nettie watched anxiously from her high chair. She was frightened and began to cry.

"ENOUGH!" boomed Jacob's voice. "If you want to fight, get your boxing gloves!"

As the boys got up and glanced toward the table, they saw their mother sitting with her elbows on the table and her hands supporting her bowed head.

"Oba kjinga, oba kjinga!" she said in a soft sad voice, "vout vaut daut met yount noch aula voren?" (translation: Oh children, Oh children! Whatever will become of all of you?) It was a comment heard often by the squabbling children.

Jake, Julius, Lena and Annie, glanced at each other then back at their mother. Their faces were somber and their eyes filled with regret. What an unnecessary waste of a good day. Tomorrow they would start off the day in better spirits.

WEDNESDAY NIGHT CHILDREN'S HOUR

CHAPTER 16

Tena and Christine sat with other children in the balcony of the Osler Church and watched intently as Stella Rempel moved Bible character figures around on the flannel background of an easel. The flannel cloth pictured a blue sky with clouds above a hill on one side and a rock cave on the other, and distant buildings showed behind them.

The story of Easter came alive for the children as Stella talked about why Jesus came to earth. She placed a cross on top of the hill and explained that he died for everyone in the world, even though he hadn't done anything wrong. Three days later he rose again from the dead and now if they asked him, he would forgive the wrong things they had done and help them live they way they should.

Tena and Christine and several friends decided to go to Stella's home after the story hour was over and pray to Jesus.

Then special meetings were held in the Osler Church for several Sundays and the Friesen family attended. They listened to the same messages about forgiveness of sin and believing that Jesus is God's Son who loved them all which gave them the hope of heaven some day.

Annie listened intently and decided this was what she wanted. She stayed to pray after a service. When she studied the

Bible with Stella and other friends, Annie had a sense of peace and belonging.

At home at the farm, Helena was concerned about Annie jumping into something not quite like what she had been taught when she was young. She had always had a deep reverence for God in her heart. He was held up as being holy, mighty and to be feared when one did wrong.

When one looked closely at the words of the catechism and church hymn book of the old colony church where they used to attend, it was much the same message her family had just heard again in the Osler church. However she had also been taught that one could not be sure of heaven. To say one was sure sounded like pride and pride was a sin. To Helena it seemed safer to stay with those old teachings. Old things felt safe. Following rules felt safe.

"Annie, how can you be so sure that you will be in heaven some day? That is for God to decide," Helena told her.

"But Mom, the Bible says we *can* know for sure," Annie replied and showed her mother a scripture that said, "I write these things to you who believe in the name of the Son of God so that you may know that you have eternal life." Helena was soon digging into the scriptures herself to find out if it was true.

Jake pondered all of this quietly. He was not ready to take the same steps his sister had taken. Stella Rempel's father, George, made Jake a priority in his prayers, walking the floor at night and praying for this young man who had so much potential.

Lena told the family that her Sunday-school teacher had explained all of this to her when she was just a little girl. Lena had prayed with her but hadn't understood what it meant at that time. Now it all made sense and she too was drawn by the love of God.

A job became available at the local telephone switchboard and post office and Lena was glad to be able to work so close to home. This made it possible for her to join Stella in teaching Wednesday Night Children's Hour and she also taught Sunday school.

Telephone switchboard at Osler, Sask. Historical Museum

In the evenings, at home, the four youngest gathered around as Lena read stories to them from Hurlbut's Stories of the Bible. It was a big, blue, hard cover book with many beautiful pictures. The bright, colourful copies of famous bible story paintings made the stories even more interesting. After saying their prayers, the children fell asleep confident of God's love and care.

TRAINING FOR WAR

CHAPTER 17

Osler Aerodrome built one mile east of Osler. Note wooden steps over fence near right side of hangar. Friesen family photo.

The airport was nearing completion and there was constant activity as small yellow planes took off into the air, turned around and practiced smooth landings.

Jacob was upset at times with the mischievous young pilots in training, who thought it was funny to swoop low over a herd of milk cows and send them running in fright. Chasing milk cows was not something dairy farmers ever did. Stressed cows would not produce much milk.

As he and his helpers worked on the airport fencing near the hangar one day, several small planes came down low and zoomed over his dairy cows. They stampeded toward a barbed wire fence as the planes buzzed over them. Jacob dropped his post-hole digger and watched in frustration.

"It's about time those airmen stop that foolishness. It's bad for the cows and dangerous for the pilots themselves," he said. Other farmers also complained. Jacob wondered if marching into that hanger to have a word with those in charge would do any good.

The Friesen family often watched as groups of small planes in formation circled high up, did roll-overs and zoomed back down.

There were times when the larger khaki bombers flew in from a north-west direction at such a low altitude, the Friesen children ducked, afraid the planes would hit the barn roof but they always landed safely.

There were red and white wooden markers near the runways showing the pilots where to land, and windsocks flying on poles showing the direction of the wind. The children sometimes walked through the pasture to stand near the fence for a closer look.

One day Tena and Christine walked to the airport, even though they had been told not to go alone and were given a tour of the buildings by a few airmen. They were complete gentlemen and treated them with respect but the girls knew their parents would not have approved.

As the activity at the Relief Aerodromes across Canada continued, there was hope that perhaps the war with Germany might be nearing the end. But more disheartening news shattered hopes for peace: On December 7, 1941, Japanese pilots flew over Hawaii and bombed Pearl Harbour. Battery operated radios blasted the news amid crackling static and newspaper headlines were in large, bold print.

Soon there was news of the government rounding up Japanese people in British Columbia, taking them away to camps for security reasons. They were Canadian citizens, people who had been born in Canada and had lived in the country for years. They now had their property confiscated and were regarded with suspicion because of their nationality and were referred to as Japs.

German-speaking people across the country and in the Osler area could relate to this as there was a stigma attached to them as well because of Hitler's army. Because of their connections to the German language, they were sometimes regarded with suspicion as well and called Krauts.

Jacob wondered how much longer this war would last.

THE CHOCOLATE MILK VENTURE

CHAPTER 18

As Jacob and the men worked on the fence, they often chatted with the young pilots-in-training. On summer days the airmen worked up a thirst as they inspected and repaired planes and practiced flying. With no shade on airport property, temperatures of more than 30 degrees made the work difficult. Pails of lukewarm drinking water were provided and town people brought soft drinks but the men were still often thirsty for something else.

Helena decided to take advantage of their need for cold drinks. She had lots of pint size glass cream bottles with cardboard lids.

"I think I'll make chocolate milk for the airmen and sell it to them," Helena remarked at supper one day. "We have those pint sized glass bottles in the cellar and lots of extra milk. Those young boys might enjoy a treat."

"That's a good idea!" Jake exclaimed, "I could deliver it to them."

So the plan was brought into motion. The girls brought the jars up from the cellar and washed and scalded them. Helena made chocolate syrup with water, cocoa, sugar and vanilla. After bringing the mixture to a boil, she added milk until it tasted just right. The girls carefully filled the bottles and capped them with the cardboard lids.

They placed the drinks in wooden apple boxes which were placed in the cooling house for use the next day. It was cold in the cooling house. Water in the trough came from deep down in the well and it was where cans of milk were cooled. The boxes of chocolate milk were placed on the cool cement floor.

In the hottest part of the afternoon, Jake hitched a team of horses to the wagon and loaded up the boxes of cold chocolate milk. He took the team to the far side of the airfield where the pilots and maintenance men were working. As he approached, the airmen looked up from their work and Jake called to them, "Would you like a cold drink?"

"Yes! What do you have? How much are you charging?" they called back. Jake sold the chocolate milk to them for a few cents a bottle.

"Here! Catch!" the men called, and they tossed their empty glass bottles to Jake. He caught them easily and repacked them to take home.

"You're good at catching!" one of them said. "Do you play ball?"

"Yes, I'm on a team in Osler," he replied. Jake climbed back on the wagon, waved to them and returned home.

"The airmen really enjoyed the chocolate milk, Mom," Jake reported at supper.

"That's good – after we're done chores and dishes, we'll make another batch for tomorrow," she replied.

For several weeks the heat continued and the chocolate milk sales brought in a little extra income for Helena to use where it was most needed. There was always a need for cloth for dresses or wool to make sweaters. She was thankful.

PREPARATION and ANTICIPATION

CHAPTER 19

At 5:30 a.m. on a Saturday morning, the birds were singing and Jacob was up. He called up the stairs, "Get up! It's time to milk." Jake, Lena and Annie slowly emerged from their upstairs bedrooms, sleepily crossed the kitchen and trudged to the barn.

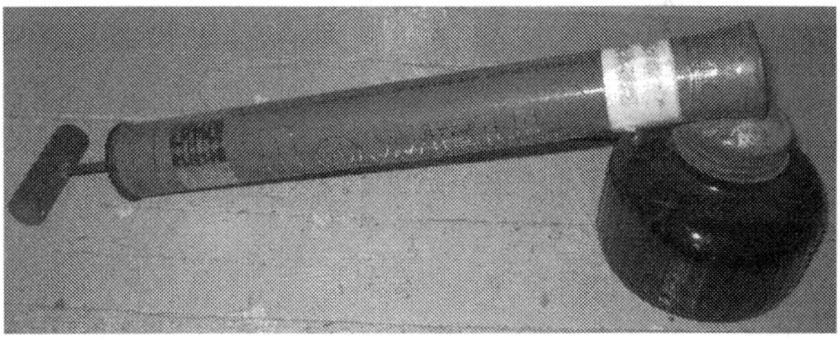

Pest sprayer at Osler, Sask. Historical Museum. (DDT – a harmful chemical now banned. In the 1940's salesmen tasted the chemical to prove to farmers how safe it was!)

Jacob opened the back door of the barn wide, spraying DDT on the cows' backs as they eagerly walked in single file to their stanchions, their udders swollen with milk. The DDT would keep the flies from irritating the cows. Jake tossed scoops of grain into the feeding troughs and closed the stanchions to hold the cows in place while they were milked.

Lena and Annie fetched clean pails from the cooling house and low milking stools from the lean-to. They tied up the cows' tails on strings that hung down from the ceiling before sitting down. There was nothing worse than being whipped in the face with a cow's dirty tail. Holding metal pails between their knees, they began to milk rhythmically while Jake set up the milk strainer in the cooling house. Soon he returned to the barn and joined in the milking.

It wasn't long before the barn cats emerged from the loft and sauntered over to watch, meowing piteously. "You want milk?" Annie asked as she aimed a stream in their direction. The cats were quick to open their mouths and lick the milk as it squirted into their mouths, over their faces, and onto the cement floor. Lena joined in with another stream aimed at the cats. The girls laughed at the comical sight.

It was going to be a busy day. Inside the house, Helena made the bed, set the table and pulled the blinds down so the house could stay cool. Then she went out to the summer kitchen, where she lit a fire in the old cook stove so she could make coffee and breakfast. Once the blocks of wood were burning well, she filled the kettle and set it on to heat. Helena was thankful to have the old summer kitchen to cook in during hot weather. Her house would remain clean and cool.

Leaving the summer kitchen, she admired the sunrise while walking to the chicken barn. What a glorious day it was!

She carried a pail of grain from the barn to the chickens' feeding trough and opened the door to the hen house. The cackling hens rushed out noisily, while the rooster flapped his wings and crowed loudly. As they pecked at the grain, Helena made note of which chickens were the plumpest. She would need at least eight for the big event tomorrow. It was hard to decide. After raising and becoming attached to them, making fried chicken out of them wasn't easy. She gathered eggs from their nests before returning to the house to wake Julius.

Once the milking was done, the eight-gallon cans of strained milk were lifted into the cooling trough. There were several full cans of ice-cold milk from last night's milking. Ben Ens' milk truck would be there on Monday, to pick them all up and take them to the Dairy Pool in Saskatoon. Businesses were not open on Saturdays and Sundays.

Julius walked outside rubbing sleep from his eyes as his dad, brother, and sisters walked toward the house.

"You're late," the girls said, "the cows are still in the barn."

"Open the stanchions and chase the cows out of the barn and into the pasture, Julius," Jacob told him. "And make sure you close the barn door!"

After scrubbing their hands and faces, the family sat down at the table in the house. Helena carried in a pot of porridge from the summer kitchen. Julius soon joined them. The family bowed their heads in a quiet prayer of thanks for their food and dug into their breakfast.

"We have a lot to do today," Helena said as she looked at her family. "You girls do the cleaning while I get the dough ready for buns. Then we need to pick gooseberries and other fruit."

There were groans of protest and disgust at the mention of gooseberries. No one wanted to sit at those thorny bushes and pick gooseberries! Helena shook her head and sighed. Her guests would purchase the berries and it would give Helena a bit of spending money.

"Can we help?" asked Tena and Chris, as they came down stairs and went to the wash basin.

"You can help inside by wiping the cupboard doors and chair rungs and doing the dusting," their mother told them.

"Mama!" a small voice called from the bedroom.

"I'll get her," Lena said, as she rose from her chair and walked out of the kitchen.

Lena put Nettie in the high-chair between her parents and Danny followed carrying a blanket. He climbed onto a chair on the other side of his dad, who ruffled his hair.

After the dishes were done, Helena, Lena, and Annie put on their fruit aprons and filled the large pockets with ripe plums, cherries, and gooseberries. They carefully filled pails with fruit and carried them into the cellar, to keep cool until Monday. There was still fruit left on the trees for the relatives to enjoy at the reunion.

Jacob and the boys raked the yard near the house and by mid-afternoon they had finished. The house was clean and Helena shaped dough into buns to be baked in the summer kitchen stove. A large canner full of water simmered on the back of the stove.

Jacob and the boys went to catch chickens and Helena followed them to choose the ones she thought were best.

They soon had eight headless chickens. Picking them up by the feet and wings, they brought them to the outside of the summer kitchen where big pails stood. Each chicken was dipped in boiling water and held for a few moments so the feathers could come out easily. The children sat down on overturned pails and began plucking the feathers, stuffing the soft breast feathers into a flour sack. These feathers would be dried and used in making pillows. Large wing and tail feathers were discarded. The smell of wet chickens was disgusting.

Helena put more wood in the stove and held the naked chickens over the open fire, turning them from side to side to singe off any hair and feathers missed in the plucking. The summer kitchen filled with the smell of burning feathers and hair.

Annie filled a big basin with cool, soapy water and washed the chickens well, rinsing them in another basin of cold water. Now they were ready to be eviscerated. Helena took a sharp knife and made a slit below the chickens' ribs. Then she slipped her thumbs into the slit and pulled the skin apart to pull out the insides. The smell in the summer kitchen got worse as she deftly pulled out the intestines and dumped them into a slop pail. The heart, liver and gizzards were kept to roast along with the rest of the meat. The feet were stripped of the outer skin and would be roasted as well.

By bedtime the buns were baked and the summer kitchen was clean. Chickens parts were waiting in a covered basin of cold water in the cooling house. The younger children were bathed and in bed and the older ones waited for their turn in the metal bath tub. Kettles of hot water from the summer kitchen were carried back and forth to the house for the baths.

Jacob and Helena relaxed in the living room with Helena's sister Margaret, who had arrived earlier by train. Tomorrow was a big day: Helena's relatives would come for her birthday and enjoy their once-a-year family reunion.

BANMAN BIRTHDAY BASH

CHAPTER 20

Sunday morning dawned with a beautiful deep rose, red and orange eastern sky as the sun rose, then burst forth in a huge fiery orange ball. As it heaved upward, the sky changed to a lighter blue and the sunrise faded from bright to light.

The cows were gathered near the barn, mooing loudly, waiting to be milked. Soon the barn door creaked open as Jacob swung it back to let the cows in. Pushing and jostling each other, they found their own spots and eagerly bent into the manger to munch on the grain Jake poured in for them.

Jacob urged his children to get the milking done quickly so they could to go to church with him. Jake, Julius and their two younger sisters, Tena and Christine, joined their dad to attend the service.

After the church goers left the house, Lena and Annie washed and dried the dishes, then carried big dish pans out to the garden to dig for fresh potatoes and carrots. While the girls and Aunt Margaret peeled mounds of potatoes and scraped and grated the carrots, their mother arranged the chicken pieces in a large roaster. After spreading dried apples, raisins, prunes and apricots around the chicken, she salted and peppered the meat and pushed the heavy roaster into the oven. The fat from the roasted meat along with the fruit cooked with it would be used as gravy for potatoes.

Helena added more wood to the fire and walked out of the summer kitchen, the screen door slamming behind her as the spring pulled it shut. Breathing deeply of the fresh air, she walked to her garden admiring her hedge of cosmos flowers, the tiny white flowers of the low alyssum borders, brightly coloured portulaka, wispy clouds of baby's breath, tall stocks of gladioli and multi-coloured bachelor buttons. She continued on to the cabbage patch where she found several fairly large heads. Helena cut them off at the stem and walked back to the summer kitchen.

"I'll chop the cabbage," Aunt Margaret offered. Helena agreed and went to the house to set the table. Margaret pulled off the outer leaves and examined them for little green worms that often hid between them. She took an enamel dish pan from a shelf, rinsed and dried it, then pulled a slop pail near the table.

The two youngest children wandered into the old kitchen shack and knelt on old chairs to watch her chop the cabbage. As Margaret got close to the core, the children crowded closer.

"Medo tek!" Nettie said, reaching toward the cabbage head.

"No – don't come so close! The knife is sharp," their aunt told her.

"What is a medo tek?" she said to herself while she continued to chop. Finally she was done and filled the enamel bowl with the chopped cabbage. The children watched silently.

Margaret held the slop pail up close to the edge of the table and swiped all the extra leaves and cores into the pail. The children's faces crumbled and they began to cry. Puzzled, their aunt tried to comfort them but they would have none of it. Annie and Lena turned from their work to see what was wrong.

Margaret asked "What on earth is a 'medo tek'?

The girls laughed, "They wanted the 'meddle schtek' – the middle piece – the core of the cabbage head. They love to munch on that." Margaret was relieved to have the mystery solved! Next time she would know what to do.

Soon the potatoes were boiling in the big pot on the stove. The cabbage was chopped, mixed with diced apples, grated carrots, sugar and cream. Annie carried the bowls of coleslaw to the cooling house, while Lena washed the summer kitchen table and utensils. On Annie's return to the summer kitchen, she picked up the slop pail of peelings, carrying them to the pig pen where the grateful animals pushed their noses into the trough, munching noisily.

"When you're done cleaning up girls, fill those large bun pans with knackzote (sunflower seeds), salt them a bit and set them on the back of the stove. When the chicken is done we'll roast the seeds in the oven," their mother told them as she popped in to check on the food.

Helena went back to the house, leading Danny and Nettie. She thought it would be a long day for them and a nap would help, so she lay on her bed to keep them company until they fell asleep. It was a relief to lie down for a little while but she got up quietly once they were asleep and closed the bedroom door softly before she resumed setting the table in the kitchen.

The house door slammed and she heard, "MOM!" as Tena and Christine returned from Sunday school. Helena put her finger to her lips as the girls ran into the kitchen. She hurried to the summer kitchen as the girls followed.

Helena opened the oven door and checked the chicken. It was well done and smelled delicious. She pricked the potatoes and found them soft. Adding more wood to the cook stove, she quickly filled several kettles with water to heat for coffee.

Lena with jar on her way to the summer kitchen. Relatives cars in background.

The rest of the Banman clan would soon arrive. Helena, Margaret and the girls quickly changed their clothes, and hurried to finish setting chairs and benches around the table in the house for the first group of relatives that would eat. On the cupboard countertop in the house stood the big 'bahk kom' (dough tub), filled with buns. The girls put bowls of buns on the table along with sugar cubes. Lena went down to the cellar and brought up a few jars of pickles.

Jake carried an old wash tub to the melon patch, calling Julius to help. They tapped watermelons with their knuckles to see if they sounded hollow – that meant they were ripe. If the muskmelons were yellow in color and had a musky odour, they pulled them off the vines as well. The boys each picked up one side of the tub and carried it to the cooling house where they floated the melons in the cold water trough. As they left, they heard the "Oooga, Oooga," sound of car horns as a stream of cars came down the long driveway.

The cousins were here! Tena and Christine ran eagerly to the road in excitement. Helen, Beth, Gertie, Christine, Katie... there they all were, jumping out of the cars and hurrying toward them with

In this photo: cousins Elizabeth Peters, Beth Braun, Christine Buhler, Tena and Christine Friesen

big smiles on their faces.

Jacob shook his brothers-in-law's hands while Helena hugged her sisters and brothers. The older cousins along with Helena's youngest sisters Eva and Margaret gathered around Jake, Lena, Annie and Julius.

Helena's sister Anna Buhler led Maria who was almost three years old. Sister Katherina Klassen followed with two and a half year old Agnes.

Another sister, Elizabeth Braun, walked toward the house with Anne who was almost two and a half, while sister-in-law Anne Banman tried to catch up with two year old Jimmy who ran ahead of her.

Another car arrived on the scene and Helena's brother Peter's wife, Mary, got out of the car with two year old Julia and baby Lawrence. Soon two more sisters, Agnes Neufeld and Susanna Peters, arrived with their families. Susanna's children climbed out of the car and joined their cousins, while Agnes and Susanna walked toward the house carrying one year old Mary Neufeld and one year old Alvin Peters.

After the aunts and uncles assembled around the table, they all bowed in silent prayer to thank God for the food and enjoyed the meal, along with conversation and laughter.

The younger children played outside in the garden, picking plums, gooseberries, cherries, raspberries and currants while the older folk ate. The children followed their noses to the house from time to time, to see if there would be any chicken left. There was lots of food and finally the children sat down to enjoy the meal while the men gathered outside to smoke and discuss the war news and the airport next door. It was Sunday so the planes stood silent. After a while, the men walked through the pasture to take a closer look at the planes lined up near the hangar.

Back in the summer kitchen, there was laughter and chatter as the older cousins and the youngest aunts busily washed and dried dishes.

One of them looked out of the window and mentioned the little two year old girl cousins with their mothers in Helena's flower garden.

Cousins Marie Buhler, Nettie Friesen, Julie Banman, Nettie Klassen, Mary Neufeld, and Anne Braun (old barn in background)

"We should get a picture of them!" Aunt Eva suggested.

The little girls' mothers soon rounded them up among the cosmos flowers to pose for their picture.

Tena and Christine, along with cousins their ages, spent time sitting on the wide cement sides of the cattle trough, talking. Cousin Katie got up and walked around on the trough walls, gazing down at the water which mirrored the fluffy clouds and sunlight from the sky above. A breeze moved the water, causing ripples in the reflections. Lost in the moment, Katie suddenly lost her balance. With a gasp and a short scream, she landed in the trough with a splash and jumped up sputtering, completely drenched. The cousins stared for a moment and then doubled over with laughter.

"It's not funny!" Katie said, embarrassed. Some of the girls ran to get Katie's mother from the garden.

"Katie fell into the cattle trough!" Her mother and Aunt Helena hurried to the water trough.

"Tena, take Katie to your bedroom and give her some of your clothes to wear," Helena said.

"But she's smaller than I am!" protested Katie. Humiliated, she followed her cousin into the house and attempted to sneak unnoticed past the twenty aunts and uncles and around thirty-two cousins milling around the house and yard. Upstairs, Tena handed her a towel and the biggest dress she had. It was very tight-fitting, but Katie followed her cousin back down the stairs and outside. She took her own clothes out to the line to dry and hoped no one would notice. elen Hlena

Katie and Tena turned toward the garden to join the others on the stone-pile among the trees and took turns on the swing. After an hour or so, they checked on the clothes on the clothes line. They were dry. Gratefully, Katie rushed back into the house to change.

Helena's youngest sisters: Margaret & Eva

Later in the afternoon, the tub of watermelon and muskmelon was brought out to the veranda and everyone enjoyed slices of melon, along with roasted sunflower seeds.

Helena's younger sister Eva finally remarked, "I am so full of melons, I need a cork to keep it all down!" As her sister Margaret and young nieces and nephews chuckled at her remark, she walked into the kitchen and came out eating a bun. The size of the 'cork' brought more laughter.

The big day was over too soon. Arms waving and horns honking, the relatives made their way down the driveway. The Friesen family waved and watched until the dust of the last car disappeared. Jacob turned toward the house to change clothes and reminded the children, "Its milking time."

PURCHASING 80 ACRES

CHAPTER 21

That fall was busy at the Jacob W. Friesen farm. The old barn became more unusable and unsafe. It needed to come down and they would need help. Jacob called several of his young Janzen step-brothers from Blumenheim and two of his Regier nephews from Warman. They, along with Jake and Julius, would tear it down.

Starting on the roof, Jacob nailed two-by four boards to make a ladder to the top and the boys helped pry the old wooden shingles off, tossing them over the edge. The lean-to had been removed earlier to be used for a chicken barn.

Over and over, Julius filled the wheel barrow with shingles and dumped them near the wood pile. The siding boards would later be sawed into stove-size pieces and be used for winter fuel.

It took several weeks to demolish the barn. The days were hot and tiring, but the evenings were filled with music. Between the Janzen boys, Regier boys and the oldest Friesen children, the music of guitars, mandolin, banjo, violin and autoharp filled the air in the early evenings. Some of their favourite songs were "Turkey in the Straw", "When it's Moonlight on the River Colorado" and other cowboy songs.

As fall became winter, preparations were made for the family Christmas celebration. With all of the family home, they discussed the situation they were in after losing half of the land they farmed to the airport. Now that they had only 80 acres of land to farm it would be a challenge to feed 10 dairy cows, four horses and several colts, pigs and chickens as well as a large family. How could one run a farm properly on such a small plot of land?

"What are we going to do, Dad?" Julius asked.

"Well, when I'm done with construction at the airport I hope to get a job as a carpenter in Saskatoon," Jacob replied.

"What will happen if Mr. Driedger sells these 80 acres as well?" Lena asked. "We wouldn't have a place to live. Maybe you should try to buy the land."

As the discussion continued, all agreed it would be wise to purchase the land they were farming and that Jacob should contact Abram Driedger and the bank about that possibility.

Abram agreed and Jacob sent a letter to the National Trust Company about his desire to buy the 80 acres. He received a reply in the mail a few days later. It suggested that he come to the city to make an application for a loan to purchase the land. Jacob took the train to Saskatoon to meet the bankers and was granted a loan of $750.00.

"We need to give them $150.00," Jacob told his family after returning from the city, "and they will allow me to make payments on the remaining $600.00. I thought I might sell two of our horses to make the down payment."

"In August, when the Banman clan was here, Uncle Dave Buhler was interested in those two dark brown horses – maybe he would want them now," Julius offered.

"But those are two of the young horses and they're beautiful!" Annie protested.

"Well, they are also very strong and would be more valuable than our old Babe and Topsy," Jake said.

Julius holding horses, Jacob with Danny and Nettie. Note Jacob's Bennett wagon with rubber tires.

As Jacob and the boys left to feed the animals, Lena sat at the table with her mother and sisters.

"If Uncle Dave buys the horses, how will you make the rest of the payments?" Lena asked.

"We could use the cheques we get for shipping cream," her mother replied.

"If you can save all the cream cheques and if I give you some of my pay cheque," Lena said, "we can make the payments. Now that I'm working in Osler I won't have to mail it." It was a good plan and they decided to go ahead. Helena hoped one day to have the farm paid for. What a relief that would be!

Jacob contacted his brother-in-law, David Buhler, at his farm near Aberdeen and the men agreed on the sale. Jacob and Helena took the caboose and travelled across the river ice road with Babe and Topsy pulling the sleigh and the two brown horses tied at the back. It was hard to give up the horses Jacob had raised and trained from colts, but now they had the down payment they needed. It would still be difficult to run a dairy farm and feed a family of ten on 80 acres, but at least they were assured of a place to live.

LOVE THY NEIGHBOUR

CHAPTER 22

Almost everyone in the area was poor due to the long years of drought in the province of Saskatchewan. Although Jacob and Helena's family didn't have everything the few more well-to-do families had, there were others in the farming community who had much less. There were times when Jacob hired men to work for him simply because they were in desperate need. Potatoes and other vegetables from the cellar, along with a little smoked meat and cash paid for their work.

One such hired man was Dietrich Fehr, a neighbour who worked for Jacob off and on. Dietrich, his wife, and eight of their nine children lived in a drafty run-down house on a small rocky sliver of tree-less land, a few miles east Osler.

Jacob was often concerned about them since aside from their garden area, the land surrounding the Fehr's few buildings was too full of stones to be cultivated or seeded. As with much of the area east of Osler, the hot wind of many years of drought had blown away much of the top soil and it seemed that no matter how many stones were picked from the land, more were exposed. Because of these conditions, Mr. Fehr and his oldest children worked for other farmers and in the city. The oldest two boys, Abe and Isaac, often herded cows for Jacob. The children contributed as much as they could to their parents and younger siblings. It was what Jacob's own children did as well. So with little land and little income, the

Fehr family east of Osler continued to be in need. Then disaster struck.

In the dark of the early morning on January 2nd, 1941, Jacob was on his way to the house for a kettle of hot water to thaw the windmill pump when he heard something. Looking eastward toward the airport, he saw two figures running across his pasture, their hurried steps crunching on the snow. As they crossed the snow bank covering the barbed wire fence, he saw it was young Abe and Isaac Fehr. With chests heaving and breath coming in gasps, they stopped in front of Jacob.

"What's wrong?" Jacob asked as he saw the expressions on their faces.

"Our dad had an accident, he's hurt," Isaac answered.

"How bad is it?" Jacob inquired.

"He couldn't use his right leg and arm and he talked funny. Then he fell into the cellar," Abe filled in.

"I'll get my team hitched up right away. You go in and warm up until I'm ready to go," Jacob told him. "Jake," he called to his son coming out of the barn, "go get some straw to put on our sleigh floor. We have to go to Fehrs' house. Dietrich is hurt. We might need to get him to a hospital."

The Fehr boys hurried to the house where Helena met them at the porch door and heard their story. She gave them each a cup of hot coffee and watched as they paced back and forth from the warm stove to the window, waiting for Jacob. The other Friesen children watched in concern.

Soon Jacob entered the house and requested warm blankets. Helena turned from the stove and hurried to the bedroom, calling Annie.

"Annie, get an extra quilt from upstairs and bring it down," she said as she pulled out another from the downstairs bedroom. As the blankets were piled in his arms, Jacob suggested they might be gone a while.

"If we can, we'll try to get him on the morning train to the city and to a hospital. Jake can take us to the station." Then he motioned to Abe and Isaac who abruptly set their cups on the table and hurried out the door without a goodbye. They all hopped on the sleigh and Jacob urged his team ahead. Helena watched as the horses trotted briskly down the snowy driveway.

At the Fehr home Jacob found Dietrich alive, but unresponsive. They lifted him out of the cellar and laid him on the floor. Looking around at the family, Jacob said, "There is still time to get him to the Osler train station. He needs to be in a hospital, so we'll take him there now."

Osler train station – Osler Historical Museum photo

"I'll go with him too," Abe said and Jacob nodded. They wrapped Dietrich in blankets, carried him to the sleigh and laid him on the bed of straw. Jacob snapped the reins. The horses leaned into the harnesses and briskly trotted the two miles to the station. Jake helped his dad and Abe carry Dietrich to the train and then turned the horses toward home.

Steam Train – Osler Historical Museum photo

Helena met her son at the door with a concerned expression.

As they sat around the table for the noon meal, Jake filled them in on the situation.

It was the day after New Years and they had been celebrating the holiday with their special New Year's fritters. Now, as they occasionally grabbed another fritter to munch on while they did inside chores, their thoughts were not on celebrating – instead they thought of that man in the hospital.

Helena looked at the clock after supper and turned to Jake. "It's almost time for the evening train. You'd better get the team hitched up."

Jake turned to his brother, "Julius, come give me a hand hitching up the team." The boys left the house and soon Jake was on his way, while Julius prepared to milk the cows along with Annie and Lena.

Later in the evening, Jake brought his dad home. When they walked into the house, Helena noticed the serious expressions on their faces.

"We took Abe home first," Jake said, "That's why we're a bit late."

"So what happened?" Helena asked in concern.

"Mr. Fehr died at the hospital this afternoon. He had a stroke." Jacob answered. There was shock on the faces of his family. Helena was silent for a moment and then said, "I want to go down there to see Mrs. Fehr. Whatever will she do now?"

"Yes, we should go. We'll go right after we've had supper," Jacob agreed. "The Fehr family all know now - Abe phoned his oldest sister, Mary, when we were in Saskatoon."

After supper Helena opened the trap door to the cellar in the living room and went down to pack some vegetables and canned meat for the Fehrs. Going down those steps gave her a strange feeling. How awful for Mr. Fehr to have fallen down his.

Jacob hitched the team to the cutter and Helena joined him, carrying warm blankets. Jake followed with a pail of vegetables and a dishpan with jars of meat wrapped in towels. He set them on the floor of the cutter as his parents wrapped blankets around themselves. With a snap of the reins, the horses started off down the dark snowy road.

Entering the Fehr home, they observed the quiet grief stricken faces of the children. They spoke to the older children about funeral plans and Helena asked about their mother.

"She's in the bedroom. She's sick," eleven year old Helen answered. Helena rose and walked to the bedroom, following Helen. She found Mrs. Mary Fehr sitting on the bed, looking very ill and grief stricken. They discussed a few details about having a funeral and Mrs. Fehr's concern that the children did not have good Sunday clothes to wear to the funeral.

Back in the kitchen, Helena instructed the children how to prepare the food they had brought. Then, bidding the family goodbye, they returned to their sleigh for the ride home.

It was much darker outside now and the stars were bright in the night sky. In the north, the beginnings of a northern light show sent flickering waves of colour across the dark expanse. It was a refreshingly beautiful sight amid such a sad situation.

"We need to do something more to help," Helena said as they drove. "That poor mother hardly spoke and just sat on the bed looking very depressed. She's been sick for such a long time and there are all those children to look after. What will they do now?"

"I'll call Reverend Pauls about a funeral," Jacob said. "The family will need help to get ready for that." After a pause he added, "Dietrich was not a very tall man; I told Abe I'd make a casket."

"All of the children and Mrs. Fehr need something nice to wear for the funeral." Helena commented, "Mary and the girls don't really have good Sunday dresses. The boys' shirts and pants looked worn too."

They sat in silence listening to the creaking of sleigh runners and jingling harnesses and thought of ways to help. The family would need more food, of course, and many in the area would be willing to bring meals, Helena was sure. She spoke up, "I wonder if I could sew an outfit for each of the children before the funeral."

Jacob turned toward her, "That is a lot of sewing in a very short time. This is Thursday and the funeral will probably be early next week."

Pulling into the yard, Jacob brought the horses to a halt beside the barn and proceeded to unhitch them while Helena walked toward the house.

The children sat at the table eating night lunch and looked up as she entered the kitchen. After hanging up her coat and reaching for a cup of hot coffee, Helena sat down with them. The questions came quickly.

"How are they? When will the funeral be?" the children asked. Jacob joined them and a discussion soon arose as to how the grieving family could be helped.

"Well, I've offered to make a casket for Mr. Fehr," Jacob said. "I'll have to see what they have available at the lumber yard."

"I would like to sew new outfits for all of them," Helena said, "but there are eight children and the mother to sew for."

"How about having other ladies bring their sewing machines over here? With several ladies sewing, you could get a lot done," Annie suggested. That sounded like a good idea and Helena decided to make some phone calls.

Jacob called Reverend Pauls about the situation and plans were set in motion for a funeral for the following Monday. Many phone calls between Helena and other church ladies that same evening brought them to the conclusion that they would get together at the Friesen home on Saturday, two days before the funeral, and sew an outfit for each child.

Helena and Jacob travelled back to the little farm the next morning to discuss the funeral details and to tell them of the planned sewing bee. Helena looked around at the children and wrote down their ages and approximate sizes. She looked at their shoes and had each of them stand on a piece of cardboard to trace around their bare feet, just in case she could find used shoes that would fit.

Helena phoned the ladies who were willing to sew, and the ages and approximate sizes of the children were discussed. The women decided to bring the patterns they had for their own children and modify them as needed. Material would be donated. Socks for the boys and stockings for the mother and girls would be bought at the local store. If anyone had shoes their children had outgrown, they could bring them.

(Treadle machine – Osler Museum)

Very early on the morning of the sewing day, vehicles began arriving on the Friesen yard. It was still dark outside as men and women carried treadle sewing machines into the Friesen living room and kitchen. Mrs. Katherine Peters, Mrs. Maria Buhler, Mrs. Maria Neudorf, and Mrs. Justina Kruger put their coats on Helena & Jacob's bed and sat down in the kitchen with cups of hot coffee to discuss how to organize the sewing bee.

Each lady pulled out the fabric they had brought and looked at the sizes Helena had written down. They decided which children each lady would sew for and the house was filled with their chatter as they cut patterns on fabric on the kitchen table. Soon the whirring sound of treadle machines was heard as outfits were made for each child and the mother: underwear, slips and dresses, shirts and pants.

Jacob's team pulled the big sleigh to the Monarch Lumber Yard to purchase the lumber to build the casket. Once home, he carried it to the shop behind the horse stall in the barn and then went to the house to call some neighbours willing to prepare Mr. Fehr's body for the funeral. At the barn he measured and sawed the boards the right length and began nailing them into place.

While Jacob hammered and the women sewed, Lena and Annie prepared a big dinner of canned chicken, potatoes and mashed turnips for everyone. They ate in shifts because they couldn't all fit at the table at once.

As the sewing bee wound down, the ladies admired each other's work as they looked at the warm underwear, slips and pretty long sleeved dresses for Mrs. Fehr and girls, and blue flannel shirts and denim pants for the younger boys. It was late and the ladies left for home to prepare for Sunday.

Jacob lined the casket with white material and brought it to the Fehr farm. Dietrich's body was laid into it and the closed casket put in a shed until Monday.

Because of the shortage of water and the hard-to-heat Fehr house, the grieving wife and her daughters were brought to the Friesen home on the morning of the funeral. The boys of the family were helped at another home.

The Fehr's oldest daughter, Mary, who was married and lived in the city, came to help. A round metal bathtub was placed near the kitchen stove and surrounded with sheets hung on chairs for privacy. As each child was bathed, they were dressed in their brand new outfits.

At the funeral that afternoon, the family followed the casket to the front of the church. The children's faces were sombre and tears ran down their cheeks, but their heads were held high as they walked to the front and sat down in the pews. Helena's eyes filled with tears as she saw them walk in. She glanced around at some of the women who had helped sew for the family and caught their eyes. They all dabbed at tears, but smiled slightly and nodded at her. How thankful she was for the way the community had come together. Wasn't this what God commanded? "Love thy neighbour as thyself".

(Names of this family have been used with permission)

Note: Jacob Friesen and other men in the area persuaded a bachelor in Osler to give up the place he was renting. He reluctantly agreed and moved elsewhere. Mary Fehr and her children moved from their drafty farmhouse to this house in Osler where they lived for some time.

Some years later it was discovered that Mrs. Fehr had diabetes. That was the cause of her many years of illness. Helena met her on a city street later and was amazed and thankful at the change in her. She looked strong and happy!

CONSCRIPTION

CHAPTER 23

On April 27, 1942, the Government held a Canada-wide vote for Army conscription. Quebec was against it, however the rest of the Provinces voted in favour. Even though the Prime Minister had wanted to avoid conscription, as the war dragged on there were not enough volunteers for the armed forces. Conscription would not happen immediately, but citizens could be drafted if the need arose.

It was against what Jacob and Helena and many others in the Osler community believed. To live in peace was a motto most Mennonites lived by. Regardless of their beliefs, local young men would have to enlist if they qualified. If they refused on the grounds of being Conscientious Objectors, they would be sent to work camps. Young Jake travelled by train to Regina, along with many others, to go through numerous medical tests to see if he was accepted. Helena and Jacob were relieved their son Jake did not pass his physical. His eye-sight was not good enough for him to go.

There were friends and family members who also had to take tests and some of them passed. Jacob's step-brother, Ike Janzen, entered the air force. Several of young Jake's friends from church were conscripted, but ended up serving in Alternative Service in the forest industry. One friend died in the war. Cousins Henry and Isbrand Regier served in the army.

Helena's own brother Julius became an air force electrician and her sister Eva worked in a munitions factory in Alberta. There were many goodbyes said in those years as some went to war and some were sent to camps to work for the country.

Meanwhile, there were bright spots that brought joy and relief to the family. The Osler Church held baptism classes that spring and on May 31st 1942, Lena was baptised and became a member of the church.

Since his work at the airport was finished, Jacob applied for a construction job in Saskatoon and was hired. With the impossibility of making a living on the few remaining acres, he was thankful for the opportunity. He was creative and enjoyed working with wood; this was a job that appealed to him. It meant getting up very early in the morning and walking to the highway where he got a ride with another farmer, Mr. John Driedger.

Helena's flower garden, with old summer kitchen top right.

While Jacob worked in the city, Helena made sure all the barn chores were done. There was also the large garden that constantly needed weeding.
This year the rains came! The crops were beautiful and the garden had never looked so lush. Helena loved walking through the rows of large healthy plants, vines heavy with peas and beans, and bountifully laden fruit trees. Then there was her flower garden – it had been years since there were so many flowers.

"Girls," she called to Tena and Christine one day, "come pull weeds in the pea patch rows. Be careful not to pull up the plants. Julius, the potato plants need to be hilled and if you see any potato bugs, pick them off and put them in this old tin can. You can pour oil on them later."

"Where's Annie?" asked Julius.

"I'm over here, picking gooseberries." she replied. "Do you want to switch with me?"

"Not likely," Julius answered, as he grabbed a hoe and the tin can and walked off to the huge patch. With a sigh he decided not to look at the whole field at once. That would be discouraging, but if his mind concentrated on the story he was writing it wouldn't seem so boring. His younger sisters followed, grumbling to each other. Weeding was just no fun at all! Besides that, the sun was hot – it made them sweaty and irritable.

Helena at her gooseberry bushes. Nettie behind her.

Helena joined Annie at the gooseberry bush row and sat

down on a stool with a pail. The berries needed to be picked and cleaned for her customers. A number of women in the area liked to make gooseberry jam and moos (fruit soup). After a while she stood, held the pail about two feet above a big empty dish pan and poured the berries into it. The wind blew away the leaves among the berries. After pouring them back and forth several times, the berries were free of leaves and small stems. Since she wanted to finish, she sent Annie to the summer kitchen to start supper.

Tired of weeding, the younger girls noticed Julius was at the far end of the potato patch with his back to them. Annie was on her way to the summer kitchen and their mother was winnowing gooseberries.

"Let's cool off in the trees for a while," suggested Christine. The girls got up from their knees and walked into the shade of the trees to sit on the stone pile. It was cooler there. After a few minutes Christine decided to sit on the swing. The light breeze caused by its motion made her cooler. Tena gazed up at the big branches swaying above her and decided to climb the tree. It was easy to climb and soon she was far above her sister on the swing. Suddenly her foot slipped and she began to fall. She tried to grab branches as she fell, but couldn't stop. She landed on the stones below and groaned as she held her knee.

"Are you hurt?' Christine asked anxiously.

"Yes, but don't you dare tell mama!" Tena told her. They were supposed to be weeding. After a few minutes, Tena got to her feet, winced at the pain in her knee and walked back to the pea patch. They saw their mother carrying two pails of berries to the summer kitchen.

As supper and chores drew near, Lena walked through the gate on her way home from work in Osler. The children in the garden saw Mr. Driedger's car stop at the highway and their dad get out of the car. Helena glanced at the driveway on her way to the summer kitchen and saw Jacob walking toward home.

"Danny, Nettie," she called to the youngest two playing in the veranda, "Papa is coming home."

Danny ran down the long driveway with Nettie following as fast as her legs could take her. As they neared their father, his face broke out in a grin and he grasped their hands as they continued toward the house.

Jacob was tired and hot. He walked into the living room and lay down on his stomach on the cool linoleum floor, resting his head on his arms. As soon as the little ones saw him down on the floor, they were on top of him, sitting on his back and legs. As tired as he was, Jacob enjoyed their attention. It was good to be home after a hard long day at work, to sit down for supper with his family, and hear about the activities of the day.

PESKY PIGS!

CHAPTER 24

That fall, Osler area farmers were thankful for a bumper crop. It was also time for neighbourhood pig butchering. Neighbours helped neighbours with their big day so Helena and Jacob had lots of help butchering their two pigs. The hams and sausage were hung in the smoke-house and bacon slabs were cured with salt and smoked. Head cheese, lard and cracklings were stored in syrup pails in the cellar.

The pig barn and pen were now empty and Jacob wanted to buy a couple of young piglets to fatten up over winter and butcher the next fall. A local farmer called one day with piglets for sale, so Jacob agreed to buy them. He would pick them up the next day. In the meantime there were repairs to be made to the pig barn and pen, and fresh straw brought in for their bedding.

As Jacob worked, he heard a car coming down the driveway. The children spilled out of the house to see who was visiting. As the vehicle came to a halt near the house, the dog barked furiously and jumped at the car door as the driver began to open it. There was a look of hesitation as he saw the barking, snarling animal.

"Smokey! Down!" yelled Julius as he hurried to the car and scolded the dog. She slunk away growling. The man opened the door completely as he got out.

"Thank you. That dog doesn't seem to like me much." he said.

"Oh she wouldn't really hurt you, she just doesn't know you," Julius answered.

"Well, is your dad or your mom around? I'm with the Western Producer News Paper and I wonder if your family would be interested in buying a subscription."

"I don't know, but here comes dad now," Julius answered.

Jacob walked toward them, taking a break from the repairs at the pig pen. He pulled off his barn gloves and shook hands with the stranger who introduced himself and explained why he was there.

"My name is Allen Kordinsky," he said, "I'm in the area selling Western Producer News subscriptions." (*fictional name)*

"We already have several newspapers," Jacob told him, "but since it's nearly supper time, why don't you join us for the meal and we'll talk about it?"

As they walked into the house, Helena glanced at the door and told Annie to get another place setting out of the cupboard. Lena carried bowls of food from the stove to the table. As Annie set the extra spot at the table, the News Agent introduced himself to Helena. He was invited to sit down to eat with the family for a simple supper of fried sausage, cooked carrots and noodles with cream gravy and fried onions.

"We've bought a Western Producer paper at the store several times," Jacob told the Agent as the conversation turned toward the purpose of his visit.

"Well, with the war on and with so many other world news stories, it might be a good idea to get a subscription and have the paper in your mail box every week," Allen said. "Besides, it looks like you have quite a few young people who might be interested in the Young Cooperatives Column."

"I read those stories and poems every time we get the paper," Julius said. "I really enjoy them. I wish I could send in some of my writings."

"That would be great! What kind of things do you write?" Allen asked.

"I write poetry and stories too, about everyday life and what I see and think," Julius replied.

"Sounds like you have a writer on your hands," Allen said, with a smile at Jacob.

"Would you like some more noodles or sausage?'" Lena asked the guest as she passed the bowls around.

"No thank you, it was very good. But I would like another glass of milk, please," he said.

"We have lots of that," Jacob said as he passed the milk jug to the man. "Now as to the subscription – how much does it cost?"

"It's $1.00 per year," Allen said, "$1.50 for two years and $2.00 for three years."

"Money is a bit scarce right now," Jacob said after a slight pause. "Maybe we'll subscribe at a later date."

The children were disappointed. It was an interesting paper.

"All right, here's what I'll do. You have given me a great meal, you've been very friendly and if you will also give me a quart of milk to take home, you can have a one year subscription!" Allen told them.

Jake grinned at his dad, "Well, dad? It can't get much better than that, can it?"

Jacob looked at his son and thought it over for a moment. "Well, that is very generous of you Mr. Kordinsky so yes, we'll take a subscription to the Western Producer!"

The subscription application was filled out, and as the salesman turned to leave, he looked at Julius and said, "Get busy writing and become a member of the Young Co-operators Julius!" With that he left, walked toward his car, gave the dog a pat as he walked by, got in and drove away.

Julius, Jake and their sisters watched him leave, already looking forward to finding their first Producer in the mailbox. As Julius went up to his bedroom to leaf through all the things he had written he wondered – which article would be his first submission?

The next day Jacob brought home two squealing piglets that darted around in the wagon box. He backed the wagon up to the gate of the pen and as the children gathered round to see the animals, he opened the gate to the pen and then lifted the tail-gate of the wagon.

Julius and his dad got on the wagon and grabbed the panicked pigs as they tried to get away. They lifted them down and carried them to the small pig barn inside the pen and closed the door.

"Let them get used to their barn before they run in the pen," Jacob explained. "You can let them out later this afternoon."

At milking time that evening, Helena looked after her chickens; then went to check on the pigs. They were not in their pen or their barn and she discovered a small hole under the fence where the pigs managed to squeeze through. She looked around everywhere, but couldn't find them. After a while, she gave up and walked into the cow barn where Julius and the others were milking.

"The pigs got out of the pen," she told her children. "After milking you can look for them."

Julius was the first one done. He carried his full pail to the strainer and then looked around the yard. He was soon joined by his younger sisters. They discovered one piglet in the field behind the barn and another in the neighbour's field.

After two hours of chasing and with the help of Jake who had returned home with a load of hay, they finally succeeded. The pen was repaired with long boards and lots of nails. They were determined not to go through that again. The pigs were definitely prisoners now.

As the family gathered around the table that evening, Julius examined the bruises on his elbows and felt the welt on his face where he had landed heavily when trying to capture one of the pigs.

"I know exactly what I will write about for my first article for the Young Co-operative Column," he stated, "those pesky pigs!"

Each week the family read the Western Producer news paper. It was filled with news from around the world and of course the children all enjoyed reading the Young Co-operators page and the cartoons. They eagerly searched the column to see if Julius' first story was published. One day they were rewarded.

"Julius!" Annie called as she and her younger sisters scanned the page. "Look, here's your story!" They crowded around as Julius read his first published story aloud.

"The Pigs Get Out" – published October 1st, 1942:
Dear Co-ops,
The other day we bought two young pigs, put them in the pen and all went well until milking time. Mom came into the barn and then told me to help catch the pigs. They had climbed out of the pen.

The pigs separated and ran over hill and dale, with me hot on their heels. Soon I lost the black and white one in some tall grass. My younger sisters saw it in the feed yard again.

At this point my brother came home with a load of hay. He told them to stop running after it and let it get though the fence. They stopped and then they lost it. I was strolling along in the pasture hoping to see it again, when nature came to my aid. One of the heifers was looking at a certain spot and pretty soon both calves were chasing the pig. It ran into the neighbour's oat field and my brother caught it with a nicely timed leap.

In the meantime Sis had been chasing the other pig across country. Now she came back empty-handed. We set out for it again and pretty soon a grunt and a squeal told us our dog had found it.

We ran after it and soon it, too, got into the neighbour's oat field. Running about three feet behind it, I made a spectacular power-dive and since I missed the target by a few inches I skidded along on my nose for several yards. I got up and tried again. I was just about to dive again when the pig ran through a fence. In order that I would not take the fence along with me, I threw myself on the ground, making a perfect one point landing on some stones. Then, after chasing it a great distance, we cornered it against the neighbour's hedge. We

caught it there and carried it home. All this took two hours, and needless to say, I was grateful when I got into bed.
A Co-op, "Hawkeye" (14), Osler, Sask.

"That's very good!" Lena said, after hearing the story. Everyone complimented him on his writing. Julius was thrilled and decided to send more stories to the paper as soon as he could.

STOOKING

CHAPTER 25

After the horse-drawn binder finished cutting and binding all the oats, it was time to stook the oat sheaves by standing them up in a tee pee formation with the grain stalks at the top. If the weather turned to rain, the water ran off and didn't damage the grain.

The Friesen children gathered in the field after school and faced with dismay the long rows of sheaves. With a sigh, Annie reached for the binder twine on two sheaves and began. The oat straw scratched her bare arms and legs, but that was part of stooking. She ignored it and kept going. (*binder twine; the string that held the sheaf together)*

Julius half-heartedly picked up two, swung them under his arms and with a single left motion he stood the sheaves on end, leaning one against other. A gust of wind blew by and they fell over. He was disgusted, but tried again and got four placed. They fell over again.

Helena walked over to the field and began stooking as well. She glanced over at her son as he grabbed the fallen sheaves and started over, muttering to himself.

"Vaut es lous? (What's wrong), Julius?" she asked.

"They won't stand up," he said glumly. Annie was working near him in the next row and offered to help.

"No, I'll do it," he replied. Finally he completed a stook and surveyed it with satisfaction. Now he had a rhythm in his method and kept going until he finished his entire row. Annie was done hers and was on to the next when mother called to Julius.

"Julius, it's time to get the cows for milking," she said. He gladly left the field, climbed through the barbed wire fence to the cow pasture and walked over to the far end where he rounded them up and headed them toward the barn. He glanced up as a plane landed on the airport side of the fence. At the barn, he opened the door and let the cows in, hurrying to close their stanchions.

After supper, Jacob walked over to survey the stooked field the children had worked on while he was in Saskatoon at his job. He stopped at Julius' row and called to the children in the yard.

"Who stooked this row?" he asked. Julius noticed where his dad was standing and walked over.

"I did, why, what's wrong?" he asked his father.

"I'm sorry son, but rain won't run off the peaks you have on those stooks. You'll have to do them all over again." As Julius groaned in frustration, Jacob offered to help him get it right.

Lena walked out to give Julius a hand too and just before bed time, he was finished. He washed the dust off and after some night lunch, lay down thinking that bed had never felt so good.

There were several more days of stooking and pitching hay and Julius wished his big brother was home to help.

Meanwhile, Jake was away working on the fall harvest for a family farm at Glamis, Saskatchewan. There were long days on the combine leaving him with many hours alone with his thoughts. He wondered about home and how the harvest was going there. Would his younger siblings be able to get it all done while their father worked in the city?

As he thought about his siblings, he couldn't help but realize there was something different about his sisters. He remembered those special meetings in his home church. The more he thought about it, the more convinced he became that he needed to make some changes in his own life.

Alone in the bunk-house in the evening, he pulled out his Bible and began to read and understand what he needed to do. As the sun went down and light faded, he knelt beside his bed and quietly reached out to God.

COURTING AUNT MARGARET

CHAPTER 26

Helena's youngest sister Margaret found work as a maid at the J.B. and Margaret Boldt farm west of Osler. While there, she met the hired man. His name was Henry Klassen and he soon showed an interest in the pretty young woman serving their meals.

As they became more acquainted, Margaret suggested that they visit her sister Helena and family on their days off. Saturday evenings and Sundays were free for them and as it was just a short drive, some Saturday evenings they drove out for a visit.

Travelling in a Model T Coup was not comfortable in the winter and they were cold when they arrived. It was also possible that the car might not start in that kind of weather. Henry had a solution. He had a pail with him into which he drained the water from the radiator and kept it warm in the kitchen while they visited. With warm water in the radiator, the car started easily when they turned the crank at the front of the engine.

On bitterly cold days though, the engine oil was so thick that the car wouldn't start at all. When visiting on days like that, Henry filled his pail with glowing coals from Helena's cook stove and built a small fire under the car's oil pan until it warmed up. One day, the light coating of oil on the sides of the engine caught fire. Henry and Jacob worked frantically, scooping up pails of snow and throwing them on the flames until it was out.

Spring travel was less complicated and the family looked forward to Saturday evenings and seeing that Model T Ford Coup with the top down come bouncing, horn blaring, down the rutted driveway.

Back of a Model T Coup with the top down

Margaret laughed as the Friesen family streamed out of the house to meet them. Henry Klassen, her fiancé by that time, grinned, a cigarette dangling between his lips. After they came to a stop, Henry lifted out a special treat – a basket of concord grapes for the whole family to enjoy while they visited.

The Friesen family teasingly sang a special song for their aunt, only changing a few words;

"Margie, Margie, give me your answer do!
I'm half crazy all for the love of you.
It won't be a stylish marriage,
For I can't afford a carriage.
But you'll look sweet upon the seat
Of a Model T build for two!"

Wedding Photo of Margaret and Henry Klassen

That July 18, 1943 there was much excitement as Aunt Margaret and Henry Klassen were married. Henry got a job at the gas station west of Osler on Highway 12 and the visits continued to be a weekend highlight for the Friesens for quite some time.

QUARANTINED

CHAPTER 27

Six year old Daniel wasn't himself. He was hot and feverish and didn't want to eat anything. Helena tried coaxing him to drink milk and water. She made butta zup (potato soup with butter added). This was usually made for anyone in the family who was sick, but he wouldn't eat that either.

By the evening of the first day of his illness, his fever rose and Helena noticed his rapid breathing. It was the custom in those days to cover people to sweat out the fever. Danny thrashed about at night throwing off the covers that felt like a huge heavy thing holding him down. His dreams were frightening and he kept trying to run away, but his legs wouldn't move.

"Danny, Danny." He heard his mama's far away voice and shivered as he felt a cool wet cloth wiping his face. He opened his eyes and felt his mother lift him as she pressed a glass of water to his lips. He drank it down – he was so thirsty.

When morning dawned, Helena took one look at his face, lifted his night shirt and saw the red speckled skin. Ah, that explained it! Danny had caught the measles from his sisters who had just recovered. Nettie woke up and after climbing out of bed, walked over to her brother.

"No, Nita! (*low German for Nettie*) Don't go near him. He has the measles and is very sick. I don't want you to catch the measles," her mother told her. Helena firmly led the little girl away to the kitchen for breakfast.

At breakfast that morning the family was all cautioned to stay away from Danny. By noon that day his fever went down, but since he was also coughing Helena pulled the old crib close to the stove in the living room and after lifting Danny into the crib she put a pot of boiling water underneath it and covered the crib with a big sheet to steam him. Now it was a matter of trying to get him to eat.

Jacob went to the store and bought two of Danny's favourite things: an orange crush soda pop and a real orange. Danny was coaxed to try them, but they just didn't taste the way he thought they should so he only drank a little of the pop and ate just a few orange sections.

Four year old Nettie watched all the attention her brother was getting and asked for some of the pop and orange slices.

"No," her papa told her. "They are for Danny, because he's sick." Nettie was disappointed and a little jealous.

The next few days Danny was miserable. He itched all over and still didn't feel like eating. Helena was able to coax him with a little soup and water. Jacob again tried to cheer up his little son with special treats.

Nettie wished she was sick too so that she could get those special treats. When her mother's back was turned one afternoon, Nettie quietly slipped into the living room where her brother was quarantined, to touch him and play with him.

"Nita! Get away from him. I told you not to do that or you'll get sick!" her mother said as she spotted the little girl's disobedience.

"But I want to be sick too," Nettie said.

"Oh no, you don't!" her mama told her.

A few days later Nettie was fussy and weepy. She cried about everything. Nothing was going right and the food at mealtime tasted terrible. She refused to eat.

"What is wrong with her?" her older sisters complained. "She's such a cry baby today!"

"She's just plain spoiled rotten," her older brother commented. This made Nettie sob even more. She didn't know what was wrong – she just felt awful.

Helena felt the little girl's forehead and sighed. "Well, looks like she'll get her wish. I think by morning she will have a speckled body, just like Danny did."

That night, Nettie's fevered mind dreamed about huge monsters floating around her. At the foot of her bed sat an old woman and Nettie was so afraid of her she covered her head with the blankets. When she woke in the morning she looked at the foot of the bed and saw her mother's big lily plant. It was shaped like an old woman with long hair.

"Mama?" she called.

Helena got up to check on her and found the fever was down, but there in the bed sat a little girl with bright red speckles all over her body.

Over the next few days she was coaxed to eat orange sections and to drink the orange crush pop her father bought for her, but nothing tasted right. The itching and coughing were no fun either. She wished she had stayed away from her brother like Mama said.

CAUGHT IN A SNARE

CHAPTER 28

Julius sat in his desk near the window in school, listening to the familiar drone of airplanes landing at the aerodrome next to the family farm. A small plane passed low over the school.

The sky was cloudy and snow began to fall. As the plane disappeared from view, he thought about soldiers and pilots who trained and went to war; some returned and some did not. Four years of watching planes circle overhead and land close to the farm. Four years of war news in the papers and on radio.

He sighed and watched dreamily as heavy snowflakes floated slowly down to the ground. He watched in fascination as the flakes chased each other in the light gust of wind. Julius rose up to take a closer look at the school yard and noticed the grass was nearly covered with a thin white blanket of snow.

The breeze turned stronger and soon the snow swirled as the wind howled around the school building. Julius couldn't see the trees at the other end of the school yard. He heard the scratching of his friends' pens as they did their work, but couldn't seem to get his mind away from the war and changing weather on the other side of the window.

"Julius," his teacher said, unaware of his student's deep thoughts, "Keep your mind on your lessons and leave the scenery to itself!"

Red-faced, Julius turned his attention back to his history book. By the time school was dismissed the wind had stopped completely. A vast expanse of white rolled endlessly eastward to meet with the horizon. Ridges of hard snow ran along the road and the last few clouds disappeared revealing a clear blue sky.

While Julius trudged home with his siblings, a rabbit, still brown, hopped across his path. As his sisters chatted about their day at school, Julius had an idea. Some time ago, his dad and several cousins had taught him and his brother Jake how to make rabbit snares. It might be a good way to make some money if he could sell the pelts.

Arriving at home he dropped his books on the table, grabbed a cookie and went back outside. He noticed several more planes land at the airport as he wandered through the pasture and climbed the steps over the fence to get a closer look. As he neared the side of the hangar, he saw something white hanging over the edge of the airport garbage bin. It was a discarded flight suit. As one of the workers passed by, Julius asked for permission to take the suit home.

"Sure, if you want it. Otherwise this stuff will all be burned."

Julius walked home with the suit as his strategy began to take shape. He neared the house and heard Annie calling. "Hey! You didn't do your chores. The pigs still need feeding!"

Although he was eager to show his parents his flight suit, it would have to wait. At supper he told them about his find.

"What do you want with an old discarded flight suit?" Annie asked.

"I'm going to set snares in the pasture and catch rabbits. This suit will be like camouflage because it's white like the snow and I'll be warmer because it's big enough to fit over my parka."

"What will you do with the rabbits you catch?" asked Tena.

"I'll sell the fur," he answered

Jacob held out his coffee cup, suggesting as usual, "Half full", and Lena got up to fill it. He took a sip of it and remarked, "This coffee is really weak – did you just hang a coffee bean in front of the kettle?"

Lena and Annie glared at him as he grinned. He turned to Julius and suggested he find out how to prepare the pelt before he snared the rabbits. There would be a lot of work involved.

"I'll see if there is something about that in the books at the school library, or maybe the teacher has some information," Julius said.

"I don't think you should trap them," Christine argued. "They're such pretty animals. Leave them alone."

"I know they're pretty," he replied. "That's why ladies like wearing things made from rabbit fur! If I can make a little money, why shouldn't I?"

Julius found some articles about tanning hides and what kind of wire to use for the snares. And so the trapping experience began. He trudged out in all kinds of weather, wearing the white flight suit and setting traps. Some days, he caught a rabbit or two. He worked hard to prepare it for sale. It was a lot of work for a fourteen year old boy. He skinned the animals, stretched the skin on a board and scraped it. Then it was dried and softened.

One day Christine and a friend heard a squeaking noise on their way home from school and found a rabbit in a snare. They released it and Christine told the story at supper. Julius was upset with her.

"What did you do that for?" he asked in disgust, "that's one less rabbit for me."

"We felt sorry for the poor thing!" Christine answered.

Some days Julius was surprised to find a fox or a weasel. He wondered if those pelts would bring in more than a rabbit pelt.

One day in spring his trapping experience came abruptly to an end. He found a skunk in the snare. It was not dead and he was suddenly overcome with the horrible fumes, but knew he couldn't leave it alive and suffering. The skunk was not impressed with the snare or Julius' sympathetic attempt to end its life. He hurried home, fully doused with the overpowering odour and feeling sick.

Helena met him as she carried in a basket of eggs from the hen house and knew what her son had come in contact with.

"Take off that suit and bury it!" she told him. "I'm not washing that! As for you, I'll bring out the round bath tub and you can bathe in the barn lean-to – with the window open."

Julius hurriedly shed the suit and grabbed a spade to bury it out in the back yard. He found the tub in the lean-to, ready with warm water, soap, a big towel and clean clothes.

For some time he had no desire to do any more trapping. Instead, as summer neared, Julius thought of building bird houses. Working with nature to help her creatures seemed much more satisfying than trapping them. But for now, he was more interested in making model airplanes. He ordered several aircraft kits and set to work. Some of these little planes were made of thin balsam wood and some of paper. A rubber band could make them fly, but the planes were fragile so he handled them carefully.

With the airfield next door to the farm, it was interesting to see different types of planes coming and going. Julius built several models; A Messerschmidt Me-109, an Airacobra and a Westland Lysander. By the month's end he had a fleet of six different planes. Unfortunately, five year old brother Danny took a keen interest as well and picked up three of the fragile machines, not understanding how easily they would break. After the disappointment passed, Julius created more planes.

Since he hadn't composed anything for the Western Producer for a while, Julius again picked up his pencil. There was a lot to write about, including his trapping experience, but as he waited for a story to form in his mind he heard the sound of planes flying overhead. He was reminded again that the world was still trapped in the snare of a war that seemed to have no end. As his thoughts centered on the world situation, he began to write;

HOPE

The sun sets on a world of strife, and Death, War's silent wife
Clad in black garb, stalks through the night
Diminishing to a spark the light of human happiness and good.

Seducing men to ways of hate, Red War, Death's mumbling mate
Screams and rumbles over the field while Hate peers over a rusty shield of lies and horrors yet to come.

Yet somehow I have a notion that after Hate's commotion,
Comes a time of clear blue skies when Peace shall lighten all our eyes and happiness again shall reign.
(published in the Western Producer in August of 1943)

INVENTION OF THE HAYDOZER

CHAPTER 29

With Jacob's work in the city, much of the haying was up to his son Jake. He hitched two horses to the mower and drove out to the airport landing field to cut the long grass growing on runways and on the land surrounding it.

Horse-drawn mower

Getting the horses lined up for the first cutting, he pushed the lever down so the blades were close to the ground, then snapped the reins on the horses' backs as he urged them forward. They set out and he kept them going at a slow steady pace so the grass would be cut evenly.

Jake sat forward on the metal seat, holding the reins, his arms resting on his knees. The hard seat had no back to it and he would need to change position several times to ease his aching body as he bounced over the field.

He glanced down often to make sure he wasn't hitting stones or other obstacles in the path of the blades. Sharpening dull blades took a lot of time away from harvesting.

It was sweaty and dirty work with the hot sun and wind blowing dust around the mower and yet it was pleasant to be outside alone with his thoughts.

His team was easily visible to the pilots that took off and landed on the runways near him because a red flag was attached to the mower. It was a requirement for all farmers who cut hay on airport land.

As the sun rose higher in the sky, Jake stopped the team, knowing it must be almost dinner time. The noon meal was the big meal of the day and he was hungry. He unhitched the horses, leading them back to the farm and the water trough, where he paused to let them drink deeply before tying the reins to a fence post. He walked to the summer kitchen to wash up for the noon meal.

It was cool in the house, a relief from the hot sun. As the family sat down to enjoy potato salad, cold ham and carrot salad, Jake turned to Julius.

"I've got quite a bit of hay cut now, so how about coming out with the other team of horses to rake the hay? We could get a lot done before dad gets home from work."

"Sure, I guess I could," Julius answered, "if I can leave off working in the garden." He glanced at his mother who nodded. "How about switching teams though? I'll use Babe and Topsy and you can use the other team," he suggested. The older dapple grey horses were evenly matched and easier for him to manage. The boys hitched Babe and Topsy to the rake and Jake led the other team back to the airfield as Julius followed.

Julius lined up his team over the first swath of hay and urged them forward, lowering the rake tines to the ground. It wasn't long before he needed to raise the lever to lift the rake, leaving a small hay mound lying behind him. Dropping the tines again he kept going. By supper time there were many small mounds in neat rows on the field and as Jacob walked home from the highway he saw his sons off in the distance driving their teams and machinery home. He decided to walk across the field toward the boys to see how much hay was cut and raked.

"You've done a lot today," Jacob commented as he looked over the field.

Supper time included the topic of haying and how much they might get for the winter.

"Hopefully we can get the hay home before it rains," Helena said. So far the weather was good.

"I've been thinking about how to push those little mounds together so we don't have to stop the horses as often when pitching the hay on to the hay rack," Jacob replied. "It would hurry things up a bit."

"Do you have an idea in mind, Dad?" Annie asked.

"Yes I have, and I plan to build something on Saturday to see how it works. I'll draw it on paper first to decide on the design."

The following Saturday morning Jacob took a quick trip to the Monarch Lumber Company in Osler for the boards, poles and planks he would need. And so was "born" Jacob's Four Horse Reversible Hay Dozer.

By late afternoon the dozer was assembled and he was eager to try it after supper and chores were done. One team was hitched to the left evener and another team to the right. Jacob grasped the reins firmly in his hands and glanced at Jake to see if he was ready with the other team. With a nod at Jake and a "Giddyup!" they both snapped their reins and urged the horses forward while they walked behind the dozer.

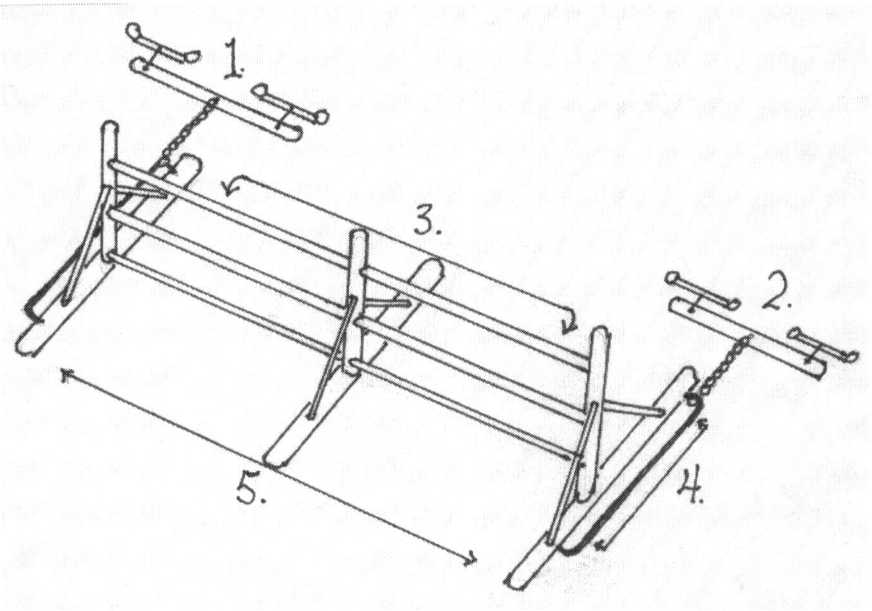

***1&2**: Two-horse eveners.* ***3**: Back stop to hold hay swath.*
4**: Elongated "u" bar(2 directional pull). Evener chains slide to opposite end to pull away from hay stack.* ***5**: Dozer base built on three smooth poles as runners. Outer poles 12 feet apart.* ***Drawing by Jake Friesen

Julius followed, eager to see the contraption work. Jacob watched as the hay piled up against the back-stop. When the hay stack became too high, they turned the horses to the side and walked them to the other end of the dozer, as the large ring on the evener chains slid along the bar and to the other end.

There the horses were driven back a bit and turned around, taking the dozer ahead of the big stack and on to move more little stacks into larger ones.

Helena and several of the younger children walked through the pasture to watch. Her husband was full of ideas and his invention worked beautifully.

Once all the hay was pulled into bigger piles, the teams were hitched to hay racks. The boys and older girls followed the racks, pitched the hay onto it with pitchforks and took it home to the feed lot.

As the stack on the feed lot grew, Danny and Nettie climbed up and slid down the piled hay. They laughed and tumbled around as their father and siblings tossed hay on top of them. Finally Jacob called them to stop. The hay needed to be neatly stacked so rain would not soak through. No more sliding or making holes in the stack – but it had been fun for a while.

READING AND 'RITING AND 'RITHMETIC

Chapter 30

Finally the day had come! Danny was starting school, which he had looked forward to for a long time. With his older siblings reading books at home, it hadn't taken long for him to learn. Danny followed the words and pictures intently as Lena read in the evening from Hurlbut's Stories of the Bible. He was so engrossed in the stories that he leaned in close to follow. She had to remind him to move his head so she could see the page. Danny was often found with his nose buried in a book his siblings had brought home from school.

"What's in my lunch kit?" Danny asked, looking forward to carrying a lunch to school. It would be like going to a picnic, he thought.

"You've got a boiled egg, buttered bread and two cookies," Tena answered, "just like the rest of us."

He ran ahead of his siblings as they walked toward the town. This was an exciting day. He heard the familiar sound of an airplane coming in for a landing at the Aerodrome and craned his neck to find it. It was frustrating to hear it but not be able to see it, especially if his siblings could see the plane and tried to point it out. As he neared the school, he hung back just a bit to let the others catch up and walked into the school with them.

There was a big Union Jack flag on the wall above the blackboard with blue, red and white criss-crossed stripes on it. The whole class stood at attention, facing the flag as they sang God Save the King and Canada's national anthem.

After singing, and praying the Lord's Prayer, the grade one students were given a "High Roads to Reading Book 1". It had colourful pictures and was a story about a boy named Jerry, a girl named Jane, a black dog named Laddie and a white cat named Snow.

As other children quietly paged through the book and looked at the pictures, Danny read to himself, "The little toy cat and the little toy horse were in the wagon." These were easy words. Reading was easy.

After a few weeks at school, the teacher had Danny read aloud to him from the grade one reader. Danny read the story of the Lost Cat: "One day Jerry said, 'Good-bye, Labbie! I am going to school now..."

"No, Danny," the teacher corrected him, "the dog's name is Laddie – you've got your b and d mixed up. Try that again."

Danny continued reading, but inwardly he thought Labbie was a much better name for a dog.

The teacher was impressed with his abilities and chose him as an example to older children who struggled with reading. Danny was asked to read a simple story they had trouble with and he did well.

One day a boy from a higher grade came over to Danny's desk during class time and showed him some words on a piece of paper.

"What does that word say, Danny?" the boy whispered.

"That's easy!" Danny replied, "it's two words, Nova and Scott-ia."

Later, as the teacher taught that boy's class, Danny overheard him use the word, 'Scoshia', and realized he didn't know all the words. His pride went down a bit but he enjoyed learning so many new things in class. Outside at recess it was hard to see the baseball thrown toward him when it was his turn to bat. He enjoyed soccer more as the ball was bigger and easy to see.

Nearly a year later, a nurse came to school to test all the children's eyes. When she tested Danny, Tena and Christine, the nurse wrote out a note for their parents. These children definitely needed glasses.

Glasses for three children would be expensive but Jacob was concerned they'd be able to see clearly. Although he and Helena had perfect eyesight, his father and some of his family did not. It was obvious some of his children had inherited the problem.

With a sigh, Jacob put down the note and said, "I'll make an appointment with Dr. Sharf in Saskatoon and we'll get your eyes tested." He called the doctor's office and arranged to bring the children to the city the next week.

"Will we go on the train?" asked Danny.

"Yes we will," his father answered. Danny looked forward to his first train ride. He was excited.

The day finally arrived and Jacob drove to the station with Tena, Christine and Danny. The big steam train arrived with the usual loud chugging noises and squealing of metal brakes on the metal wheels. Jacob led Danny to the train steps and lifted him onto the first step while the girls followed.

Danny pressed his face against the window and watched the countryside speed by in a blur of fall colours as they passed yellow fields and trees filled with orange, brown and yellow hues.
As the train arrived in the city, he was surprised by all the houses close to the train tracks. They all looked the same to him. They were wartime houses – all built according to the same plan. Some were painted different colors, but all had doors and windows in the same places.

The train came to a halt at the Saskatoon station and they made their way through it. Danny hung on to his dad's hand as they walked through the big building and out to the street. It was noisy and busy.

"Where is the doctor's office?" Tena asked.

"Right across the street, at the Canada Building," Jacob answered. "Be careful when you walk across the street. Don't hurry, it's more dangerous to run because then the drivers might not be able to stop in time." He placed his hand in front of them to stop the children as a street car hurried past the corner they stood on. It rode on tracks and a long antennae on its' roof reached up and touched
wires that hung above the street.

Photograph ID : LH 5033 by Leonard A. Hillyard. Permission courtesy of Saskatoon Public Library, Local History Room

They crossed the street and walked up to the door of the Canada building. Danny was surprised to see that the doors were made of glass. None of the doors at home looked like that. He turned back to look at the busy street on the other side of the glass and bumped his head on it. Tena looked up as they entered and squinted at a sign. "Doctor Sharf: Eye, Ear, Nose and Throat, Second floor" she read out loud.

They walked up a set of stairs. Jacob opened the door to the doctor's office and told the children to sit down in the waiting area while he went to the receptionist's desk to let her know they were there for an appointment.

There was a fan whirring fast in the corner to provide a bit of coolness to the room. Danny heard it and walked over to check it out. As he bent down close to it, people in the waiting room gasped and put their hands over their mouths, afraid this boy would get cut. The fan had no protection over the metal blades. Tena reached out and grabbed Danny away from it.

The doctor examined all three children and spent a few minutes alone with Jacob, informing him of the condition of his children's eyes. Jacob looked over the selection of frames and saw several different kinds of wire frames. He picked out three pair that had wire all around the lens instead of just at the top. They were also less expensive. The glasses would arrive in the mail within a few weeks.

They had time on their hands before the evening train took them back to Osler so they went down the street to explore several stores, stopping in at Kresgies Five and Dime where Jacob bought each of the children a small trinket, and then on to Eatons. Danny enjoyed looking in store windows as they walked down the sidewalks. There were mannequins in many windows, dressed up in the latest fashions. There was so much to see. At lunch time they were hungry and Jacob took them down First Avenue to the Commerce Cafe for vegetable soup and cheese sandwiches.

On the way home, Danny fell asleep as the train swayed and the wheels clattered on the tracks.

The children waited eagerly for their glasses to arrive in the mail. Finally, the parcel arrived. As they were each handed their pair, their faces showed surprise and delight at how the world really looked. They gazed around the kitchen and out the window and then walked around outside slowly because things looked closer through their glasses. It took a bit of balancing to get the feel of it.

"Look at the trees!" Christine exclaimed. "There are so many little leaves and they're all separate!" Trees had always seemed like one big green or colourful cloud around the branches.

Tena gazed around in silent appreciation at the brilliant colours everywhere and Danny walked around in wonder as he spotted small things he had missed before. He crouched down on the ground as he spotted a beetle scurrying close to his shoes. There were more beetles and ants – so many tiny creatures. A yellow airplane flew over the farm and Danny looked up, able to see it clearly.

Helena and Jacob watched, partly in sadness that the children hadn't seen these things before, but also with joy as the delight showed in their faces.

"I'll be able to see the baseball when we play at recess!" announced Danny. All three children enjoyed school much more with better eyesight. As Danny progressed with reading and arithmetic, Tena and Christine enjoyed literature and music appreciation classes the most. At bedtime, Danny could now rest his head against Lena's shoulder for the Bible stories and pictures he enjoyed so much.

SEWING LESSONS

CHAPTER 31

Lena was eager to earn a higher wage than the Osler Post Office could pay so she went to the city to apply at the Veterans Hospital. While waiting for word about the job, she heard about sewing lessons offered by a lady from her church. She decided to check into it.

Mrs. J.J. Neudorf, who lived out on a farm near the village of Schlorrendarp, invited young women to her home to spend a few weeks learning to sew.

Lena, along with other friends, travelled to the farm and stayed two weeks, going home for weekends. Mrs. Neudorf patiently taught them how to measure and make their own paper pattern pieces. Next they used those patterns to create dresses, blouses, skirts and underwear out of fabric they brought.

L to R: Lena, Mrs. Neudorf, and sewing classmates.

Along with the lessons, this gracious lady cooked three meals a day for the girls and only charged them $35.00 each. The girls all enjoyed their time at the Neudorf home and returned home as capable seamstresses.

Helena was impressed with Lena's abilities when she made identical dresses for Tena and Christine, as well as outfits for others in the family.

Meanwhile, Annie enjoyed getting together with girls her own age in their church Junior Ladies Aide where they did embroidery, sewing, and crocheting. It was a great time for visiting and laughter, as they compared their work on tea towels, pillow cases and doilies.

Junior Ladies Aide: Annie is in the back row, third from right. Osler Museum archive photo

The day came when Lena was to begin work in the city and took the train to Saskatoon to work at the VA Hospital. She found a room to rent, and soon enjoyed the work and time spent in the city. On her days off, she returned to the farm and filled the family in on her work.

"So what was work like this past week, Lena?" her siblings questioned her one day.

"I really enjoy working there, bringing meals to the patients. Some of them have lost a leg or an arm because of the war and are having a hard time. I'm glad to help them with their meals," she replied. "I usually get along very well with the matron, but today she was upset with me."

"Why?" asked Christine.

"I was already in the hallway with the meal wagon, when she came to check the dishes on it. She found a cracked cup on the cup tray, picked it up, and threw it as hard as she could down the hallway. Then she glared at me and left!"

"What on earth made her do that?" another sibling asked. "Did you have to clean up the broken glass?"

"I don't know why she did it, but maybe I'm supposed to check for cracked dishes before I serve the men their meals. I didn't know I was supposed to, but I did clean up the glass, because I couldn't just leave the mess there. The matron was friendly again before I left to catch the train."

"She was probably happy you cleaned up her mess!" Julius chuckled.

"Do *you* have a job yet, Annie?" Lena asked.

"I'm planning to go to the Wilkin Hospital in Warman to see if I can get a job there," Annie announced.

"That's a good idea – you would make a good nurse," her mother told her.

"Well, I wouldn't be a nurse, but maybe a nurses' aide. I think I'd like working there," Annie replied.

In a few days, Annie was granted a position at the hospital in Warman. It wasn't easy work and being a compassionate and sensitive person, it was hard for her to see people in pain.

After working with women who gave birth to babies, Annie wasn't sure she ever wanted to be a mother. However, she learned to cope and tried to be an encouragement to the patients there. The family enjoyed more stories around the weekend supper table from both girls in their new jobs.

DO DOLLS GO TO HEAVEN?

CHAPTER 32

It was the week before Christmas and everyone was home! It was a busy time as Helena and her oldest two daughters baked piles of pressed flower-shaped ginger cookies, cream cookies with icing and coconut, and lots of buns and bread. In November they had baked Christmas cakes filled with green and red maraschino cherries, nuts, and candied peel. Now the cakes had aged enough to make them soft and tender.

"Dad, may we go Christmas shopping in Saskatoon?" Tena and Christine begged. They wished to buy a few gifts too, even though they had no money to spend.

"I won't have time to take you," he replied.

"I'll take them," Lena said. "I plan to go on Saturday anyway. They would enjoy seeing all the lights and decorations in the stores."

"All right," Jacob agreed, "but it costs 65 cents per person to get there and back."

"I just got paid so I'll have enough," Lena offered.

The girls were excited and they looked forward to seeing the many Christmas decorations in store windows. But they wished they had their own money to spend on gifts.

The day finally came and Jacob handed Tena and Christine each a 50 cent piece. Their eyes lit up with delight.

"Let Lena take the money in her purse so you don't lose it," their dad told them. They handed the money to Lena who put it in her change purse and then bundled up for the ride to Osler.

Jake took his sisters to the railway station with the horses and cutter. They climbed out of the sleigh and made their way into the station to buy their tickets. Lena decided to pay a one-way fare instead of a return and handed 98 cents to the Station Agent.

Soon they heard the train whistle as it came down the track from Hague to Osler. They hurried out to the platform and stepped back as the train ground to a halt with a loud chugging noise and bursts of steam. The chugging noise slowed down but continued as the conductor climbed down to the platform and walked into the Osler station to hand a delivery list to the station manager. A few parcels were dropped off and some were put on the train.

Soon the conductor was back outside calling, "All aboard?"

Lena and her younger sisters climbed up the steps and walked into their coach car for the 25 mile trip to the city. The chugging noise of the train sped up as the train picked up speed.

The girls found a seat and took off their coats as the conductor walked down the aisle collecting tickets. They wore the floral green dresses Lena had made for them in her sewing classes. The conductor stopped at their seat, reached for the tickets and then looked at the girls with a twinkle in his eyes.

"You must be the "gold-dust" twins," he commented, "you two sure look alike!" (*Gold Dust Twins was a term for people who were closely associated and originally was the name of a washing powder that featured a set of twins on the box)*

Tena and Christine had been mistaken for twins before. Lena turned and smiled at her sisters. They did look a bit alike and the dresses suited them well. Lena enjoyed watching their faces as they saw the winter landscape pass by. The train stopped briefly in Warman where more passengers got on, then continued.

"Button up your coats and put on your scarves and mitts," Lena told them when they arrived in the city after their forty-five minute ride. She made sure they were warm and then put on her own scarf and gloves.

Saskatoon Railway Station: ID – QC-27. Permission courtesy of Saskatoon Public Library, Local History Room.

They stepped down to the platform and then walked to the Station doors. They headed down some wide steps to the basement underneath the Station and then back up to the main floor. The Station had high ceilings and their voices echoed as they talked.

As they stepped out of the station and onto the sidewalk, they met with lots of traffic noise. Car horns honked and street cars clanged as they turned the corner. The cars halted to allow the many pedestrians to cross the street. It seemed everyone was out to finish their shopping.

As the girls walked down the sidewalk toward Kresgie's Five & Dime store they saw the big Bessborough Hotel at the far end of the street through the falling snow and haze of car exhaust.

"Look! There's the Bessborough. It looks like a storybook picture," Christine said. They had seen it before in the few times they had been to the city but it was always an interesting sight.

Kresgies was crowded with people looking for last minute gifts, but the girls enjoyed the crowds and all the shelves filled with clothing, dishes, tools and many other interesting things. After a while they decided to check out the Woolworth store.

By eleven thirty the girls were hungry and Lena took them back to the Kresgie lunch counter where they each had a serving of tomato soup with a cracker.

"Now that we've looked around at prices, let's pick up a few things here," Lena said, "and then we'll go to the big Eatons store and look at all the decorations there."

They walked back to some shelves where they had seen lovely lace handkerchiefs.

"Let's buy Mom a lace hankie," Tena suggested. The cost of the hankie was 25 cents.

"What about a neck tie for Dad?" Christine asked. "That's 25 cents too."

"Why don't you give the gifts together?" Lena asked, "Those two things will cost 50 cents, so you'll have another 50 cents to spend.

After purchasing those items, they walked past a toy shelf where Tena spotted a small spinning top for 10 cents.

"Look at that blue and red-striped top! Danny would love that!" Tena said. She tried spinning it and the colours shimmered together.

"Ok, that's 10 cents, so how much do you have left now?" their big sister asked.

"40 cents!" Christine replied. The girls found a pretty red butterfly hair clip for Nettie which cost 5 cents. Then Lena pointed out a few inexpensive combs.

"They're two for 15 cents." she said, "You could get Jake and Julius each a comb."

Tena counted out what they had left and whispered to Christine, "Get another two for Lena and Annie!" Chris handed the combs to the cashier while Lena pretended not to notice. They had 5 cents left and eyed the penny candy counter, looking at Lena questioningly.

"Go ahead, it's your money," she told them. The girls picked out a small bag of peppermints.

"All right," Lena said as she picked up her own purchases and handed the girls their bags. "Let's take a look at the big Eatons store."

They walked down the snowy street to Eatons. The big revolving doors were a challenge and made the girls giggle as they walked through to the inside. They gazed up at the high patterned ceilings and wide dark woodwork.

"Come on, girls," Lena said. "Let's get into the elevator and check out the second floor."

The girls waited while the elevator came down and stopped to let them in. The metal folding bars of the door were pushed open while the elevator operator announced, "Going up!" The girls got into the elevator and held their breath when it moved up. It made their stomachs tickle. Going down was even more fun.

After looking at ladies and girls clothing styles in dresses and coats, they left by the south door of the store, walked to the end of the street just across from the Bessborough Hotel and stopped to let their eyes travel over the turrets and many windows.
It stood on the bank of the Saskatchewan River and was so big and grand; the girls were in awe of the beautiful building. One could easily let the imagination travel to stories of castles and princesses. Lena let them gaze at the "castle" for a little while and hurried them on.

Photograph ID: A-1762. A Leonard Hillyard Photo permission courtesy of Saskatoon Public Library, Local History Room.

"It's almost time for the train and we should start back," Lena told them.

Walking back down the street toward the railway station, they again passed by the Eatons store. Suddenly Lena stopped at the store window. There were toys and dolls displayed for everyone walking by to see. Somehow she hadn't noticed it before.

"Look at that doll!" she said as she pointed to a lovely Eatons Beauty doll. "I wonder how much it is. Do you think Nettie would like that?"

Christine and Tena stood gazing at the beautiful doll. "She would love it!" the girls agreed.
"I've got to get that for her. Come on, it's getting dark, and the store will close soon. Let's see what she will cost," Lena said, as they hurried back into Eatons.

They quickly found the toy section and looked through the rows of dolls on the shelves until they found her. Lena saw the price. It was $2.75. That was expensive! Should she, or shouldn't she spend that much? She checked her wallet and decided - yes, she had enough and took the doll to the check out. With their arms full of packages and Lena carrying the big box the doll was in, they hurried toward the train Station. It would soon be leaving for Osler and they couldn't miss it.

Eatons Doll 1943 Catalogue.
ID – F229-1-0-148
Used with permission from Sears Canada. Ltd.

Once inside the station they went to find the bathroom before boarding the train. Each stall needed a dime in the slot so the door would open. Lena counted her money – no – she did not have a spare dime, so when a lady walked out of a stall, Lena quickly grabbed the door before it closed.

"All right, let's hurry!" Lena said, as she led the way to the ticket counter. She reached into her purse and counted out the money. That's when she realized she didn't have 98 cents left for their train fare home. She was 15 cents short. It was too late to return the doll and they needed to get home. Embarrassed, she explained her problem to the ticket agent.

"Well," the man at the ticket counter said, "I'll let you go to the train and you can ask the conductor if he will allow you to go."

"Thank you," Lena sighed and hurried the girls down the stairs to the basement and then back up to the outside platform. They walked quickly to their train car and Lena approached the conductor to explain their situation.

"So you bought a doll for your little sister and now you don't have quite enough for the fare for the three of you?" The man paused for a moment and said, "If you promise to meet me at the Osler Station tomorrow morning when the train goes back to the city and give me what you owe me, I'll let you board."

Lena promised and handed him the amount she had left. They hurried up the steps and into the train. She sighed with relief as she sank down on the seat with her sisters and all their packages.

Their father Jacob was there to meet the train and the girls got into the cutter. "Giddyup!" he called to the horses as he snapped the reins. As they drove through the deep snow, Lena explained the ticket situation.

"I'll give you the money to pay back tomorrow," Jacob said. Lena was relieved and enjoyed the ride home as her sisters told their dad about their big shopping day. Next morning Lena bundled up and walked to the train station to pay the conductor. He met her with a grin and wished her a Merry Christmas.

Christmas morning dawned a few days later and the children came down to see what "Santa" had put on the plates they put on the table the night before. Along with a few peanuts and an orange, the younger children received a small glass train car filled with candy and a small unlined notebook and pencil, while older children received socks and handkerchiefs.

After a few quick bites of the treats, the older children trudged out into the snow with their father to attend to the chores. Once the milking was done, the boys gave each cow a pail of water to drink, cleaned the manure out of the barn and spread fresh straw for the animals to lie on.

Helena fed the chickens and Annie gathered the eggs. This morning there were quite a few eggs and Helena was thankful, since she used so many for Christmas baking the week before.

When the chores were done and breakfast cleaned up, the family gathered in the living room before they got ready to go to Church. Jacob read the Christmas story from the German Bible and then the family handed their gifts to each other. Lena brought out the big box for Nettie. Five year old Nettie stood beside the warm pot-bellied stove and looked down at the gift on the floor.

Tena nudged Christine, who fairly bounced on her chair with anticipation. Their eyes shone with excitement as they waited for their little sister's reaction to her gift.

"Open it, Nettie," Lena said. The whole family watched with smiles on their faces. Nettie tore off the wrapping paper and then lifted the lid of the box. She stopped, her eyes widened and her mouth opened in a gasp of delight mixed with tears.

"A doll!" she cried and reached down to pick her up. As she did so, the doll's eyes opened and it cried "mama". Nettie stared at her eyes which had real eyelashes, and at her open mouth with its little red tongue and two little white teeth. She was beautiful. The doll was dressed in a white frilly dimity dress, with red dimity trim and lots of lace. On her head was a matching bonnet, with ruffles and lace. She had a pretty slip and underwear, white socks, and little black button shoes on her feet.

Nettie laid the doll down in her arms and it fell alseep. She lifted her up and the eyes opened and she cried 'mama'. The family watched as the little girl stood transfixed, staring at the doll with a look of wonder on her face. Lena thought of how worried she had been about not having enough money to get herself and her sisters back home on the train. Seeing the delight on her baby-sister's face made it all worth it.

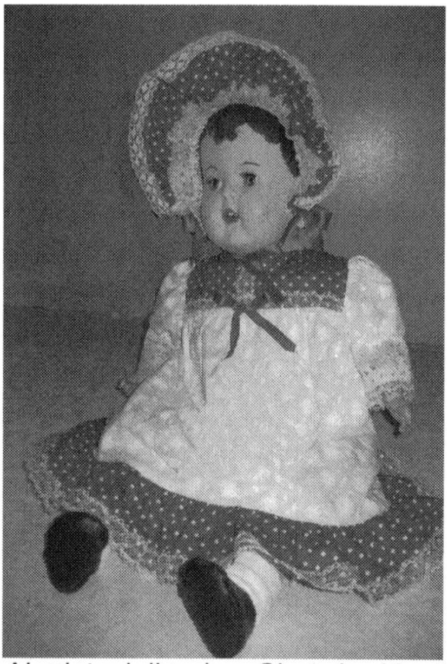

Nettie's doll today. She's had brain surgery, has false teeth & tongue, false eyelashes and two prosthetic arms. Not bad for a 71 year old!

Nettie finally turned toward her family and asked, "May I take this doll to heaven with me?" They smiled and chuckled at her question.

Annie answered, "No, Nettie, you can't take the doll to heaven. Heaven is for people, not for dolls."

Nettie frowned and said, "Then I don't want to go to heaven." This brought a round of laughter from her parents and older siblings.

As she got older, she changed her mind about not wanting to go to heaven, but the doll was a favourite for many years.

WILL THEY SINK?

CHAPTER 33

In spring Helena ordered baby chicks from the hatchery as she usually did, but a few weeks later decided to hatch more from her own hens. While feeding her hens she heard several of them "clucking" while they ate instead of the usual "crrrrr-crrrr" sound they made while contentedly eating their grain. That meant they wanted to build a nest and sit on their eggs until the chicks hatched.

If Helena didn't set them on eggs in a chicken run, they would make their own nests away from the barn yard – probably in the hay stacks or bushes. That made them easy prey for foxes, skunks, weasels and crows.

Chicken Run drawing by Nettie Balzer

Jacob helped Helena build a box with four runs a foot high and covered them with chicken wire on top, nailing it to the sides of the boards. At one end of each run was a lid over a straw nest for the hens. An old metal bowl for water was placed in each run.
Helena chose eight eggs and gently arranged them in the straw nest in a chicken run. She caught a clucking hen and placed her with the eggs. The hen soon discovered them and settled over them to keep them warm until they hatched.

Helena also decided to try hatching goose eggs and found a neighbour willing to trade them for cream. The goose eggs were much larger than hen eggs, so she placed only four in one of the nests.

After several days, she had four setting hens on 24 chicken eggs and four goose eggs. She looked forward to the time baby chicks and goslings would appear. It would take 21 days for the chicks and 30 days for the goslings to hatch. Once the babies grew into hens and geese, there would be lots of eggs and meat for the family.

Every day, Helena and the children fed the hens as they sat patiently and quietly, getting up every once in a while to eat and to turn the eggs over with their beaks, then spread their warm feathers and settle over them again.

After fourteen days, Helena decided to check to see how many eggs had survived. She took a bowl of warm water to the chicken run, knelt down at the first nest, lifted the lid and reached under the hen to pull out an egg. Carefully placing it in the warm water, she watched to see if the egg would float and bob on the water, or if it would sink to the bottom of the bowl. If it floated and bobbed, she knew it held a live baby chick, so she quickly put it back under the hen. There were three eggs that sank like stones, so she knew they were rotten and needed to be discarded.

Danny and Nettie loved to watch their mother check the eggs and one day, while playing near the chicken run, they decided to help mama by checking the eggs themselves. Danny hauled up a pail of cold water from the well and they took four eggs from under the hens. They sat down beside the well with their pail and carefully lowered the eggs into the water. Each one of them sank to the bottom. They were disappointed. Just then Helena walked by to check what they were up to. "What are you doing?" she asked them.

"We're checking to see if the eggs float, but they must be rotten because they sank down to the bottom," Nettie said.

"Where did you get the eggs?" their mother asked with a sinking feeling.

"We got them from under the setting hens," Danny answered.

"Oba Nay! (Oh no!) That's cold water! You've killed those baby chicks inside the eggs. Don't ever take eggs from those hens again!" Helena scolded, taking the pail away from them. She was relieved the children had not taken the goose eggs.

Danny and Nettie felt terrible. They thought they were helping their mama, but had only disappointed her.

A week later the baby chicks hatched and they watched 18 fluffy yellow balls scurry after their mothers on spindly legs. The nest with the goose eggs hatched nine days later.

The children enjoyed watching the hens teach their chicks how to scratch the ground and peck for bugs and grain. At any sign of danger the mothers clucked warnings and the chicks scurried to hide under their mother's feathers.

The poor mother hen who hatched goslings was often in a state of panic. Her babies followed her everywhere but didn't peck and scratch, they gobbled the grain. They didn't seem worried about danger, but took shelter under the hen at night to keep warm. When it rained, instead of running for cover, the goslings delightedly headed for the nearest puddles. The frantic hen ran around the puddles, scolding her babies for splashing in that dangerous water. Besides, she was getting wet while the rain ran off her babies' backs.

As Danny and Nettie watched and laughed at the comical sights and sounds of their mother's "bird herd", the cold water sinking of eggs became a distant memory.

REGISTERING FOR FAMILY ALLOWANCE

CHAPTER 34

Since well water was used to water the garden, the fall harvest yielded a lot of potatoes and carrots. However, the fields didn't produce much grain or hay as drought conditions continued. The snows came soon after and the weather was cold and windy.

On a chilly November day, Helena opened the oven door to pull out four big loaves of fresh bread and turned them over on clean tea towels on the cupboard counter top. As she turned back toward the stove, she heard something outside. Six year old Nettie heard it too and ran to the kitchen window to look out. The warmth of the room on the cold window pane caused it to fog up with a thin layer of ice. Nettie scratched the ice off with her fingers to make a clear spot to look through. She spotted a sleigh.

"Mama – there's a lady with children on a sleigh," she said as Helena joined her at the window, moved Nettie aside and peered though the clear spot.

She hurried to the door as the woman and children got off the sleigh. They looked cold.

"Hello! Welcome! Come in," she called as they walked toward the house. Three children followed the woman who carried a baby wrapped in a blanket.

"Hello. My husband slipped on the ice near the barn and hurt his back. He couldn't get up to walk so he crawled to the house. I thought I'd come here to see if Mr. Friesen can help," the lady offered in explanation.

"Here – take off your coats and warm up by the stove. I'll go get Jacob from the barn," Helena said as she quickly added wood to the fire and moved the kettle on to heat. As the family gathered close to the stove, she hurried into her warm coat and left the house. Nettie watched curiously from a safe distance.

Jacob had heard the sound of the sleigh and horses and was on his way to investigate. As he stood near the lady's horses, Helena caught up to him.

"A neighbour's wife is here with her youngest children. Her husband had an accident at their place and is hurt. She needs help," she explained to Jacob and then turned back to the house.

Jacob followed her into the house and asked a few questions. He offered to head out to their farm to see what he could do.

"Why don't you stay here and warm up until I get back," Jacob suggested to the lady and her children huddled close to the stove.

"I'll make some faspa," Helena said as the lady agreed to stay. She set the cups and plates on the table along with homemade butter and turned to the cupboard to cut thick slices of warm fresh bread.

As the family gathered around the table for faspa, Helena took the baby from his mother and sat down in a nearby chair. It wasn't long before she coaxed him to smile. He cooed and gurgled as he reached up toward Helena's face. She giggled at the baby's response and kept him entertained until the mother was done eating.

Soon they heard Jacob's team and sleigh returning. He unhitched the horses, took them to the barn and then walked into the house. As he took off his coat, Helena and the woman turned to him questioningly.

"His back is hurt pretty badly and he won't be able to do his chores for a while. I'm willing to look after your animals, but he should see a chiropractor. I'll take him to see one tomorrow. It shouldn't be too long before he's healed up."

"Dank Schoen (*thank you)*," the lady said. She rose, turned to her children and gave them their coats. "We need to get back home," she told them.

"Wait a moment," Helena said as she walked over to the kitchen cupboard. She reached for a large paper bag from a drawer and slipped a warm loaf of bread into it.

"Here, take this with you. And do you need anything? Could you use some potatoes and carrots? We have lots in our cellar," Helena offered.

"Yes, we could use some vegetables," the mother answered. "Our garden didn't do very well. Thank you so very much!"

Jacob took a pail down to the cellar and came back up with potatoes and carrots and a jar of canned beef. The lady thanked them over and over for their generosity and returned to her horses and sleigh for their drive home.

Jacob washed his hands and sat down at the table. He grinned at Nettie who joined him, then turned to look at Helena near the stove. "Na Hehya (well, dear), how about a couple of slices of that fresh bread?" Jacob suggested. "And make sure they are "Banman" slices – not wood shavings!"

he joked. (This was Jacob's description of thick or too thin slices of bread). Helena chuckled and cut two very thick slices and handed them to him on a clean plate.

After Jacob returned to the barn, Helena sat down to mend a pair of socks and thoughtfully mulled over the condition of that young mother and her family. There were others in the area that had a difficult time making a living during those years of drought and war. It would be nice if more financial help was available for everyone.

A Radio broadcast on March 22, 1945, brought welcome news to many families in Canada who were struggling to make ends meet. The government passed the Family Allowance Act, which would provide a monthly allowance of five to eight dollars for the care, education and training of all children age 16 and under.

Since the average yearly wage of Canadians was only $2000.00 per year and in many cases much less than that, this would be a big help for many citizens of the country.

The Friesen family heard the radio broadcast as they sat at the supper table. Jacob raised his eyebrows and glanced at Helena who had a questioning look on her face. When the News Broadcast ended, Jacob reached over to turn off the radio.

"Does that really mean we'll get money from the government every month?" Helena asked.

"Mom, that's what it sounds like," Julius commented. He had been listening intently as well.

"But it won't be for another year, if I understood what he said," Jacob added.

"How would you register us?" Tena asked. "Do we need birth certificates? Do we have birth certificates?"

"No, we don't have them for all of you," Jacob answered, "and apparently we will need them to qualify for the allowance."

"Lena and Jake were registered in 1940 during the beginning of the war, weren't they?" Julius questioned.

"Yes, they were," Jacob answered.

"But the broadcast said only children 16 and under can receive the payments," added Annie who was home for a few days.

"I guess I'd better stop in Warman sometime soon to get you all registered," said Jacob.

In the war time registration, Jake had been registered as Jacob (his real name) and Lena had been officially listed as Helen instead of Helena. At home they were still called Jake and Lena. It was easier for other people to remember whom they were talking about when the Friesen family was mentioned.

After hearing the new Family Allowance Act announcement, Jacob registered Annie as Anne and had no problem remembering how Julius was to be registered, or Danny – his name was Daniel Peter. However when it came to his three youngest daughters, he forgot what they had been named at birth and instead wrote down what they were called at home.

Tena officially remained Tena on her certificate, although she had been named Katherina; Christine remained Christine, instead of her given name of Justina; Nettie remained Nettie, instead of Agenetha.

Helena looked forward to having a bit more money to spend on material for clothing and school supplies for her family. Because they grew their own food, the family had enough to eat but Helena was thankful to be able to trade food stamps and fresh eggs and cream for things like flour, sugar, coffee and tea, as well as other necessities.

Shoe repair foot; Osler Museum

But there were things they couldn't grow or trade for. She looked at the row of shoes often passed from child to child. Jacob kept shoes repaired by putting new soles on the bottoms and patching holes with leather. His iron "upside down foot" often held a shoe he was working on.

In the meantime, the cold winter kept Helena busy as she knit mittens, sweaters and socks and sewed warm clothing. Old winter coats from a bag of Salvation Army clothes were taken apart, turned inside out so the material looked new again and made into ski pants and parkas.

The children kept the wood box and coal bin filled so the fires would not go out in the stoves. Helena sat knitting zocken (warm wool slippers) near the living room pot-bellied stove and allowed her mind to drift at times to when that first allowance cheque would arrive. How much would it be? What extras would she be able to buy with it? A thankful soft-spoken, "Danke, Gott" (thank you God) escaped her mouth as she twisted the yarn around her finger for the next knit row.

THAT LEFT OVER LAND

CHAPTER 35

As Western Allies began making advances in Europe against Hitler and his armies, fewer aircraft flew over the Friesen farm. The war was winding down and on March 30, 1945 the Osler Aerodrome was closed. Finally, in the beginning of May of that year, Germany surrendered to the Allies and to the Soviet Union.

The war between the United States and Japan was still going on and continued until the month of August, when the United States dropped an atomic bomb over Hiroshima, causing horrific casualties. The Japanese government surrendered on September 2, 1945.

"THE WAR IS OVER!" shouted the newspapers and radio broadcasts. There was rejoicing all over the country and the world. What a feeling of relief! However, disturbing stories of dead and injured soldiers and civilians on both sides of the conflict continued to be reported on the radio and read in news-papers. The crimes Germany committed against Jewish people was unimaginable – so much destruction, so much heartbreak in so many places.

Slowly, the aerodrome hangar at Osler emptied of aircraft. The barracks no longer housed air force pilots or maintenance workers. There were no small yellow planes or larger bombers landing on the runways and things seemed very quiet to the Friesen family.

When everything had been moved out, Jacob became the caretaker of the buildings. Haying on airport property was still allowed for the local farmers.

The younger Friesen children enjoyed going with their father when he looked after the buildings. The long hallways and empty rooms of the barracks were a delightful place to run and to play hide and seek. Their voices echoed as they ran from room to room and the empty hangar seemed huge to the children.

Jacob gazed over the many acres which made up the property and wondered if there was any way for him to regain the land he lost to the airport and perhaps purchase more.

Helena and Jacob held a family discussion about the possibilities of increasing their land. Jacob decided to write to the government to see if the land would become available. He received a reply, but written on the open envelope were the words, "opened by mistake". Someone else had read his letter and it disturbed him.

Around the Osler District, many desired to own more land and the fact that a three-quarter section with buildings stood vacant made it a favourite topic of conversation everywhere. It soon became known that the CCF Government of the day (Co-operative Commonwealth Federation) encouraged farmers to become involved in Co-operative Farming ventures, and abandoned airfields seemed the perfect places to make this happen.

In light of the many years of drought it was thought that farmers banding together might make them more prosperous. However, to those Mennonites who originally came from

Russia, it was a reminder of the collective farms in that communist country.

At the store one day, several farmers voiced their desire to get some of that airport land and the co-op farm idea was discussed among them. It sounded like a good idea to some and others objected.

"What do you think, Jacob? Would you be interested in being part of a co-op farm?"

"I probably would be. How many others are interested?" Jacob asked. He had been thinking along those lines for a while.

"There are quite a few who want to talk about it. Maybe we should meet for discussion." So it was decided and a meeting was set up for September 25th 1945 at the Friesen home.

Julius was very interested in co-operative ideas ever since becoming a member of the Young Co-operatives in the Western Producer at the age of fourteen. Most of his published articles contained the words, "We Co-operate." He decided to look into the Co-op Farming idea and became excited about it.

"Dad, this could work, if other people in the area are interested in it too," he told his dad after a discussion about the possibilities with the family.

"We'll see what happens at the meeting," Jacob answered.

Neighbours called other neighbours and four interested farmers arrived at the Friesen Home to discuss the situation. Present were George Hein, Henry Martens, P.J.W. Peters, J.M. Dyck and Jacob.

Since Jacob had taken night classes and was good at writing, he wrote a letter to Mr. Alex Turner of the Department of Co-operation, telling him that a group of farmers in the Osler area were interested in taking over the Aerodrome for a Co-operative Dairy Farm.

Mr. Turner replied that the Aerodrome had not been declared a surplus by the Department of Reconstruction and was not yet available.

While they waited for the aerodrome to become available they made plans to proceed, inviting a member of the Mackintosh Co-op Farm near Hepburn for information. He explained how to best organize and work such a farm and contacted Mr. Alex Turner about the eagerness of the farmers to begin.

Over the next months, discussions were held at several meetings to decide what they should do. The cost of the Airport, once available, would be approximately $5,500.00 and establishing a Dairy Branch would cost approximately $10,000.00. The amount was overwhelming.

If they went ahead with the farm, it would have to be a chartered organization. The cost of the charter was $4.50. Each farmer donated 50 cents to the Hepburn Co-op member who agreed to apply for them.

There were many things to be considered, including what each farmer would donate in cows and equipment, as well as the problem of there being no well on airport land. Cooling milk might have to be done at the Friesen farm, since it was the nearest and the Friesens had a windmill well.

At the January 21st 1946 meeting, seven hopeful farmers, three of the wives, as well as Julius and Jake Friesen, met with Mr. Harold E. Chapman of Regina who told them the success of the farm depended on the farmers working together and they should carefully consider the potential problems and responsibilities before jumping in too deeply.

In the discussion, young Jake boldly asked, "Since none of you are very successful farmers, what makes you think you can make this work?"

Another man agreed, saying, "Yes – let's hear more of that and discuss it." Still another farmer suggested holding a meeting to see how deeply they should plunge into this venture. In the meantime, Jacob was chosen as chairman and Julius as secretary.

The day after the meeting, the phone rang and Julius answered. It was one of the men who had been at the meeting. He was concerned about the possibility of the Co-op Farm not working out. Since the man spoke in Low German, Julius attempted to answer him that way.

"Yo, Vann daut opp latst aules voat derchfaul jeven," Julius began. The man on the other end of the phone line went silent. What Julius meant to say was, "If by chance there is a possibility that everything falls through." Unfortunately it was not what he said.

Helena paused abruptly from punching down the dough in her dough tub, and gasped in surprise. "Na oba, Julius! (Oh Julius!)," and then burst out giggling. Julius looked baffled and when the conversation ended, he hung up.

"What's so funny?" he asked. By this time his sisters were also laughing.

"You said," Annie giggled again, "you meant to say "derch faulen" which means to "fall through" but you said "derchfaul jeven" which means to have diarrhoea!"

"Well I can't help it if some of the words sound so much alike!" Julius protested, turning red with embarrassment. He raked his hands through his hair and commented, "Oh boy – I wonder what that man thinks."

"He's probably laughing too," said Helena. Julius' mistake was hard to live down. Whenever he made plans, his siblings reminded him to be careful - his plans might "fall through".

As the farmers continued to meet, they decided that 22 cows should be pooled in order to start the dairy with each farmer donating three cows. However, a lot of work would need to be done to the hangar to make it a cow barn. The airport transmitter shack could be used to store grain.

The meetings became filled with many uncertainties and disagreements between the farmers. Jacob decided to let someone else be in charge. He resigned as chairman at the end of January 1946. He would help in any way he could and continued, along with Julius, to send minutes and reports in to the government.

Borrowing money was daunting for all of the farmers, but eventually a man in Saskatoon was willing to loan the money needed once the airport became available.

In March of 1946 Jacob travelled to Regina by train to meet with Mr. Chapman and on March 22nd, **The Turner Co-operative Association Ltd**. was incorporated, with bylaws drawn up and plans for the farmers to become shareholders in the association – eight shares being worth $25.00. They discussed leasing the land until it was available for sale and each farmer took out a personal loan in order to pay back the money borrowed.

At the April meeting, the men could not agree on how to distribute the hay they would be cutting in the haying season.

Any extra hay that would not be needed for the co-op farm could be divided among the share holders.

"How are we going to divide it up?" one farmer asked. "Why should two members of one family each get a share of hay, when others only have one member in the group?"

"We're all equal share holders, so it should be divided equally," another reminded the group.

"I don't think so, that means that Jacob and his son Julius each get a share of the hay and the same with P.J.W. Peters and his son, while the rest of us only get one share each," another one said.

"It doesn't really matter to me," Julius replied, "I don't need the hay." He glanced at his dad, realizing too late that his dad could use extra hay.

"I move we push out the single farmers and that will leave more for the rest of us," the first farmer moved.

"I second that," another said.

"All in favour?" asked the chairman. The voter and seconder were the only hands raised and the vote was defeated. The two men looked at each other and both decided to bow out of the association. Another member withdrew the following morning. That left only five people in the group, but more were interested and the farmers continued to plan for the future.

NEW BEGINNINGS

CHAPTER 36

Jacob continued working at carpentry in the city while the Co-op Farm plans were being discussed. Work was begun on the airport property and he helped with the venture in the evenings and on weekends.

At seeding time, Helena and Jacob said goodbye to Jake, as he left to work at the A.B. Jones farm near the town of Clavet, Saskatchewan. It wasn't too far from Saskatoon so he would be able to visit from time to time.

Jake at his bunkhouse

He soon knew his way around the farm and machinery and enjoyed his work. Mr. Jones was a good man to work for and he appreciated Jake. The couple's dog Daisy became a constant companion.

As he sat on the machinery out in the fields and relaxed in his bunk house in the evenings, Jake remembered
his decision to become a believer in God, while he had worked at a farm near Glamis several years before. Over

time he had thought of this often and decided, on his next visit to Osler, to speak with Reverend Pauls about baptism.

The family was happy to see him and at the Saturday dinner table, the subject of baptism came up.

"I'm taking catechism classes at church," Annie said.

"Good for you," Jake replied. "When is the baptism service going to be?"

"It's on June 16th," Annie replied. Jake commented that he had decided to be baptised as well and hoped to speak with the pastor at church the next morning.

"Reverend Pauls," Jake said, after shaking the pastor's hand, "I would like to be baptised in June as well, but I won't be here to take the classes. I'm working near Clavet for most of the spring and summer. There is a little country church there called the Pleasant Point Mennonite church. Would it be possible for me to take the catechism with the pastor there? His name is Rev. Gerhard Zacharias."

"I'm sure that would work," his pastor said. And so arrangements were made for Jake to take the classes while working at the Jones farm. He began meeting with the Clavet pastor and memorized the entire catechism booklet. It was all in the German language.

Back at Osler, June exams were looming for Julius, Tena and Christine, and studying between and after chores took most of their time. It was hard to concentrate both in school and at home with the birds singing in the trees and the smell of freshly cultivated earth in the fields. They all looked forward to summer and the end of school.

Baptism Sunday arrived and Jake and Annie, along with others from their church, were baptised by Bishop Johannes

Regier and welcomed as members of the Osler Mennonite church. Each received a "Taufschein" (certificate of baptism). Jacob and Helena became members of the church as well.

Baptism photo:
Jake – last row, far left.
Annie – second last row, far left

When exams were finished, Julius, Tena, Christine and Danny returned to their home, delighted to be done with school. There would be chores and gardening but there would also be many hours of freedom to enjoy.

Julius was now finished with his high school and filled out an application to attend Normal School in the fall. The province was desperate for teachers and set up a six to eight week course in education which provided an interim teaching certificate. Students could begin teaching immediately after finishing, but had to agree to take summer school in order to upgrade that certificate.

"I hope I'm accepted," he said after mailing the form. Teaching was a career Julius was very interested in. His dad had been a teacher in German schools and encouraged higher education for his children.

Julius walked to Osler many times to get the mail and if someone else brought mail, his first question was, "Did I get a letter?"

In the beginning of August Julius walked to Osler and opened Box 52 to get the mail. A big grin spread over his face as he spotted his letter.

"I'm accepted at Normal School!" he announced excitedly as he entered the house. He was hot and sweaty after the fast walk home in the heat of the day, but none of that mattered.

"Good for you!" his sisters exclaimed.

"And Mom," Julius said as he handed his mother an envelope. "Here's a letter for you too. It looks like a cheque."

While her son and his siblings talked about Normal School, Helena opened the envelope to find the first Family Allowance payment. She smiled at the thought that each month an allowance cheque would arrive.

At the supper table Jake mentioned the Osler church elders and pastor had suggested he attend Bible School in Rosthern, Saskatchewan.

"I think I will apply for that and go after I'm done harvesting at the A.B. Jones farm. I'll be about a week or so late but I can't leave until the harvest is finished," he said.

"Well, I hope the crops around Clavet are better than around here," his father said. "We'll barely have enough oats and hay for our own cows and the Co-op farm has the same problem."

As her older children made plans to attend school away from home, Helena watched her last one excitedly skip down the trail in the neighbour's field toward Osler with her brother Danny and sisters Tena and Christine.

It was the beginning of September and Nettie was starting school. Like the others before her, she already loved to read thanks to the coaching of Julius and other siblings. She could hardly wait to join her friends. Her one complaint was that her father made her wait until she was seven to begin grade one. That meant some friends her age were a grade ahead of her. Jacob had the idea that age seven was soon enough to start school. He was in no hurry to see his children leave their early childhood and liked to keep them close to home as long as possible.

Grade One Reader: FUN WITH DICK AND JANE Image from Osler Historical Museum

Nettie's grade one class had a different reader than Danny had when he started. Now it was "Fun With Dick and Jane". These two story characters had a baby sister named Sally, a dog named Spot and a cat named Puff. The stories were interesting and the repetition of words made learning easy for everyone.
"Look, look, look. Look and see. See, see, see. See Sally run. Run, run, run."

For Helena, the house seemed empty and very quiet with all of the children away during the day and she looked forward to four o'clock when they arrived home from school. When she needed a break from the daily house and garden chores, Helena relaxed in the quietness of the living room, creating fancy crocheted doilies for her plant-stands and for the back and arm rests of the sofa.

At a Co-op farm meeting in October, Julius announced to the members that he had started Normal School to become a teacher and would only be home on weekends. Another farmer, Jacob's brother-in-law David Janzen, joined the group. When it became possible for them to begin shipping milk on the aerodrome property in November of 1946, the Janzen family moved into the barracks and David began to manage the farm. A well had been dug and now there was water on the property.

For the Friesen children, it was exciting to have their cousins living next door and the path through the Friesen pasture became well travelled as they played at each other's homes and walked to school together.

A CHALLENGE FOR JACOB

Chapter 37

Jacob had a habit of leaving his cigarette dangling from his mouth even when it was not lit. He had been smoking for many years and lately it was uncomfortable to hold a cigarette between his lips. There was a cold sore on his bottom lip that would not heal. He tried every ointment he could think of, but nothing worked.

Sitting at the table one day, he placed the tobacco on the paper and rolled a cigarette. Licking the edge of the paper to make it stick together, he again placed one between his lips. He winced.

"What's wrong? Is that sore getting worse?" Helena asked him.

"The whole lip is sore now and it feels like it is getting worse all the time," he replied.

Tena looked at her dad and suggested, "Dad, maybe you should go see the Doctor in Warman to have him look at that lip. It looks very sore."

"Well, I have to go to work in the morning but I'll see if the driver is willing to stop by the doctor's office on our way home," he answered. "Maybe he can give me something that will heal it up."

The next evening when Jacob returned home, he told his family he had been laid off work for the winter.

"On our way home I thought about the possibility of selling Watkins Products. I may try that," he said.

After a bit more discussion on this new development, Helena interrupted the conversation with the question that was uppermost in her mind. "Did you go to the doctor?"

"Yes I did. He's very concerned about my lip and wants me to see a doctor in Saskatoon. He says it isn't just a cold sore. It may be something worse."

"You should make that appointment as soon as possible," Helena said. Jacob made the call and had an appointment with Dr. Peterson the next week. After examining the sore closely, the doctor expressed his concern about what he saw.

"Well, Mr. Friesen," he said, as he straightened up. "This looks like cancer to me. I want you to go over to the cancer clinic to see a doctor there. He will probably want to remove it but you need to stop smoking immediately."

Jacob's heart sank as he heard the dreaded word "cancer", but he agreed to go and an appointment for surgery was made. A week later Jacob travelled back to Saskatoon by train and after the doctor froze his lip, the cancerous part was removed. As he lay in the hospital waiting for the surgery, he remembered the verse in John 6:37 in the Bible. "Whoever comes to me I will not turn away." This was a situation that Jacob knew he had to go to God with. It was a saving, calming moment for him. He chose to trust in God.

He returned home on the evening train and walked home from town. As he entered the kitchen, the family turned to look at him. His eyes were filled with pain and as he removed the scarf from around his face, they saw his swollen lip was covered with a small bandage.

By morning the bandage was off and the swelling was worse. Jacob sat down to breakfast, but could not open his mouth for the food. One of the children quickly opened the cutlery drawer and brought him a straw. He carefully pushed the straw into the healthy part of his mouth and sipped his coffee.

Jacob went to the cancer clinic for numerous radium treatments after the surgery, so until the lip healed, he was on a soft food diet.

The experience created a sudden desire in Jacob to quit smoking. He had always wanted to, but it seemed too hard to break the habit. Somehow quitting didn't seem so hard anymore and he never smoked again. He urged his children to never take up the habit. It also brought him to a place of surrender to God.

As he healed from the surgery, he decided to sell Watkins Products in the winter and was given a large territory to work in. Jacob bought an old horse-drawn Bread Wagon from Saskatoon to which he hitched his trusty dappled grey horses.

He began traveling the countryside to visit many farm families around the Osler area and across the river near Aberdeen, selling spices, pie fillings, ointments and other goods. The Friesen children found some of the descriptions of spices interesting. Paprika had this description: *"Adds piquancy and zest to all kinds of insipid foods"*. On the coldest days Jacob used his closed in sleigh with its wood burning stove to travel down the snowy country roads.

This was a new turn in the road of life for Jacob. He was now a cancer survivor and learned to live without smoking. That habit had been more than just the tobacco; it was the automatic reaching for something to relax with and the camaraderie with other smokers. Instead of working as a carpenter, Jacob became a salesman who sold spices door to door. All of this was a challenge but again he chose to trust in God.

RUNNING WATER

CHAPTER 38

When extreme winter weather made travel on his Watkins route too difficult, Jacob stayed home and began a project he had been looking forward to. Over time he had collected a used water heater tank, a porcelain bathroom sink and a large enamel kitchen sink. He decided now was the time to put in running water – at least in the bathroom.

He measured how much room was available behind the kitchen stove. The younger children stood watching, curious as to what their father was making.

"Dad, what are you doing?" asked Danny.

"I'm going to build a tank to fit behind the cook stove," he replied.

"Why?" Nettie asked.

"So we can fill it with snow to melt for water and we won't have to have a water barrel taking up space in the kitchen. Besides, I plan to connect it to the stove and bathroom sink, so we can have hot running water," their dad explained.

Back in his shop in the barn, Jacob welded together a galvanized steel tank which he placed back of the stove and connected to a pipe circulating through the stove fire box.

From the fire box he led a pipe to the bathroom sink on the other side of the kitchen wall and installed a hot water tap.

Setting the old water heater tank upright beside the bathroom sink, he connected it to the sink as well, adding a cold water tap.

"All right children," he said when he finished. "Now you can bundle up warm and bring in pails of clean fresh snow and fill the tank behind the stove."

The children trudged in and out with their pails, carrying in 15 pails of snow which filled the tank. Behind the warm stove, it melted to much less so the children bundled up again and more snow was brought in. The water from the barrel in the kitchen was emptied into the tank in the bathroom and the barrel removed from the house. Pails of melted snow water were added to the bathroom tank until it was full.

Helena walked into the bathroom and turned on the taps. "Look at that," she said as Jacob and the children watched. "It works! We don't have a sewer, but that's all right. We can still carry out the slop pail like we've always done."

Jacob smiled with satisfaction. It was a big help, even though the children tired of all the snow and water they had to bring in.

A few days later after returning from another sales trip, Jacob built a stand for the large enamel kitchen sink, making rounded corners to match the curve of the sink. He made a door at the front to hide the slop pail underneath.

Although their kitchen sink did not have running water, Helena and the girls enjoyed the luxury of being able to wash dishes in a large sink instead of in dish pans on the table. They enjoyed these modern conveniences. Jacob had again come up with something to make life easier at the farm.

WHO'S NOT GUILTY?

CHAPTER 39

"Last tap!" Danny said, as he slapped Nettie's arm and ran away. It was a warm summer day and Nettie turned to chase after him. He had long legs and could run much faster. Nettie knew that but was determined to catch him and have last tap.

Nettie on rope swing. Danny next to her.

After a few minutes, she gave up, pushed her hair out of her face and wiped off the sweat. She would get him when he wasn't looking, she decided.

Trying to appear as if she had forgotten about him, Nettie walked into the garden, pulled a carrot and sat down on the swing to eat it. As her brother wandered into the garden, she moved back to the shadows among the trees to wait for an opportunity.

As Danny bent down to pick some peas, his sister dashed out, slapped his arm and ran away calling, "Last tap!"

Unfortunately, he easily caught up to her, slapped her arm, laughed and said, "Now you don't have last tap!"

The two chased each other around the yard, with Nettie becoming more and more frustrated. Soon it became an angry pushing and shoving match. As their voices rose louder, Helena came out of the house and stopped them.

As they stood before her, she looked down at them sternly and asked, Na – veah es u-schuldig? (Well – who's not guilty?)"

Eager to blame her brother, Nettie's arm flung out as she pointed to her brother and said, "Danny!"

She saw her mother raise her eyebrows and Danny's mouth turn into a smirk and realized what her mother had asked.

"No! I mean – I'm not guilty – Danny is," she said, trying to correct herself, but it was too late.

Helena firmly grasped both children's arms and led them into the house and toward the living room.

"From what I heard, I think you are both guilty," she said as she reached for the strap from the large middle drawer of the chest of drawers. *(a leather strap was used for spanking when necessary)*

Danny stood meekly and bent down to receive his punishment. Nettie saw this as an opportunity and bolted out the door and out of the house. She ran around the house and to the chicken barn, and hid under the chicken roost.

She stood for some time and became very itchy and uncomfortable as tiny chicken mites began crawling all over her.

Suddenly the chicken barn door opened. Tena and Christine looked in at her and laughed.

"We found you! We're going to tell mom where you are!" they taunted. After a few minutes of this, Nettie forgot why she was hiding and longed to get even with her big sisters. Besides, she needed to get away from the crawly mites.

She left her hiding place and ran to the house to complain to her mother about her sisters.

"Mom – Tena and Christine were teasing me!" she said. Helena reached out, took her arm and led her back to the living room for her just desserts. After the tears were dried mama led her to the bathroom where she gently scrubbed her head in the sink, and poured water for a bath.

It felt good to be clean again and it was a relief that the fighting was over. Maybe tomorrow she and her brother would get along better. At least, they would try.

A NEW SCHOOL FOR OSLER

CHAPTER 40

For quite some time the idea of building a new two-room school in Osler had been tossed back and forth at local school board meetings. Jacob was on the board at that time and was hoping it would become a reality.

On September 5, 1946, a board member spoke up after more discussion and said, "I move we build a new two-room school."

"I second that," Jacob added. All were in favour and soon plans were drawn up. Construction would begin in the spring of 1947.

In between his Watkins area trips and helping at the Co-op farm, Jacob took part in the Board meetings and looked forward to a completed project by the next school year. There was much to plan in order to make the new school as modern as possible.

The big basement would be separated with a middle wall so the boys had one side and the girls the other. Each side would have an indoor bathroom.

In the spring of 1947, Jacob was back at his job in the city but spent many evenings and weekends on the building of the new school, joining other local workers to get it built in time for the fall. Once the basement was poured, construction of the walls and roof began. The work was watched with excitement by the school children who saw it take shape while they studied and played.

Before the area around the basement had been backfilled, several young boys played around the building, including Danny. Chasing another boy too close to the hole, Danny suddenly found himself tumbling down the slope. He was unhurt and ran back up the incline left by the grader to find his friends. The dirt was soon pushed back into the hole so no one else would fall into it.

Throughout the summer the new two room building was completed and in the fall was ready for the new school year. A bell tower was placed on top of the roof at the west end of the school and a rope for it was hung down into the classroom below.

At the beginning of September, Nettie, Danny and Christine carried their school supplies and lunch kits to Osler and walked into the new building which smelled of freshly painted walls and oiled wood floors. The sweeping compound used on the floors had a fresh clean smell. When it was time to begin class, the teacher pulled on the tower rope and the clanging bell announced all over town that school was in session.

In the school basement there were hooks lined up on the walls and each child was given a place to hang their coats. Lunch kits were placed on the ledge above it.

The classrooms were so much bigger than in the old school and here the grades were divided. Grades one to four had one room and grades five to ten had the other. A small room at one side of the school was a library and held space for science project equipment.

For the Friesen children there was a feeling of pride, "My dad helped to build this." Of course there were so many others, but to them, their father's involvement was most important.

New two room school

RUNNING AWAY

Chapter 41

Julius at boarding house in Glaslyn

After finishing Normal School, Julius taught at Glaslyn, Saskatchewan until the month of June and returned home to attend a few weeks of summer school in the city. He completed the course and was hired to teach in the town of Guernsey, Saskatchewan. In the middle of August, Julius was home for a break and to prepare for his new position.

Annie had a few days off from her job at the Warman hospital, Jake was back from working for a farmer and Lena had some time off from her job at the Veteran's hospital in Saskatoon.

It was the second last weekend in August and they all busily prepared for the annual Banman reunion. Everyone looked forward to Sunday.

Eight year old Nettie wandered around the yard, looking for something to do and followed her sisters into the garden.

"May I help pick cabbage?" she asked her sister Annie.

"No, just stay out of the way," Annie said as she picked cabbage heads for the Sunday coleslaw. Nettie wandered over to the swing. As she moved the swing slowly back and forth she spied Danny eating ripe gooseberries.

Running over to him she asked, "Will you play with me?"

"Not right now," he said, through a mouthful of berries.

Tena and Christine were busy pulling carrots for the big meal and had no interest in a bored little sister.

"Here, have a carrot," Tena said and added, "Don't bother us."

The girls brought their carrots to the summer kitchen and washed them. Then, whispering to each other, they quietly left, climbed through the fence and walked toward the little pond in the neighbour's field. Nettie wandered back from the garden and spotted her sisters. She ran to the fence, rolled underneath it and ran after them. As she caught up, they turned around.

"I told you not to bother us!" Tena said.

"Yeah! Scratch! Scram!" Christine added.

Nettie turned around with a frown. There was nothing to do and nobody wanted her around. As she returned to the house, Jip the puppy met her eagerly, wanting to be petted. She sat down beside the house with her arms around the dog still wondering what to do. Maybe if someone noticed she was unhappy, they'd feel sorry for her.

She walked into the house and to the living room, sat down in a chair and sulked. No one noticed. Finally she decided to ask if she could go to Osler and visit friends in the afternoon.

Everyone was inside. The older girls set the table for lunch while Julius played the accordion. Jake joined him with the violin. Tena, Christine and Danny washed up for the meal and Julius and Jake joined them. Jacob walked in after working in the barn and got cleaned up for the meal as well. The kitchen filled with laughter and conversation.

To Nettie, it seemed all of her tall family members talked above her and around her but never to her. She approached her mother who was busy at the stove.

"Mama, I want to go to Osler to visit friends after dinner," she stated.

"No, you can't go to Osler. We'll be busy this afternoon and you can help."

Nettie turned around with a pout and walked to her parents' bedroom. It was obvious that no one loved her. She thought of running away but she needed a suitcase. As she sat on her parents' bed, she looked into the living room and spotted Julius' accordion case. That would do it!

She hopped down off of the bed, opened the case and struggled to lift the heavy 120 base accordion out of it. She put her Eatons Beauty doll in instead and closed the lid. The bulky, oddly shaped case was heavy and banged against her legs as she walked past her family, out the door, through the caragana hedge and towards the gate leading to the neighbour's field.

Annie noticed Nettie's determined little face as she passed through the kitchen and watched her walk to the lane between their garden and the neighbour's field.

"Mom!" Annie called. "Look at this! Nettie is running away!"

Helena stopped her work at the stove and all of the family gathered at the west windows of the house. They watched her walk down the lane struggling clumsily with the heavy case and soon they were all doubled over in laughter at the comical sight. Helena sank down on a chair unable to stop for a while. "Oh, the poor child," Helena said as she caught her breath and wiped her eyes.

Meanwhile, Nettie trudged resolutely toward Osler. As she neared the large hedge close to the neighbours' farm house, she wondered where she should go and what she should do. The train would cost money and she didn't have any. Well, she would go back and her mama would have to give her money. She stopped to catch her breath and turned around.

As she neared the house, the family quickly went back to their places. Helena was again stirring something on the stove and the girls put bread, salt and pepper on the table.

"Mama," Nettie said emphatically as she stopped at the stove, "I want some money for the train."

Helena turned and looked down at her. "Little girls who run away from home don't deserve money for a train," she said.

Nettie broke into tears and ran to her parents' bedroom. She unpacked her doll from the accordion case and lay down on the bed crying angrily, saying, "Mama doesn't love me! God doesn't love me! No one does!"

Helena heard her and paused to listen. She shook her head and sighed. Tears formed in her eyes.

Tena walked into the bedroom and said sternly, "Stop this at once! You're making Mama feel bad!"

Nettie stopped crying. She thought she was the only one who was sad. Knowing mama felt bad too made her think about how she had behaved. As Tena turned to leave, Nettie buried her head in her arms and told God, "I'm sorry. I don't want to make mama feel bad."

She dried her tears and joined the family for lunch. After the meal, she saw her sister Lena walk upstairs and knew her big sister would be kneeling beside the bed to read her Bible and pray. She followed her up and knelt down beside her.

"What would you like?" Lena asked her.

"I want to ask Jesus to forgive me and live in my heart," Nettie replied. After praying with Lena, Nettie felt so clean and happy, she ran downstairs and handed her mother a penny she had been saving.

"Here, mama, you can have this," she said.

Helena smiled and replied, "That's all right, you may keep it."

The next day, the family enjoyed the Banman extended family at their annual reunion. Nettie had swept out the winter caboose and put all her doll furniture and dolls into it. She and her cousins had a wonderful time playing house.

1947 CROP FAILURE

Chapter 42

The Turner Co-op Farm dairy venture was not going well. The whole Osler area needed rain desperately. While they hoped and waited for a crop for the fall, the Co-op farm cattle received very little nutrition from the oat straw and rationed grain they were being fed. However, they were still shipping milk and now a new trucking company came to pick up their milk. Ben Ens Trucking became Lobe's Transport and Albert Lobe began making the rounds to all the dairy farms in the area.

The Co-op farmers kept meeting together to try to come up with more money to buy feed but banks and people in general were tight fisted with money during these times of drought. Then there was the problem of how to pay back the loans when there was more expense than income.

On a hot evening on July 7th 1947, another meeting took place and Julius withdrew from the association, taking $20.00 of his $25.00 share capital. He would begin a teaching position in Guernsey, Saskatchewan in fall so would no longer be available for meetings. He wrote to Mr. Chapman of his decision and another member took over the secretarial duties.

On August 23rd, a large group of dairy farmers in the Osler and Warman area held a meeting to discuss the extreme feed problem in their district. They decided to send two delegates to the Dairy Pool in Saskatoon to discuss the problem. Unless feed could be bought somewhere, very little milk would be going to the Dairy Pool. The Pool agreed to help the farmers financially, if they would buy oats.

At the end of the month, one of the other Turner Co-op members, Mr. John M. Dyck, moved onto the Co-op farm with his family and lived in part of the barracks. He contributed six cows and twenty loads of feed. They planned on raising hogs at the farm and the feed was very helpful at this difficult time.

In October, the Osler Aerodrome Title would finally become available; however the group did not have enough money to pay the final amount and struggled on to find solutions for the shortage of feed and money.

While Jacob and Helena worried and wondered about that group farm venture, they still had their own farm to look after. The family fed their animals chopped oat straw mixed with hay and chopped thistle, as well as some grain. Pails of well water were carried to the garden fruit trees. Jacob was again working in construction in the city.

In spite of the heat and drought of the summer, the children found things to do to keep occupied and happy. Now there were more children at the Co-op farm to befriend and to walk to school with in the fall.

When summer was almost over Julius packed his clothing, accordion, and books and left for the town of Guernsey. It would be a new experience for him to be in charge of a classroom of children and teenagers, but he felt he was ready at 18 years of age and well prepared after eight weeks of Normal School, the few months he taught in Glaslyn and a few weeks of summer school.

Back at school in September, Christine enjoyed figuring out songs on the school piano and asked for permission from her teacher to stay indoors to play, instead of going out for recess. He gave permission and after a while realized how well she played. She was playing by ear in 5 flats with both hands. He saw talent and potential in this girl. When he met Jacob in town one day, he suggested Christine take piano lessons from Mrs. Bessie Rostek. Jacob agreed to the idea and Christine took a few lessons. She caught on quickly and was able to read the notes, but her father told her he just could not afford the 35 cents per lesson each week. It was disappointing, but she kept playing the piano during recess, praying that someday the family would have their own piano.

As the youngest three settled into school, Lena took the train to Rosthern a few weeks later to attend Bible School. Annie left for Tabor Bible School in the town of Dalmeny.

The house felt empty to Helena, but it was also a relief to have some quiet time for a few hours a day.

The first few months in Guernsey flew by for Julius as he studied in the evenings and taught during the day. Being a teacher was challenging work but he enjoyed it. The first week of November he wrote to his parents and family at home and it seemed he was a bit lonely.

Guernsey, Sask.,
Nov. 8,1947

Dear Folks,
Received your long awaited letter at last. Thanks heaps!

How are the meals at home, Danny? Judging by your letter that seems to be your favourite pastime; not to mention kicking over telephone poles. How is your teacher treating you?

Did Jake forget to write his brother? What are you doing now to keep out of mischief?

How are Lena and Annie getting along at Bible School? Tell the three of them I'd appreciate hearing from them sometime before Christmas.

So Tena is the 'biggest girl' at home now. How is work? Nettie must have a good teacher (ahem!) – she's writing very well for a grade 2 girl. Chris seems to be developing quite a sense of humour. The teachers can't be that bad, give them a chance, eh Chris?

Did you get your hammer-mill, Dad? I think that would be a good idea, it would save money in hauling and be less expensive than baling. Do you think you will have enough feed for the winter? How is the Co-op Farm running?

I acquired a sheet of plywood today for our school wood work. We have a nice line of tools for a school. Drew a few designs for the kids to use in their woodwork period. If my old woodwork patterns should show up at home, I could do with them.

I must begin work on the Christmas concert soon. As you will know by the time you receive this, I won't be home for Remembrance Day. But Christmas isn't so far away.

A friend in here offered me an organ, in good shape and tone, for a very small sum of money. But not having any too much cash and no way of getting it home, I had to decline.

*Und wie ist Mutter?(*And how is mother*?) Sie mussen mier ein brief schreiben. (*you should write me a letter*) Ich Korrigiere Hoch Schul Deutsch fur sechs schuleren. (*I am teaching High school German to six students.)

Winter has apparently set in here, so would you kindly 'ship' my fleece-liners up here? Also, 'Julius Caesar' by Shakespeare, and if you run across any good Christmas Concert material, let's have it!

Nighty night,
Joe (a name many called him)

As the winter snows came, some farmers in the area felt helpless as the reality of a complete crop failure sank in. For the Co-op Farm members, milk production was low which meant small milk cheques, debt was mounting and each of the farmers struggled to make payments on the loans they had taken out to buy the Aerodrome land. On top of that, they still didn't have enough feed for the cattle. Discouragement hung over their heads as they plodded through the winter months hoping for a better spring and summer.

For Jacob, as depression sank in, there was comfort in the Scriptures in the Bible and in prayer as he often knelt beside the bed, or the sofa in the living room, to bring his concerns to God.

HOLIDAYS

Chapter 43

A highlight of summer, for the youngest four, was taking turns spending a week at Aunt Margaret and Uncle Henry's place west of Osler. This time it was Christine's turn and she was excited about being away from home and spending time with her aunt and uncle.

Meanwhile, Julius and Tena stayed home to herd the cows as they grazed in ditches near the 'lienye' (highway) where there was more grass. One day as Tena sat beside the fence next to the ditch, she saw one of the cows wander on to the road. She heard a car coming and ran to chase the cow back.

"Hey!" she yelled at the cow as she ran. She suddenly stumbled and fell, landing on a rock with her knee. Julius came running to check on her as she rocked back and forth in pain.

"Sis' you had better go home. I'll look after the cows," he told her as he helped her stand. She could hardly put any weight on her leg, but limped home and lay down on the sofa in the living room.

"What happened?" her mother asked as she checked Tena's knee. After hearing the story, Helena told her to rest.

"I hope you'll be all right tonight. There is church tonight, remember? The rest of us will go, but you stay home."

Tena tried to rest the knee, but the pain was getting worse and the knee became very swollen. By the time the family returned home she was in tears, moaning in pain.

Helena hurried to the telephone and called Jacob's step-brother, Peter Janzen, to come with his car because Tena needed to see a chiropractor. Peter arrived quickly and they drove away to get help. When they got there, the chiropractor told Peter to pull on Tena's legs while Helena held her shoulders. As they pulled, the chiropractor worked on getting the knee cap back into place. The pain was almost unbearable. She was given a pair of crutches and told to stay off the leg.

At home again, she took some aspirin and lay down for the night. As she slept Jacob and Helena discussed the fact that since she couldn't herd cows, why not let her take her turn at Aunt Margaret and Uncle Henry's place and have Christine come home to herd the cows.

It seemed like a good arrangement for Tena and next morning Christine noticed her dad drive on to the Klassen yard with her sister.

"What happened to you?" Aunt Margaret asked in concern as Tena was helped down from the wagon and handed a pair of crutches.

"I hurt my knee trying to chase a cow off the road," Tena replied. "Chris, I guess you'll have to take my place herding cows. Dad says I have to take my turn now so my knee heals. You can come another time." After Aunt Margaret agreed to the arrangement, Tena was taken into the house.

Christine was disappointed but concerned about her sister so after a short visit between her father, Uncle and Aunt, she carried her suitcase to the wagon and left, waving goodbye as Jacob snapped the reins on the horses' backs. She didn't look forward to herding cows but hoped her sister would soon be able to walk without crutches.

Several weeks later it was Danny's turn to have his holiday and he enjoyed listening to Uncle Henry's gramophone. He learned to put the records on, carefully place the arm with the needle in the first groove of the record and turn the crank at the side until it was wound up. The songs of Hank Snow blared out of the big horn speaker as he and his uncle sat back and enjoyed the music. Over and over, and over again, Danny played Uncle Henry's favourite tune:

"Lonely Cattle Call".
The cattle are prowlin' the coyotes are howlin'
Out with the doggies bawl
Where spurs are jinglin' a cowboy is singin'
This lonesome cattle call
(yodeling and moaning)

Wind-up Gramophone.
Drawing by Nettie Balzer.

Finally, when Uncle Henry was out of the house, Aunt Margaret took Danny outside and gave him a book to read under the trees. Henry loved Hank Snow. Margaret did not. She wasn't sure she could listen to that "Lonely Cattle Call" song again! Oh, for some peace and quiet!

A neighbour who lived about six miles away stopped by the Klassen home and saw eleven year old Danny outside with his aunt. He walked over and began a conversation with them. He talked about his cows and his hayfield and how he needed help with the haying. Then he turned to Danny.

"You're a pretty tall fellow for your age and I could use a good worker, how about coming over to help me with the haying?" "Oh, I'm not here to work," Danny replied. "I'm here for a holiday." The conversation was short-lived and the neighbour chuckled and left. But Aunt Margaret informed her nephew that the neighbour really had needed his help and would have paid him. Danny felt bad knowing he had missed his first job opportunity and disappointed his aunt as well!

The next week was Nettie's turn. She could hardly wait, and enjoyed Uncle Henry's wooden Pluto puppet with strings you could pull to make the arms and legs jump. The gramophone was fun for a while, but she loved being outside, playing among the trees and in the garden. Aunt Margaret's strawberry patch had the best tasting strawberries and Nettie ate her fill until one day her aunt took her aside to explain a few things about the garden.

"Nettie – you need to stop eating all the ripe strawberries. You may have a few, but I need the rest to make strawberry jam for the winter. Now leave them for a few days, so that I'll have enough to make jam."

It hadn't occurred to Nettie that there was any other purpose for those berries than to be enjoyed but she left them, and found other things to do until it was time to return home and prepare for school.

A CLOSE CALL

CHAPTER 44

For several years, Helena suffered with tooth aches and had several teeth pulled. Now it was getting worse. At times she groaned in pain rocking back and forth as she held her head in her hands.

Jacob saw her suffer and decided it was high time she got relief from the pain. He made an appointment with the dentist. The dentist checked her mouth and suggested pulling the rest of her teeth and putting in false ones. It would be expensive, but it was the only answer. He took an impression of her mouth and told her the teeth would be ready in a week.

A week later Helena took the train to Saskatoon for her appointment to have her teeth pulled. The freezing needles were painful and she needed several, for the roots were deep and hard to dig out of her gums. She gripped the arm rests on the chair as the dentist twisted and pulled. Her head began to ache and she wished it was over.

When the teeth were out, the dentist packed gauze into her mouth to stop the bleeding. After removing the gauze, he pushed the new false teeth into her mouth. Her mouth felt too full and she wasn't sure she could tolerate the foreign objects.

When the appointment was over, she walked to the train station to wait for the train to Osler to depart. On the way home, as the train swayed back and forth, Helena felt sick. The freezing was coming out and the pain was hard to bear. Finally she arrived in Osler and walked through the snowy street to the church where her family was attending a service. She waited in the baby nursery.

As the church service ended, Nettie walked past the nursery and saw her mother sitting there. She was shocked at the shiny swollen face of her mother. As the family gathered for their ride home on the sleigh everyone was concerned. Their mother did not look well.

Next morning the children filed into the bedroom to see her and were afraid. When Jacob returned to the house after chores, he took one look at Helena and then walked to the telephone. He called the dentist in Saskatoon, angrily told him of his wife's condition and asked what he should do.

The family did what they could to relieve their mother's pain, but for some time she could not open her mouth. Her whole face was swollen and she did not look like herself at all. Nettie often stood beside the bed afraid that her mother would die, and she nearly did. Without antibiotics an infection like that was life-threatening. It took a long time before Helena was up and healed. But once the swelling was gone, Helena had a lovely new smile.

MAKING MUSIC

CHAPTER 45

In the spring of 1948 Julius had a used pump organ delivered to the farm and moved it into the living room. Lena had played the church organ for hymns at times and now sat down at the instrument in the living room as the family gathered around for a hymn. She pumped the pedals with her feet while she played on the keys at the same time. Helena and Jacob relaxed in their chairs and listened as the family choir sang in four part harmony.

Annie, Tena and Christine had learned on the school piano and now enjoyed having those black and white keys to play on the organ. A favourite key for the girls to play in was five flats, mostly black keys. Jake played on the black keys as well, but he preferred playing in sharps. Danny followed his big brother's lead and played in the same key.

Osler,Sask. Historical Museum Pump organ

Julius tried playing as well, but preferred his accordion to the organ. Soon Nettie had figured out a song even though she didn't know how to read notes. The song she played was the old

Negro spiritual, "Old, Black Joe", sung in music class at school.

In between all the chores and when older siblings returned from jobs away from home, the sound of music filled the house. Hymns as a group, duets, trios, or quartets – how Jacob and Helena loved to listen to them.

Jacob soon began requesting his favourite hymns. "He Leadeth Me", "I Love to Tell the Story" and many German songs from the church hymn book, "*Evangliums Lieder*" (Evangelistic Songs). Songs about Jesus helped him deal with the many disappointments he had faced in life.

Christmas and Easter times became even more special as everyone came home. Music bound the family together and became a tradition of every gathering.

THE 1937 CHEVY

CHAPTER 46

To the family's relief, Jacob finally bought a car. It was a 1937 Chevy and he spent a lot of time driving around the yard and up and down the driveway. He had to get used to a steering wheel instead of reins, and a brake instead of pulling on reins and yelling "Ho!" to stop the horses. Finally he drove to Warman to get his license. Now he was able to drive to Saskatoon for his job instead of relying on others for a ride

For Helena the car was a fearful thing. She had ridden in many cars but wasn't quite sure about Jacob driving his own.

They drove to Saskatoon one Saturday with Danny and Nettie in the back seat enjoying the ride. Their own car! It was exciting, even though some families had newer cars.

Jacob stopped at a place of business in the city and told his family to wait in the car.

"I won't be long," he said.

He turned off the engine and put on the hand brake. The children couldn't resist reaching forward and grabbing the steering wheel.

"Loat daout toch! (leave it alone)," Helena snapped frantically. Even a runaway horse could be stopped eventually but what if this mechanical beast moved when Jacob was not there?

Danny and Nettie laughed, "The car won't drive by touching the steering wheel," they said. "It has to be started first!"

"I don't care. Leave it alone!" she said again, and was relieved when Jacob got back in to drive home.

Use of the car was rationed somewhat but the family found it so much easier and faster to get to the nearest towns of Warman and Hague, as well as to church. Visiting their Friesen and Banman relatives took so much less time and the visits happened more often.

Jacob liked the car to be clean so the children carried pails of water from a rain barrel, grabbed soap and rags and made it shine. Jacob was thankful for the car and wanted it to look good, but it must not become a thing of pride. He wanted to be an example of humility before God and his family.

THREE BILLY GOATS GRUFF

CHAPTER 47

It was another hot summer with no rain and Jacob and other area farmers again feared the future. There was not much grass for the cattle in his pasture. As a Co-op Farm member he could chase the cows to the Co-op pasture for grazing during the day, but those fields didn't have much either.

As another crop failure loomed for the area, the Co-op Farmers held meetings to determine what to do. Disagreements mounted as they found that bills were not being paid, income was not enough and they were getting deeper into debt. Feed for the cattle became an obsession as the amount of milk from the cows dwindled.

The Hog project had to be given up as many pigs died as a result of disease and not enough nutritious feed. It was heartbreaking to see animals suffering. The farmers felt helpless to change the situation. Some wept with disappointment.

While the Co-op Farm members struggled to come to terms with those hardships, their younger children were not aware of the problems and spent many hours playing together.

Danny and Nettie chased the cows to the Co-op pasture in the mornings and brought them home in the evenings. They

met their cousins and other children at the wooden steps that led over the barbed wire fence to the Co-op yard.
A favourite game was "Three Billy Goats Gruff". Someone would be the ugly troll under the steps and others would fearfully climb the steps and try to get down the other side before the troll chased them.

"Who is that tramping over my bridge?" the troll would growl.

"It is I, little Billy Goat Gruff. I want to eat grass on the other side of the bridge," a child would reply meekly.

"Then I'm going to eat you up," the troll responded.

The child cried out, "No! Wait until middle-sized Billy Goat Gruff comes, he would be much tastier than I am!"

After the troll allowed the first two goats to cross, the biggest Billy Goat Gruff tramped over and chased the troll. The game was played over and over as the children took turns at each role.

The fall of 1948, Tena left to attend Rosthern Junior College for grade eleven. She enjoyed dorm life and her artistic abilities were recognized by fellow students and staff, especially when she drew a caricature of one of the teachers on the black board. Since she was slim and petite she earned the nick-name "Scrawny".

Julius returned to teaching, and Lena joined Jake at the Jones Farm to finish the harvesting.

As the children left for their various places of school and employment, Jacob and Helena mulled over what the future would hold for the Co-op Farm. Jacob was frustrated and sometimes angry about the discussions at meetings.

Several months earlier one member complained that since Jacob was making good money in construction at $10.00 per day, the other members in the Co-op Farm should be paid more than they were getting. Jacob didn't think that would be fair and pointed out that at one of the first meetings, the farmers had agreed that there would be equal distribution of funds even if some of the farmers had to find other jobs to make ends meet. One day the two men had a loud verbal confrontation in the Co-op farm yard.

Helena and the children heard the voices clearly. She flung off her apron and marched through the pasture to face the two men.

"This is not the way we do things!" Helena said, as the men turned to her in surprise.

After she had her say the men apologised to one another and shook hands. Helena also admitted her own anger and asked for forgiveness.

At home, they decided it was probably best if Jacob withdrew from the Co-op Farm. He spent time searching the scriptures for guidance in his decision, and when the older children were home for the weekend he called the family into the living room.

"I've come to a decision about the Co-op Farm. I want to withdraw from the organization. There are many uncertainties and disagreements, and after reading my Bible and spending time asking God what to do, I feel that decision is the right one. But you should know that we'll lose money and cattle because of it. I will still have to make payments on the personal loan I took out for that farm."

As the family discussed what this would mean, the children admired their father for taking a stand and making a decision.

On September 20th, 1948, Jacob met with the farmers and took out his equity in the form of one cow valued at $100.00 (instead of the three cows he had brought to the farm) as well as a rusty electric gas pump (used to fill the airplanes gas tanks). It was valued at $150.00. However, he had no electricity at home and so had no use for it. It was never brought to the farm.

Jacob would still be able to graze his eight cows in the Co-op pasture but would now have to pay $1.50 per head per month. It was a sobering and upsetting time, but Helena and Jacob felt they had done the right thing.

When harvesting was done at the Jones farm, Jake left for Two Rivers Bible Institute near Carlea, Sask. Lena continued to work for the Jones family as Mrs. Jones was blind and needed help in the house.

Annie left for Kansas City, Missouri to attend candidate school at Gospel Missionary Union. She was interested in becoming a missionary to Columbia. She returned after a few months, discouraged because she was not accepted as a candidate. Since she had a very tender and sensitive nature, they felt the difficulties facing missionaries in Columbia would be too hard for her. She found a job doing day work in the city, looking after the home and meals for a doctor and his family.

As fall turned to winter, plans for Christmas concerts were again in full swing at school and at church. Helena busily sewed colourful plaid Christmas dresses for her youngest daughters, Christine and Nettie.

Nettie came home from school one day and announced to her mother, "I need a white dress for the concert too."

"Why?" asked, Helena.

"We're doing a drill and all of us eight girls have to wear white dresses," Nettie replied.

"What is a "drill"? Helena asked.

"There will be music playing on the phonograph, and we march across the stage in different lines to the tune of the music." Nettie said.

Two dresses? That would take more time, but Helena agreed and found white material. Copying the pattern from another of Nettie's dresses, she pedaled fast on the treadle machine as she sewed.

At the Christmas concert, eight girls in white dresses marched across the stage in criss-cross patterns in time to the music. Each girl carried a crepe-paper wreath of red roses.

The audience was impressed and the families enjoyed the evening. It was a treat for Jacob and Helena as well - to be able to put worries aside and watch their children at the concert.

Rose Wreath Drill

Left to right: Martha Wall, Donna Lobe, Edna Pauls, Nettie Friesen, Norma Abrams, Barbara Rostek, Connie Rempel and Tena Janzen.

Photo taken in early spring.

LATE FOR CHURCH

Chapter 48

The milking was done and breakfast finished. The girls hurried to do the dishes, so they could get ready for church. Sunday mornings were always a mad rush of vying for the one bathroom, mirror, hairbrushes, and finding a private place to get dressed.

"Are you dressed?" Lena called up the stairs to the boys. "We need to come up and get ready!"

There were only two bedrooms upstairs, one belonging to the boys and one to the girls. In order to get to their room the girls needed to walk through the boys' room. They tried to make sure they didn't surprise anyone in a state of undress.

"Yes, I'm ready," replied Jake. Julius and Dan quickly pulled on their pants as Lena started up the stairs.

The girls hurried to get their dresses on, took out their pin-curls, combed their hair and patted face powder on their faces. Lena and Annie prodded Tena and Chris to hurry.

"You have to sing this morning," Lena reminded the girls.

"We know that!" they answered. Tena reminded Lena they needed the guitar for their duet.

"I'll bring it," Lena replied.

As they rushed downstairs, Helena walked into the kitchen with Nettie, both dressed and ready.

"Is Dad ready?" Annie asked. "I hope he's not late again!"

Helena did not reply. It was hard sometimes to have older children who had their own opinions of what their parents should do and didn't mind speaking about it.

Jake hurried into the living room to grab a handkerchief from one of the two small drawers near the top of the chest of drawers. As he turned, he glanced into his parents' bedroom and saw his father on his knees in prayer beside the bed. It was a familiar sight to the Friesen children.

During the rush of family preparations for church, Jacob paused to read the scriptures and took time to pray for the young pastor, Reverend Jacob Pauls, each Sunday morning. Once his prayer time was finished and the bathroom was finally free, he got ready himself.

The family arrived at church in time for Sunday school and then the service. A few minutes into the hymn singing their father arrived and walked through the noisy swinging doors to the very front because he was hard of hearing.

Although he usually wore a white shirt, today he wore a red flannel shirt. His brown shoes were repaired with black thread. His daughters cringed because of the way he stood out in the crowd.

Tena and Christine sang their duet accompanied by Tena on the guitar, and then it was time for the message.

Reverend Pauls messages were always very thoughtfully, prayerfully and powerfully delivered. He closed the service by suggesting his favourite hymn; "Die Zeit ist Kurtz, O mensch sei weise...lazst eine gute spur zurick" (The time is short, O people be wise.... leave a good footprint for others to follow).

There was always something of the pastor's messages to take home and think about. But the children did not always consider, and others did not know, that perhaps the power in the pastor's messages was due in part to a farmer in a red flannel shirt and brown shoes repaired with black thread, who knelt in prayer each Sunday morning to pray for a young pastor with a very large responsibility – even if it made him late for church.

THE PRANK

CHAPTER 49

After Jacob's brush with cancer of the lip, he was very concerned that none of his children should smoke. Julius, however, had taken up the habit and he also played cards, which Jacob considered worldly.

The many concerned lectures from his father did not sit well with Julius who learned to keep these activities hidden from his dad.

One lazy summer afternoon, when their dad was at work and their sisters were visiting friends, Danny and Nettie had nothing much to do. They sat in the barn loft and played with kittens for a while. They played with the puppies and went to the garden a few times for a carrot and a kohlrabi.

"Where is Julius?" Nettie asked. Julius was home for the summer after his year of teaching.

"I don't know, but let's look for him," Danny suggested.

After walking to the house and looking in the rooms, they decided to check the barn.

"Maybe he's in the loft now. Let's be really quiet - maybe we can scare him!" they decided. Carefully opening the barn door, they smelled cigarette smoke and looked at each other. They had just found their brother.

The two walked softly through the cow barn and peeked around the corner into the shop behind the horses' stalls. There was Julius – deeply engrossed in a game of solitaire, with a cigarette between his lips.

Danny quietly stepped back and tugged at his sister to follow. They left the barn and came up with an idea.

Danny hauled up some pails of water from the well and they entered the barn quietly again. As they got to the door of the shop, they yelled, "FIRE!" and threw the water on Julius.

At the look on Julius' drenched face, Danny and Nettie ran for their lives. They flung the pails aside and the two raced down the driveway with their brother in hot pursuit.

Half-way to the highway they stopped, out of breath, and looked back. Julius was not chasing them anymore. They walked back to the house where Julius met them with a grin on his face as he dried himself off with a towel.

"Well, you brats - that was quite the prank! Obviously you two don't have enough to do! Come watch me finish my radio crystal set."

Danny and Nettie were relieved he wasn't angry and they eagerly watched as Julius connected the little wires. Soon they heard crackling static and then voices over radio frequencies. Their big brother was a genius!

MAYBE WE SHOULD PRAY

CHAPTER 50

After many years of swinging the agitator handle back and forth on the old washing machine, Helena finally bought a new one. It was white enamel with shiny chrome trim. With the press of a button, the wringer rollers turned and wrung water out of the clothes. The machine was mounted on wheels for easy moving and had a very loud gas motor with an exhaust hose, which was led out through a hole in the bottom of the kitchen window frame.

Washing Machine. Osler Museum

Her children helped Helena read the instructions and explained what the machine could do. She was thrilled and loved wash day after this. Of course the water still had to be heated on the stove, but it was still so much easier. Helena enjoyed wiping down the whole machine after using it. It sparkled. Not a drop of water or finger-mark remained.

The standard meal on washday was noodles with cream gravy, or rhubarb sauce. The noodle water was saved to use as starch for cotton shirts and dresses so they could be ironed crisply.

One day, Helena began her usual washday routine. She heated the water for washing in the big oblong canner. She boiled and strained noodles so the starch would be ready when she needed it and sorted the clothes that had been tossed behind a little door underneath the stairway. By the time the clothes were sorted into piles from whites to darks, the wash water was boiling.

After filling the machine, adding soap, and putting the first rinsing water in a tub next to it, Helena pulled the handle to start the machine. Nothing happened. Again and again she tried, and it wouldn't start. She was getting frustrated - the water in the machine was cooling off and the piles of laundry were still waiting.

10 year old Nettie watched and sensed her mother's frustration.
"Mom – maybe we should pray," she said.

"You go ahead and pray!" her mother tossed back, as she decided to give up for a while.

Nettie walked to the living room, knelt beside the couch and prayed for God to please help her mama start the washing machine.

"Ok, try it now!" she said, as she re-entered the kitchen.

Not wanting to appear to have no faith, her mother went along with the suggestion and pulled the handle. The motor roared to life!

"See mom?" Nettie yelled above the roar of the motor, "I prayed and it started!" And Helena couldn't deny it as she grinned, sighed with relief and tossed the first load of tea towels and white shirts into the machine.

Older siblings claimed the motor had merely flooded, but no matter how one looked at it, it was still an answer to prayer and it encouraged a little girl's faith.

TITLE TO THE FAMILY FARM

CHAPTER 51

It had been two years since Jacob had withdrawn from the Turner Co-op Farm, but he continued to hear about the difficulties faced by the remaining members of that association.

Drought conditions from 1946 to 1949 continued to plague the Osler area and grain was still hard to come by. There were few pregnant cows at the Co-op Farm and the feed still consisted of wheat straw and some oat sheaves – insufficient nutrition for the hungry animals that were expected not only to stay alive but produce milk as well.

While Jacob was thankful to not be personally involved any more, he knew how those farmers felt. He was going through the same problems with his cows at home.

Mr. E. Chapman met with David Janzen and made arrangements to turn over the assets and liabilities of the Co-op Farm. On February 2nd of 1950 it was sold to Mr. Janzen.

On February 8th, the Turner Co-operative Association Ltd. was legally dissolved. Three former members were owed money by the association. Jacob was owed $65.00.

Jacob concentrated on his own farm, his construction work in the city and his Watkins route to bring in the needed income. The family looked after their dairy cows, chickens, pigs and garden.

For years Helena had made payments at the bank in order to own the title to the 80 acres they were living on. She saved the cream and milk cheques and several of her oldest children helped out by sending her money when they could.

The day came when the last payment had been made and the Title arrived in the mail. Helena could hardly wait for Jacob to come home so she could show him.

After supper, she handed him the letter and Title from the bank. Jacob pulled the documents out of the envelope. "What's this?" he asked.

"It's the Title to our farm. It's ours now. We don't have to make any more payments," Helena replied.

Jacob stared at the document for a few moments, wondering how this was possible. When he learned that his wife had saved the cream and milk cheques in order to make the payments and that his children had been helping out, he was overcome for a few moments.

"Well – I guess you don't need me around here anymore." he said, with a bit of a smile. What a relief it was to finally own the land.

THE NINETY AND NINE

CHAPTER 52

Jacob's step-mother spent some of her winters living with her various children, at one place one winter and at another the next. This winter Helena and Jacob decided to invite her to live with them.

Grandma's bed was set up in the living room and Helena learned how to cook without salt, because grandma was on a salt-free diet.

Christine was taking her grade eleven in Guernsey with her brother Julius. She kept house for the two of them. This left only the youngest two at home with their parents.

Nettie and Danny enjoyed having grandma there. She was easy to live with. Helena enjoyed having her also. There was someone else to sit and talk with in the afternoons or evenings. They would crotchet or knit and their interesting Low German conversations flowed.

Nettie also enjoyed talking to grandma, but one day Helena took her youngest daughter aside and said, "You need to speak German to grandma."

"I can't," Nettie replied.

"Of course you can!" her mother insisted. Nettie tried, but since she and her siblings and father spoke mostly English at home, even though their mother still answered in German, she was out of practice.

Helena realized that her children were no longer fluent in the language their ancestors had spoken for generations.

One day Danny and Nettie returned home from school to find a special treat. Grandma had hot baked apples with sugar and cinnamon waiting for them. Nettie flung her arms around her grandma and received a big hug in return.

Grandma told Helena that she enjoyed living with the family, saying that Nettie and Danny were so well behaved – especially Danny. She also enjoyed the prayer meetings with Helena and Jacob's neighbours.

Grandma's night time routine included taking out her hair bun and brushing the long naturally curly hair. Nettie wished she had hair like that. When grandma was in her nightgown and ready for bed, she called her granddaughter.

"Nettie, come," she called.

Nettie walked into the living room and sat down at the organ to play the old hymn, "The Ninety and Nine". Grandma sang it in the High German language, while Nettie sang it in English. It didn't matter that two different languages were sung at the same time. This became a special memory for Nettie.

Grandma Janzen/Friesen in Helena's flower garden.

MUSIC LESSONS AND FUN AT SCHOOL

Chapter 53

At the elementary school, the younger grades enjoyed music class and the teacher sometimes had the students move to the back of the room and square dance to the song "Bingo".

"A farmer had a little dog, and Bingo was his name-o, B.I.N.G.O, B.I.N.G.O, B.I.N.G.O, and everybody changes," the children sang as they turned to move in a different direction. Of course, it wasn't called dancing back then, since most people in the Osler area considered dancing to be worldly and wrong. Instead, it was called Musical Games, but the children loved it.

Besides musical games, they listened to records of orchestra music and learned to identify different musical instruments. These were some of Nettie's favourite times.

Story time was another special time when the children listened to Cinderella or other stories while looking at a picture book, turning the pages to follow what they heard.

While "Cinderella" was the story Nettie enjoyed most at school, her favourite book at home was "Heidi". It had been her older sister Annie's book at one time. The Friesens had a good little library of their own since everyone loved to read.

Besides reading, the pump organ drew ten year old Nettie often and she played by ear using both hands. It was decided she needed to learn to read music as well, besides what was taught at school, so she took lessons from Mrs. Bessie Rostek. Nettie learned quickly and enjoyed the lessons, always wondering how the music teacher could watch her student's fingering on the piano while at the same time Mrs. Rostek's own fingers flew as she knit lovely lacy sweaters and blankets.

Nettie's first music lesson book

Excitement about the coming Christmas Concert at school had the children trying out for parts in the plays and practicing songs over and over. Each grade prepared a special song or acrostic for the program.

Finally, a week before the concert all the desks from one room were moved to the other. Wide planks were laid across saw horses at the front of the room to make a stage; a wire was strung from one side of the stage to the other and green curtains hung on it. Wide planks were also used to set up benches for the audience of parents and family who would be attending the concert. Now the rehearsing of the plays and songs began in earnest.

The grade one class practiced their acrostic while holding up the letters;
C – is for the Christ Child born this glorious day
H – for Hallelujah, sing His praise
R – is for rejoicing in our Saviour's birth
I – is for incredible merriment and mirth
S – is for Salvation, shining as a Star
T – is for triumphant shouts from near and far

M – is for the manger, where Jesus lay nearby
A – is for Angels singing praise on high
S – is for our Saviour upon whom we rely.

The classes from both rooms gathered on the stage and below it, as they sang "O Little Town of Bethlehem", "Silent Night," "Joy to the World" and "Away in a Manger". The audience joined in the singing.

The children's faces glowed from the lights on the tree and from their own anticipation of Christmas and for the gifts that lay beneath the school tree. Each child received a bag with an orange, candy, and assorted nuts after the concert.

Nettie loved Christmas, but this year she wondered if there would be any gifts at home, because she had overheard some of the family's conversation about the drought, hard winter and shortage of cash. She decided not to expect anything for Christmas. After all, she didn't want her parents to worry about gifts.

On Christmas morning, she was surprised to receive a doll with lots of clothes; a dress that matched her own Christmas dress, bonnets, a coat and several other colourful dresses. She learned that her father had bought the doll at the Thrift store for 25 cents and her mother made the clothes for it. Nettie decided this was one of her best Christmases ever.

I DIDN'T THINK THEY'D FLOAT

CHAPTER 54

As warmer weather melted the snow, winter recess games like Fox and Goose were replaced with Prisoners' Base and Red Rover at the school. The boys and girls began bringing their baseball gloves and teams were chosen as soon as the ball diamond was nearly free of mud. Everyone looked forward to the end of school and summer holidays, despite how much fun recess was.

The end of the school year brought the older Friesen siblings back to Osler and then on to their various places of work. Jake left for the Jones farm for seeding time, while Tena and Christine worked as maids for farm families in the area. Lena continued to work at the Veterans Hospital, Anne did day work and Julius took more summer school classes to improve his teaching.

At home, the youngest two had to help with the milking, gardening, housework and other chores. However, there was always time allowed for friends to visit and spend time with.

Several of Nettie's friends and cousins came over one afternoon. The girls skipped and sang rhymes to go with the jumps:

"Mother, mother I am ill
Call for the doctor over the hill
In came the doctor
In came the nurse
In came the lady with the alligator purse
Out goes the doctor
Out goes the nurse
Out goes the lady with the alligator purse"

Helena walked by on her way to the chicken barn, carrying two pails of grain. As she neared the girls, Nettie glanced her way and then turned to her friends. "My mom can't skip anymore. She's too old," she told her friends.

Fifty-two year old Helena stopped, put down the pails of grain and reached out her hand, "Give me that rope!" she commanded.
She skipped several skips, handed the rope back and said, "There!"

The girls stood in awe that someone that old could still skip.

One day, Jacob walked from the barn to the house, looked into the kitchen window, and gently knocked on the window pane. This was his way of letting Helena know he was ready for a coffee break. She saw him, nodded, and put on the kettle. After coffee time, Jacob suggested they drive to town for some supplies. Helena needed groceries anyway and agreed. Nettie asked to go with them.

When they returned from town Helena walked into the house, placed the grocery items on the table and turned toward the bathroom to wash her hands. As was her habit, she glanced under the sink to make sure the slop pail was not too full.

Danny walked into the kitchen as his mother came out of the bathroom.

"Who was here while we were gone?" she asked him.

"No one," Danny replied.

"But – there are cigarette butts in the slop pail," she said.

Danny's face turned red, he looked down sheepishly and said, "I didn't think they'd float." He turned and walked out of the house and to the barn. It was milking time.

Helena's eyes sparkled, but she bit her lip until her son was across the yard. Then her face broke into a big grin and she doubled over in laughter, her shoulders shaking as she giggled. It took a while for her to stop and throughout the evening, whenever she thought about it, she giggled again.

Jacob glanced at his wife's merriment, went to the bedroom to change his clothes and joined his son in the barn. He stopped where Danny sat milking and looked at him with concern.

"Danny, the devil never sleeps," he warned. Although his wife thought the incident was funny, Jacob was more serious of nature and his cancer made him concerned. Danny never took up the habit.

A NEW OUTHOUSE

CHAPTER 55

The old outhouse was beginning to crumble with age and a new one was sorely needed. Julius was home that summer and was interested in building a new one.

"Dad, if I can find a good deal on lumber, would it be all right if I built a new outhouse?" Julius asked.

"See if you can find a good price at the lumber yard first before we decide," his dad answered.

"I can help pay for part of it," Julius offered.

Julius hopped in the car and drove to the Osler Monarch Lumber Yard. He wandered around the lot until he came upon cedar boards. He loved the smell of cedar and checked the price. It was reasonable and available, so he returned home to make plans.

Julius and Jacob talked it over, made measurements and decided how much material was needed. Soon the back yard was a bustle of activity as Julius framed the walls, built the floor, toilet seat and roof rafters. Within the week it was covered in cedar siding and roofed in cedar shingles. Now all that was needed was a new hole. As they dug the new hole, they threw the dirt into the old hole to fill it.

Julius and his dad manoeuvred the building across the grass and set it firmly over the new hole. It was a good solid building with a clean cedar smell to it. Everyone was pleased with Julius' creation.

Summer was soon over and Julius went back to teaching. Winter quickly followed and the old cook stove burned constantly in an effort to heat the drafty house.

One morning Helena cleaned the ashes out of the stove and carried the ash pail outside to sit in a snow bank to cool off. It was important for the embers to die before they were dumped so there was no risk of fire.

It was a Wednesday and Tena was home for a few days. She spent the entire day off ironing all the shirts, pillow cases, sheets and tea towels.

"We're going to the Neudorf's for Prayer meeting this evening, Tena," Jacob said as the family sat down to a delicious meal of pluma mousse and fried ham. "We'd like you to stay with Danny and Nettie."

"Oh, and Danny, make sure you take the pail of ashes to the back yard and dump them on the ash heap before you go to bed," Helena said. The ash heap was some distance away, northwest of the outhouse.

Nettie and Danny spent the evening doing homework and playing Chinese checkers with Tena. It was getting late so after winning the last game of checkers, Danny bundled up in his warm parka and took the pail of ashes out to the back yard and dumped it on the ash heap. Soon it was bedtime and their parents had not returned. They carried their coal oil lamps upstairs and went to bed.

A strong northwest wind began to blow around the house as they got into bed. Nettie wondered if it would snow all night. She didn't like the howling sound of the wind, but snuggled under the warm wool quilt and fell asleep quickly.

At about 10:30 the phone rang. The Line Four party line rang three long rings, over and over. It was the phone number for the Friesen family. Each phone line in rural areas had many people on the same line. Each home had its own pattern of long or short rings. Tena woke up and ran downstairs to answer. There was an eerie flickering glow coming in through the curtains.

"Hello?" she said, and heard many 'clicks' as others on the same phone line picked up their phones to listen in to this late call.

"What is burning at your place?" the neighbour asked urgently.

Tena dropped the phone receiver and yelled upstairs, "It's burning! It's burning!" then turned and ran outside into the snow in her bare feet.

Nettie ran downstairs and followed her sister out into the snow, also in her bare feet. They saw it was the outhouse, so quickly ran back inside. Tena told the neighbour the outhouse was burning. Danny, half asleep with glasses askew, made his way downstairs with difficulty - his pants were on backward.

Meanwhile Helena and Jacob were on their way home. They saw the flames shooting skyward in the wind and were filled with dread. Was it the house or the barn? They hurried their horses down the ½ mile lane between the two farms. It seemed to take forever to drive the short distance.

As they reached the yard, other neighbours began to arrive. They had heard the party line ring and listened in to the conversation.

The wind blew embers onto the barn roof, so the neighbours quickly dumped snow on the outhouse and on the embers. Finally the fire was out, but the cedar outhouse had burned completely and fragrantly to the ground. Thankfully the house and barn were spared.

Next morning Danny and Nettie went to school where their teacher, John Loewen, commented with a grin, "So, we hear there was a fire at your farm last night!" At that the whole class burst out laughing at the thought of a burning outhouse.

A few weeks later, Julius returned home for a visit. As the family sat at the faspa table, Julius folded his arms on the edge of the table and turned toward Danny, "So - why did you burn down my new outhouse?" he demanded, with a grin.

"You built it," quipped Danny dryly, "I wasn't satisfied – I burned it down!"

SURPRISE DELIVERY

CHAPTER 56

Spring seeding took Jake back to the Jones farm. Lena was still employed there. She did the housework, made meals and worked in the garden. In spite of the amount of work, there was time in the evenings to relax in the living room.

Mrs. Jones had a lovely piano and enjoyed hearing Lena play. Since the lady was blind, she was no longer able to read music. She sat back to listen to the music Lena and Jake brought into the house. Lena played the piano while Jake joined her with his violin. They enjoyed singing and the Joneses enjoyed listening. The couple grew fond of the two workers.

When seeding was completed, Mr. & Mrs. Jones made a decision: the piano should go to Lena and Jake and their family. A day was set when it would be delivered to the Friesen family farm.

Lena and Jake decided to make it a surprise for the rest of the family. The piano was crated and shipped to Saskatoon by train and then on to Osler. Jake and Lena came home for the weekend with Mr. Jones' truck and Jake arranged to pick up the piano at the station. Julius and Christine also arrived from Guernsey for a visit.

Nettie stayed at school with friends for a short time that Friday while Danny returned home. He was surprised to see a truck on the yard with a big crate on the truck box. Christine was standing near it. She was excited! Could it be? Was her prayer for a piano answered? She waited to see the crate carefully removed.

Danny walked to the other side of the truck and read the big lettering on the crate; LOAD THIS PIANO ENDWISE TO THE CAR TO AVOID TIPPAGE WHILE SHUNTING. The freight train car the piano was shipped in needed to be shunted from one track to another to get it from Clavet to Saskatoon and from Saskatoon to Osler.

Finally the piano was visible. Carefully it was moved to the living room where it was opened and the perfect ivory and black keys invited someone to play.

"Go ahead, Chris," Lena suggested as she saw the delight in her younger sister's eyes.

Christine sat down and touched those keys. Soon the beautiful sound filled the living room as those who were home gathered around to hear it for the first time.

Jake glanced at the old pump organ. "I wonder if the old organ and the piano would be in tune so the two instruments could be played together." He walked over, pumped the pedals and hit a three sharp chord. Christine tried the same chord but, unfortunately, they were not in tune.

"We should give the pump organ to someone who could use it," Lena said.

"How about giving it to Uncle Henry Friesen's family? Dad said they don't have a piano or an organ," Julius suggested. It sounded like a good idea to the rest of them as well.

Nettie arrived home and was greeted by smiling family members. She walked into the living room to put down her books and turned to see her siblings following her. They were still smiling. As she was about to ask what was up, she saw the piano. It was beautiful! She sat down at the keyboard. Nettie was filled with awe at the lovely instrument and was suddenly overcome. She touched the keys and said, "But I can't play well."

Jake, Christine,Tena and Lena singing. A friend joins them

"Yes, you can," Christine encouraged.

After chores were done that evening, the family stood around the piano while Christine played. They sang hymn after hymn in harmony. That instrument became the center of many a solo, trio, duet, quartet and family choir through the years.

Along with the piano, the Joneses sent their dog Daisy to live at the farm. She was a small Jack Russell terrier, a dog used to being in the house as well as outside. It was a surprise to the family that Helena allowed the animal in the house. Dogs and cats were barn animals and that was where they belonged - this had always been her motto.

Daisy soon spent more time outdoors than in the house, as she roamed the barnyard with the other dogs and cats. After a while she became round and fat by supplementing her diet with grasshoppers of which there were always plenty. It was comical to watch her leap into the air to catch the insects.

But Daisy often joined the family in the living room in the evenings, sitting near one of the Friesen siblings, while they sang along with the piano.

The old pump organ was moved to Uncle Henry Friesen's home where it was enjoyed for many more years.

(The Piano is now in Helena's granddaughter's home in Calgary)

(Daisy with Tena and Lena)

THE JANZ CRUSADE

CHAPTER 57

In the summer of 1950, Jake built dugouts along with neighbour Jake Neudorf and others. A contractor from Hepburn hired the young men and they supplied dugouts for many farmers in the area. These holes in the ground, filled with water from snow, spring run-off and rain, were important sources of water for farm houses and cattle. The young men used a TD14 International Diesel Kat pulling a Latourneau scraper. One dugout took approximately 3 - 4 days to complete.

That summer also brought some excitement to the Osler area as the Neudorfs, who lived between the Friesen farm and the town of Osler, invited four men from southern Saskatchewan to bring special meetings. A big tent was set up in a large area next to the Neudorf house, chairs and benches were brought in, a stage was set up and the meetings advertised in the area.

Three brothers, Leo, Adolph and Hildor Janz, sang in a quartet along with Cornie Ens, accompanied by pianist Jack Simons. Leo was the evangelist. Their families traveled with them and stayed with the Neudorfs in their home and in a trailer on the yard.

Next door at the Friesen farm, the family heard the quartet clearly as they practiced during the day. With Hildor's high tenor, Cornie Ens' deep base, and the close harmony with Adolph and Leo, the songs were wonderful to listen to.

When the day's work was done and supper was over, the family walked the half mile to sing hymns, listen to the quartet and hear the preaching. The young men who built dugouts during the day were eager to attend the meetings in the evenings.

It was fascinating to watch the pianist, Mr. Simons. His fingers flew all over the keyboard while the quartet sang;
"I once was lost in sin, but Jesus took me in.
And then a little light from Heaven filled my soul.
He bathed my heart in love and wrote my name above
And just a little talk with Jesus makes me whole....."

Leo's strong voice rang out through the microphone as he spoke of the love of Jesus and encouraged people to get right with God. He explained that God came to earth as Jesus, who gave his life for our sins as he died on a cross and that he rose again from the dead. He assured people that Jesus will come again to take us home with Him some day.

Janz Quartette

HILDOR ADOLPH LEO CORNIE
JACK

Night after night the tent was packed with people, some who came from quite a distance and didn't want to miss the evenings. The messages stirred their hearts and many walked to the front to pray and get right with God. Lives were being changed. People knew they were loved and forgiven by God.

Leo Janz spoke about being sure that one could spend eternity with God when this life ends. It was a message both Helena and Jacob welcomed. Their religious upbringing had always taught them about the love of Jesus but they were also taught that they could never be sure they would be with God after they died. At the end of one service Helena and Jacob walked to the front and knelt at the stage where one of the men prayed with them.

They rose from their knees, thankful for finally being able to be sure of where they stood with God. It was an event that changed them and gave them joy and peace.

After several weeks of meetings, the tent was taken down and the Janz quartet returned home with their families. The people of the area were left with the memories of good Bible teaching and great music. They hoped the quartet would return some time.

As fall rolled into an early winter, Jake finished working on dugouts and returned to Two Rivers Bible Institute to finish his last year of Bible School.

BEST SPELLER IN THE OUTFIELD

Chapter 58

In the spring of 1951, Jake graduated from Two Rivers Bible Institute and returned for another summer of building dugouts. Christine found work at a farm near Melfort.

Danny, along with other school boys his age, was hired at the Ben Buhler farm to pick stones on Saturdays and after school to clear the fields for seeding. The hilly land had lots of small stones that could damage the drill or disker blades. Danny and the other boys collected the small stones in five-gallon pails and dumped them into the stone wagon. Ben Buhler, senior, set the pace by running, not walking, with his pail. "Schvind, schvind!" (Quick, quick) was his family motto. He got the boys working and then tended to his other chores.

As the boys rested on the stone pile after a few hours of hard work, Mr. Buhler provided Pepsi and Paulins' Chocolate Puff cookie breaks, especially welcoming after working in the heat of the day. He knew how to keep the boys interested.

At home in the evenings, Danny and Nettie practiced pitching the softball to each other. Both could pitch straight pitches, but Danny had a fast windmill pitch his older brothers admired when they were home at times in the summer and enjoyed family ball games. It was a lot of fun to practice and play with each other.

After the summer and fall work was over, Lena and Tena left to attend Bible School at Two Rivers Bible Institute. Christine joined them at the same school to take her grade twelve. It wasn't long before the three sisters' talent in singing became known. 'The Friesen Sisters Trio' took a month off of school to travel with an organization called, "Christ For Everyone'. Then they returned to school.

Friesen Sister Trio: Left to right; Tena, Christine and Helen(Lena)

Back in the Osler school, the students were all busy with various subjects. When the teacher announced a spelling bee, the Friesen children were ready and quickly chosen for sides, because spelling and reading came easily to them.

Captains were selected by the teacher and they took turns calling fellow students to their teams. Soon the teams were in place and the teacher called out the first word: "Chocolate"

"C – h – o – k – a – l - i – t," replied the first child.

"Wrong. Please take your seat," the teacher stated. The other team was given a chance to spell it correctly. One by one team members sat down as the words got harder and harder. Finally it was Danny Friesen against an opposing team mate.

"Recuperation" the teacher called out.

"R – e – c – u - p – a – r – a – t – i – o – n, " his rival spelled out.

"Wrong." the teacher said as he turned toward Danny.

"R – e – c – u – p – e – r – a – t – i – o – n!" Danny spelled effortlessly.

"Correct!" the teacher exclaimed and the team cheered. Once again Danny had won the spelling bee for his team.

"All right – it's recess time, everyone outside for some fresh air and softball," the teacher announced.

Teams were chosen and Danny's team walked out to their positions on the ball diamond as the other team prepared to bat.

Danny stood in the outfield considering the irony that since he was near sighted, he didn't have much chance of catching a ball in the outfield when he actually could have seen quite well in closer positions. Out where he was, it would be difficult to see the ball up high against the sun and sky.

He glanced around at the other players. "Oh well - at least I'm the best speller in the outfield!" he muttered to himself as he crossed his arms to wait for the game to be over.

PICKING UP POTATOES

CHAPTER 59

Each year, the schools in the area held Public Speaking Contests. Students were expected to prepare speeches to memorize and present to the class. Nettie wondered what to talk about.

When Julius came for a weekend, Nettie mentioned that she didn't know what to write about for her speech.

"I'm stumped," she said.

"Well," her teacher brother said, "How about writing about something on the farm. What do we do around here that might interest people? What things did we do to get ready for winter?"

"We picked up LOTS of potatoes!" Nettie answered, rolling her eyes. Julius grinned and chuckled.

"Yes, we sure did," he said, and added, "what is involved in picking up potatoes? How would you tell others about that?"

That gave Nettie ideas and she sat down with a notebook and pencil. She wrote about following the older siblings with a pail as they dug up the potato plants so she could pick up the potatoes, fill her pail and dump it into a gunny sack on the stone boat. Once the sacks were all full, old Babe was hitched to the stone boat and led to the west side of the house.

There they stopped and the small door that covered the opening to the cellar bin was removed. There was a metal slide inside and the potatoes were poured down the slide. The sound of those vegetables bouncing loudly down the metal was a satisfying sound. There would be lots to eat for the winter.

Julius checked on her progress each time he came for a weekend, fine tuning the story and coaching Nettie on how stand when speaking, how to hold her hands clasped in front of her and how to begin and end.

The Osler teachers listened to all the speeches in order to select the best speech from each grade. Nettie was chosen for her grade and the teacher told her, "You're going to Warman!" Then the memorizing and coaching began in earnest. Every day after other school work was done, those who were going to the contest were asked to stand before the class and say their speeches. It was probably boring for the other students; after all, they heard the same speeches over and over.

The Regional Competition was held in the Warman School gymnasium. When Nettie was called to the stage, she stood with her hands clasped in front of her, looked around at the full room and took a deep breath.

"Honorable Judges, Teachers, Ladies and Gentlemen, fellow students," she said as she glanced at the judges, teachers and audience. "Today I am going tell you about 'picking up potatoes."

She felt good about how she had done as she sat down. When the judges were ready, they announced the winners.

Nettie would be going to the provincial contest in Floral, Saskatchewan.

Floral was located about an hour from Osler, southeast of Saskatoon. When the big day arrived, her teacher, Mr. John Loewen, drove to the Friesen farm to pick up Nettie, Danny and their parents.

At this contest, Nettie was pitted against a grade twelve student who spoke about "Ju-ven-ile De-ling-quen-cee" in clipped sentences. The grade twelve contestant won. Mr. Loewen was very upset with the judges and complained most of the way home. He was sure that the winning speech was taken 'word for word' from an encyclopedia and Nettie's was an original story.

Although Nettie was disappointed she didn't win, it was a wonderful feeling to know her teacher believed in her ability. Her parents were pleased with her speech.

(Through the years Nettie continued to write and won a few more regional competitions. Many years later she spoke at a Mothers' Day Service and afterwards, her 9 year old granddaughter exclaimed, "Grandma! That wasn't even boring.")

Row of potatoes waiting to be picked up.

BACK TO SCHOOL FOR JACOB

CHAPTER 60

In spring, Jacob had the opportunity to buy a 1938 Chevy car and decided to give the old '37 Chev to Julius.

When Julius came for the Easter weekend, Jacob approached his son as he looked over the newer car.

"So you bought a different car? Looks good," Julius commented.

"Well, I'm about to start back into construction in the city and needed a better car for the job." Jacob said and continued, "Julius, you need a car of your own so I wonder if you would like the '37 Chev?" Jacob offered. "It usually starts fine, but once in a while it needs a little push to roll start it."

"I would appreciate having the car," Julius replied. "Thanks Dad!" He walked over to the older car and got in. It hadn't been started for a while but Jacob handed him the keys and Julius turned on the ignition. The motor tried to turn over but couldn't quite make it.

Julius stepped on the clutch, shifted into neutral, turned on the ignition, then opened the car door, got out, put his hands on the door frame and pushed. As the car began to roll, he jumped in; his foot hit the clutch at the same instant as he slipped the gear shift into third and engaged the clutch. The motor roared to life. Julius grinned as he took the car for a spin around the yard.

"Well, Dad – I figure if I park it on a downhill street with the handbrake on, it'll work fine!" And that's what Julius did until he got the starter fixed. The car ran well for him for several years and took him to and from his teaching positions.

As Jacob started back to work in construction in the city, he decided to look into the possibility of working for another Construction Company. He heard the wages were better than his present job and he was interested in working for the company.

"I plan to drive over there tomorrow to see if they will hire me," he told his family.

He drove his "new" car to the city for work and inquired about the new job on his lunch break.

"Do you have your papers in Carpentry Trade?" he was asked.

"No, I don't," Jacob replied, "but I've been working in construction in the city for quite a few years."

"In order for us to hire you, we need you to show us a certificate in carpentry trade." he was told.

"How would I go about getting my papers?" Jacob inquired.

The man at the Construction office reached for some papers from a desk drawer and handed them to Jacob. "Here's the address and the application form. You need to apply to the Department of Labour in Regina for the course to study. They'll send you the books. It takes about eight weeks to complete and the fee is $5.00."

Jacob decided to do just that. He took the papers home and filled out the application form, included the $5.00 fee, mailed it and waited to hear from them. Meanwhile he continued at his old construction job.

The siblings from Two Rivers Bible Institute returned home and looked for work for the summer. While the other sisters found work, Christine didn't know where to start. She wanted to work in Saskatoon but was too timid to phone or apply for a job there.

"Where would you like to work?" asked her dad while they sat at the noon dinner table.

"I've heard there might be jobs available at the Sanatorium." Christine answered.

It was a Saturday, but Jacob rose from the table and walked to the phone. He called the local telephone operator and asked for Saskatoon. When a city operator answered, Jacob asked for the Sanatorium.

"Saskatoon Sanatorium," a woman answered, "How may I help you?"

"I wonder if you have any job openings for a young woman?" Jacob asked.

"I'll put you through to the Matron's office." she offered.

When the Matron answered, Jacob explained, "I have a daughter who needs a job. She is a Mennonite girl from Osler."

"Mennonite? From my experience, Mennonite girls are good workers," the Matron said. "Have your daughter come in for an interview on Monday morning and we'll see if we can work something out."

Jacob thanked her, hung up and turned to Christine with a smile. "Well, she wants you to go for an interview on Monday morning to apply for a job. She says Mennonite girls are hard workers."
"Thanks dad!" Christine said relieved, and a bit anxious about the interview for Monday.

Christine had her interview and was hired on the spot. She would stay in the nurses' residence, wear a white uniform with a red TB emblem and her title was "Nursing Assistant". It was a job she enjoyed.

A large package arrived in the mail for Jacob a few days later and he eagerly opened it when he returned from work in the city. Several text books lay before him, along with work books. It felt a bit daunting, but he was determined and set to work.

Gas Lamp. Note silk bag tied to gas spout. Osler, Sask. Museum

One thin brown book caught Danny's eye. It explained about how to use a steel square. Danny skimmed through the book and was surprised that the square could be used for many more things than a 90 degree angle.

Jacob worked in construction during the day and studied in the evenings and on weekends. As the sun lowered in the western evening sky, Helena lit the Aladdin mantel lamp and hung it on the ceiling hook above the kitchen table to give him a brighter place to study.

The Aladden was a gas lamp with two small artificial silk or rayon bags attached near the top. The lamp was lit and the new bags burned until they were just hanging ashes and amazingly, they did not fall apart. Those mantles contained the flames within them each time the lamp was lit. Unless the mantles were bumped or a moth flew through them, they lasted many days. The lamp gave off a very bright light. After several months of study, it was time for Jacob's final exam.

"Are you nervous, Dad?" Danny asked.

"Well, maybe a little, but it is an open book exam, so I'll be able to have my books with me. I hope I do well. This is just for the Third Class certificate. If I do well, I'll try to work my way up to a First Class," Jacob answered.

He took his '38 Chevy to the city for the exam and afterwards, waited nervously to see the results. He received his Certificate of Status in Carpentry Trade on September 25th, 1952.

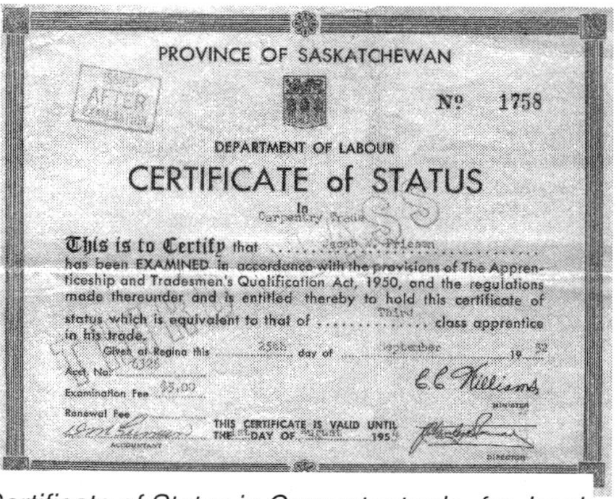
PROVINCE OF SASKATCHEWAN

№ 1758

DEPARTMENT OF LABOUR

CERTIFICATE of STATUS

In Carpentry Trade

This is to Certify that .... Jacob W. Friesen .... has been EXAMINED in accordance with the provisions of The Apprenticeship and Tradesmen's Qualification Act, 1950, and the regulations made thereunder and is entitled thereby to hold this certificate of status which is equivalent to that of ....Third.... class apprentice in his trade.

Given at Regina this ....25th.... day of ....September.... 19 52

Acct. No: ....

Examination Fee ....$5.00....

Renewal Fee ....

ACCOUNTANT

THIS CERTIFICATE IS VALID UNTIL THE ....DAY OF .... 195..

MINISTER

DIRECTOR

Certificate of Status in Carpentry trade, for Jacob W. Friesen

Jacob took the certificate to the company that had required he take the course and was hired. He looked forward to the steady job with good pay.

When he turned up at the job site, he was sent to work on the Wheat Pool Flour Mill on 33rd street. Some of the structure on the outside of the building needed redoing.

The building was high and required Jacob to work from scaffolds. He had often climbed the windmill ladder at home to stand on the precariously narrow platform so he could grease the gears while Helena stood anxiously clutching the kitchen window sill watching, praying the wind would not shift to turn the wide wooden vanes on the wheel and knock him off.

Helena wasn't here to watch and pray for him as he stood on a high narrow scaffold for long periods of time and worked with his tools. It was better not to look down. After a while he was more used to heights but continued to be cautious as he worked. At home – Helena prayed for him anyway.

MUSIC LESSONS IN THE CITY

CHAPTER 61

The next fall when the feed lot was full of oat sheaves, straw and hay stacks, it was again time for school. Lena, Tena, and Christine left to attend Bible School at Two Rivers Bible Institute and Dan went with them to take his grade eleven. All the siblings left home, except for Nettie.

Jake lived in Saskatoon and worked in the shoe department at the Bay. Julius was away teaching. Since expenses for the Friesen students in TRBI were a bit overwhelming at times, Julius and Jake sent money to their siblings when they could. Anne worked in the city and helped out at home on her days off.

With all but one of his children away, Jacob needed someone to look after the farm while he was at work. He hired a young man to help.

Life seemed lonely for Nettie with many of the family gone. Her brother Jake came home on a Sunday and spoke to her and their parents.

"Nettie, how would you like to take piano lessons in Saskatoon?" he asked his sister.

"Really? I would love to take lessons!" she replied.

"How much do they cost?" asked Jacob.
"It's all right, Dad," Jake said. "I'll pay for a year of lessons for her. I found out about the Lyell Gustin Studio in the city and it's well known for having good teachers. I know several people who have trained there. I think it would be good for Nettie to go. She would have to take the train to the city every Saturday morning though, is that all right?"

Jacob and Helena considered that offer for a moment and then Jacob consented. "I'll pay for the train fare, if you pay for the lessons. Thank you, Jake."

"I'll call home when I find out what time the lessons will be and give you the address of the studio," Jake said turning toward Nettie. "And when you're done your lesson you can walk over to my apartment and spend some time with me until the evening train."
Nettie was thrilled!

Gustin House where Nettie took lessons. :(A Michael Pomedli Photo. Used with permission.)

Saturday morning of her first lesson she took the train to the city, walked through the big doors to the busy street and walked east to Fourth Avenue where she turned south toward the Broadway Bridge. She had never walked across that river bridge before and enjoyed the pleasant walk to the south side of the city. A few blocks later Nettie turned right on 10th Street, found the Studio and knocked on the door. It was opened by a young man who smiled and led her to a room with a piano.

Mr. Gustin walked in and sat down to ask a few questions.

"How far have you progressed in Royal Conservatory music books?" he asked.

"I've finished grade four," she answered.

Mr. Gustin had her sit at the piano while he placed music in front of her. She played several of her grade four pieces and then was given grade five pieces to sight read. Nettie was already familiar with them since she had played some of her sister Christine's grade five pieces. After a while, Mr. Gustin closed the book.

"I don't think you need grade five. We'll put you into grade six," he said. Nettie was surprised, but pleased. He turned toward the young man who had invited Nettie in and introduced him.

"This is Douglas Voice. He'll be your piano teacher." Eighteen year old Douglas shook fourteen year old Nettie's hand and sat down with her on the piano bench while Mr. Gustin waved and left the room.

After a short lesson, the hour was over and Nettie left to walk back across the bridge. She could hardly wait to tell her brother Jake about the first lesson. She found his boarding house and climbed the stairs to his third floor apartment at 303 6th Avenue.

Each Saturday through the school year, Nettie took the train to the city for her lesson. Douglas Voice was a dedicated teacher and a quiet, polite young man who helped her with her coat and opened the door for her. His feel for expressing emotion on the piano pieces was something Nettie could relate to and became an even more important part of her playing. She practiced every spare moment she had and enjoyed the feel of her fingers running up and down the keys.

At home the piano became her friend in many more ways. It was there when she needed soft music to calm her soul; it was there when she needed to pound out frustrations from school; it was there for her to express joy and excitement - and best of all – it was there for her to worship God in music and song.

Helena and Jacob sat listening while Jacob read the newspaper and Helena darned socks on the wooden foot Jacob carved for her. It was relaxing and rewarding to hear their daughter's progress in music.

CHRISTMAS WEEK COLLAPSE

Chapter 62

Jacob wasn't feeling well at all. Extreme pain in his stomach caused him to double over at times and it was hard to know what to eat. Helena was very concerned and Jacob was more worried about finances. It became difficult for him to work in construction and at home. He was glad to have the help of the young hired man.

As winter set in, the three family members at home looked forward to Christmas when everyone would return. Helena and Nettie baked cookies and decorated the house in anticipation of celebrating together. There would be carol singing around the piano and lots of visiting. Nettie could hardly wait.

Finally, the four from TRBI arrived on the CPR train at Warman on December 17th. Jacob bundled up for the drive to pick them up at the station. He was cold in spite of the warmth of the car heater. As the train pulled away, the siblings saw their father's car waiting. They hurried into it.

"Hi Dad!" they said as Jacob greeted them with a hug and a smile.

"Good to see you!" he said. The siblings were glad to be on their way home to the farm and looked forward to the warm kitchen stove and mom's baking.

"How have you been, Dad?" Lena asked as the car turned toward Osler.

"Well, I've been laid off for the winter again, but I'm glad. It's so cold and I haven't been feeling well," he replied. They pulled into the yard a half hour later and all hurried into the house.

"Merry Christmas everyone!" the girls and Dan said as they walked in and removed their scarves and coats. Helena stepped forward to greet them with warm hugs. She was so happy to have them home again. They moved to stand around that good old kitchen stove as it radiated warmth around them.

As the family sat around the lunch table later, Jacob quietly looked around at his family. It was good to see them. He was also glad for more help with chores during the Christmas holiday. With Dan and the hired boy, there would not be as much need for him to be in the barn, but the boy would leave for his Christmas break. Julius would arrive in a few days and Jake would be home for the weekend as well. There would be more help. Jacob was so tired.

At the supper table, the children saw their father's drawn, tired face and noticed how little he ate before a look of pain crossed his face. He excused himself from the table to lie down.

"Mom," Lena said, "Dad looks awful! Has he been to see the doctor?"

"Yes, several times but they don't know what's wrong with him," Helena answered.

"Has he been able to work?" asked Julius.

"No, he hasn't worked for a week now and besides, he's been laid off for the winter," she answered, adding, "Maybe they laid him off because they know he's sick."

On Sunday, December 20th, the family attended the Osler Church morning Service and enjoyed seeing many friends. Jacob remained at home and in the afternoon, he sat back in the chair beside the stove and listened to his family sing. His children glanced at him at times, concerned with the look of his pale face.

Everyone pitched in to do the chores. Later in the evening, Helena and the children were gathered in the kitchen for night lunch and lively conversation when they heard a thud in the bathroom. Helena rushed to see what had happened and the family heard her frantic voice.

“Oba nay! Blous nich schtoaven! Blous nich schtoaven! (Oh no - just don’t die, just don't die!)”, she said. Several of the siblings ran to see what had happened and found Helena holding Jacob, who had vomited blood and collapsed. As he re-gained consciousness, he said, "Let me be for a few minutes."

"He needs to go to the hospital right away!" Annie said urgently. Dan hurried into his warm jacket and boots and ran out into the bitterly cold evening to start the car but it wouldn't start. He ran back inside.

"The car won't start!" Dan announced frantically.

Lena rushed to the telephone to call their Uncle David Janzen at the farm next door to see if he would take Jacob to the hospital in the city. David hurried over and the older children dressed their dad warmly and helped him to the back seat of the car so he could lie down. Helena got in beside him and David started down the road. As they reached the edge of the city, Helena feared her husband would not make it to the hospital.

"We need help now!" Helena said urgently as she held her husband's head up as he vomited more blood and then passed out again.

David turned into a Service Station yard and stopped near the door. He glanced in the back seat of the car and then ran into the Station to call an ambulance. It arrived within a very short time and Jacob was quickly transported to the hospital.

After a quick look at the patient's condition, the doctor hurried over to the waiting room where Helena and David Janzen sat waiting.

"Your husband needs emergency surgery," he told Helena. "We will operate immediately. But you need to sign some papers to consent to the operation. Please go to the nurses' desk and they will help you with this. I'll let you know how things are after the surgery." With that, the doctor turned quickly and strode away.

Helena rose and went to the nurses' station to sign the papers. Her brother-in-law stood beside her to help with translation if needed.

The waiting seemed to take a very long time but finally the doctor appeared, pulled off his surgical mask and sat down with them. He looked very sober.

"Mr. Friesen had a bleeding stomach ulcer and hemorrhaged during the operation. It was very serious and we've had to remove 2/3 of his stomach. It will be a long slow recovery process in the months ahead. When he heals up, he will only be able to eat small amounts at a time and will need to rest a lot."

"How long do you think it will be before he comes home?" Helena asked in Low German. David translated.

The doctor shook his head, "It will be several weeks – maybe a month or more."

When David dropped Helena off at the farm in the early hours of the next morning, he handed Dan a bag. "Here are your dad's clothes."

The next day David told his own family how thankful he was that he was able to be there for his brother-in-law. It was a moving and sobering time for him.

A few days later Jake took his mother Helena to Saskatoon along with Dan, Tena, Christine and Nettie. Helena stayed at the hospital for the day. On the way home, Jake fell asleep and the car hit a rock in the ditch. Tena pitched forward and hit the windshield with her forehead. Christine had been asleep in the back seat but lurched ahead and hit her head on the seat in front of her.

"Tena!" Jake said, gently shaking his sister, "Are you all right?" After a few moments, Tena nodded while holding her head. Christine's neck was very sore. Danny and Nettie seemed fine, except for Nettie's panic. Jake told her to be quiet.

After making sure everyone was all right, Jake walked to a nearby farm to ask for help in towing the car out of the ditch. The farmer declined, rather rudely, and Jake walked to Warman for help. He found a car repair shop and asked for help. The car was repaired enough to drive and the siblings returned to the farm.

The traditional Christmas Eve concert at the Osler Church was filled with beautiful four part harmony as the congregation sang German and English Christmas Carols.

The Friesens joined in the singing, but their hearts were heavy with concern for their dad.

Christmas morning was very quiet and subdued. Helena moved about mechanically doing the usual meal preparation with her daughters. Her mind was at the hospital with Jacob.

After Christmas, the Bible School siblings stayed home a week longer than planned. Everyone was concerned about how things would be at home with their dad unable to work. Finally, it was decided that Danny would remain at home to run the farm while the sisters returned to school. His education would be delayed. Julius had his teaching position to return to while Jake and Annie returned to their jobs in the city.

It was good to have Danny at home. He did the major chores about the farm while Nettie helped with milking and feeding the animals before and after school. Helena looked after her chickens and geese and at times joined in the milking.

Nettie found it rewarding to be entrusted with the care of the animals and milking. There was something comforting about walking across the cold snowy yard and into the warm barn with the familiar pungent smells and sounds of animals eating and breathing. Nettie enjoyed the rhythmic sound of streams of milk hitting the metal pail. Being responsible for the chores was something they could do to help in those worrisome and uncertain days of their father's illness.

For Danny, hauling water seemed an endless task. No matter how cold the weather was, water was needed for washing and cooking. He drove the team across the field to David Janzen's farm and filled barrels from their well and brought them home again. If the well at home froze or was low on water, he had to haul water for the cattle as well.

Every day the family members at home waited, wondered, prayed and phoned the hospital often about Jacob's condition; those who were away called home for an update on their father whenever they could. All of them hoped he would soon be able to return home. Meanwhile, everyone tried to focus on the things at hand that needed to be done. Helena gazed out of the window often, wondering what the future would hold and breathed out prayers for help.

HOME AGAIN

CHAPTER 63

In the month of March, after seven weeks in hospital, Jacob returned home, weak and pale. Sitting at the table for faspa, he turned toward Danny and said, "I've found a spring job for you. I met a man in the hospital who has a farm near Radisson. He is recovering from surgery too and needs help for spring field work."

"That's great," Danny said, "but who is going to do the work here at the farm?"

"I'll hire a young man to help again. I hope to be able to do some work myself after a while," Jacob replied. "It would be good for you to be able to earn some of your own money for a change and the man needs help."

As Jacob gained a bit of strength, he would appear in the barn at times trying to help in any way he could. However, the huge worry hanging over his head was how he was to earn a living. Finally, in spite of Helena's protests, he again took out his Watkins wagon and sometimes his caboose.

Jacob traveled the areas around Osler and across the ice-road to Aberdeen selling his wares. The roughness of the roads caused a lot of pain during travel and he was often hungry but could only eat small portions at a time. Very gradually he re-gained some of his strength but his worries weren't over yet. There were many Doctor's appointments in between his travels.

When Jacob was home, the rocking chair close to the living room stove was a favorite place for him to relax and listen to his youngest daughter practice piano. Music soothed his soul.

Spring finally arrived. Lena and Tena graduated from Bible School and returned home along with Christine.

Danny left for Radisson. He found himself on a steep learning curve and wished he had challenged his dad's protectiveness which kept him from doing heavy work at home, although he certainly proved himself capable while Jacob was in hospital.

The Friesen 80 acre farm had no tractor and few implements so he found this job exciting. Filling the seeder box with grain and sowing that first field was very satisfying. After a few weeks the farmer felt well enough to finish what was left and Danny returned to Warman on the train. Jacob picked him up at the station. It felt good to be on his way home.

"Welcome back!" his sisters said as he walked in the door. There was a wonderful baking aroma in the kitchen and he was very hungry. After the big meal, a beautiful rhubarb pie was brought to the table. Danny wolfed down three pieces.

"Boy, you must be hollowed out, Dan!" Lena laughed as she watched him eat. "Didn't those people feed you?" They had fed him well, but his mother's and sisters' cooking was always the best.

"Dan, we're nearly out of water for the house again," Helena said as they finished their meal. "Could you go to the neighbours' and fill the barrels before it's time to do the milking?"

"Sure," Dan said. He walked upstairs to change his clothes and went to the field with a pail of oats to lure the horses back to the barn. He grasped their halters and led them to the barn where he put on their harnesses.

Old Babe was too old to do heavy work and her two grown-up colts were not well matched. Danny led Pat and Jim out and backed them into place so he could hitch them up.

Pat, who was a bit of a rebel, snorted and tossed her head defiantly as Dan ordered her to back up. She was of slender build, a light grey color and somewhat mean at times. Although she was sired by a race horse, she could not be ridden. She was beautiful to watch though, as she galloped across the pasture, her mane and tail flying in the wind. She was fast.

Jim simply stood patiently as he was hitched to the wagon and leaned down to clip up a mouthful of grass. He was a heavy horse, dark brown in colour with a black mane and he moved slower than his sister. Jacob walked over to hold Pat in place while Danny hitched her up with her brother; hitching those two up to a wagon, or anything for that matter, could make things difficult.

Jacob opened the field gate as Danny got on the seat of the wagon and picked up the reins. Pat charged forward – Jim just stood there. He was bigger than she was, so her hurry didn't get her anywhere until Jim decided to move.

Holding Pat's reins firmly while she pranced about eager to be off, Danny yelled at Jim, "Hey, you blockhead! Don't just stand there like an elephant - move!" He snapped Jim's reins and the horse reluctantly lurched forward.

Jacob watched as his son drove down the road with that mismatched team. It would be good to have a tractor. He rested his arm on the gate post as he thought of the difference that would make and then smiled slightly. At least a tractor wouldn't be mismatched - both sets of wheels would move forward at the same time! Perhaps soon he would find a good deal somewhere. He turned toward the house to rest. He was thankful to have some of the children home.

EXTERNAL FACELIFT

CHAPTER 64

The appearance of the farm house was old and weather-beaten and it needed a real face-lift. After making plans to improve the place, the family members contributed both financially and physically and the work began.

Since they were planning to re-do the outside anyway, Jacob decided to do something about the veranda, which was falling apart. Helena loved flowers, both in the garden and in her house. Every window sill had pots of African Violets and Geraniums and her plant stands in the living room held more, so Jacob decided to make that old veranda into a bright room with big windows; an ideal place for his wife to have room for more flowers. If he removed part of the wall between it and the kitchen, it would add to the space in the kitchen as well.

"Na, vaut denkst? (well, what do you think?)," he asked Helena after explaining his ideas.

"Daut vood seya gout sennen, (that would be very good)," she answered. She could see it in her mind. How lovely it would be to have a bright room for her flowers and how much brighter the kitchen would be as well.

While his children prepared the outer house walls for new siding, Jacob began to take down the old railings of the veranda.

"Dad," Nettie commented as she helped to remove the old siding. "There used to be a back door in the living room and another one to the Veranda. Why aren't they used?"

"It's much too cold. It would be too hard to heat the house in winter if those drafty doors were left. That's why they were enclosed," her father answered. Nettie was disappointed. It would have been great to have the use of those doors, she thought.

Jacob built insulated outside walls to enclose the veranda. With many rest periods in between and with the help of his boys, he managed to put in large south and west windows for light. He cut an archway between the kitchen and the veranda, planning to complete it when he had the strength to finish.

After a few weeks, the roof welcomed the brightness of green painted cedar shingles while the old walls stood proudly displaying new grey brick-siding. Window frames and trim were painted white and the place was transformed. Of course, Helena wanted new wall-paper in the living room and the kitchen re-painted. The kitchen also received new congoleum flooring. Helena wouldn't have to paint the floor anymore.

1. Old house 2. House after renovation

The whole process brought a fresh feeling of optimism to the family and now they looked forward to some excitement coming up in the fall. During those few years at Bible School, both Tena and Christine met fine young men they were very serious about. Tena and Raymond Dell began dating at school, and Christine and Lorne Albertson dated as well.

In the spring Raymond visited the Friesen farm. After walking about the farm and garden with Tena, he approached Jacob and Helena.

"Tena and I would like to speak with you privately, if we could," Raymond said. They walked to the house and to the living room. Jacob closed the door to the kitchen.

Nervously clearing his throat, Raymond said, "I'd like your permission to marry Tena."

Helena glanced at Tena with a twinkle in her eye. She looked like she was about to giggle. Permission was granted and plans for the wedding began. They would be married in Osler on September 2nd.

By the month of August Jacob was stronger and while he and Helena visited her sister Agnes and husband, Frank Schmidt, in Hague one day he discovered Frank wanted to sell his Ford 8N tractor along with a cultivator. A deal was reached and Danny was given the task of driving it to Osler from the town of Hague.

Everyone was thankful for that tractor. It was so much easier to haul water and since it could pull heavier loads, extra barrels could be put on the wagon. Fewer trips were needed. On the field, it moved faster and at an even pace and made tighter turns than they could have done with horses. Work was done in much less time.

The only problem was that they didn't have a 45 gallon drum for the gas needed. They had a 15 gallon drum which of course had to be refilled many times. That meant going to Osler for more gasoline whenever the tractor ran out of gas.

In spite of sometimes grumbling about the inconvenience of having to go for gas – again, the machinery was a welcome addition to the small farm.

'BETROTTED' HUSBANDS

CHAPTER 65

A few days before Tena's wedding, her fiance Raymond Dell and his best man, brother Elmer, arrived. Christine's friend, Lorne Albertson, also arrived from Saskatoon. The house was full and the family busily prepared for the special day, along with the usual chores and fall farm work.

One of the jobs Helena needed help with was banding young chickens. In order to tell the old hens from the young, she put colored plastic rings on their legs so she could tell the difference. Lorne and Ray helped catch and band the birds.

At the rehearsal on the eve of the wedding, the bridal party practiced walking down the aisle to meet the pastor at the front. The pastor needed practice too. It would be the first English service he had ever conducted.

As he began rehearsing the ceremony, he came to the part where he asked the couple about their vows.

"Tena Friesen - do you take this man to be your betrotted husband?" Reverend Pauls asked.

The whole group burst into giggles. The Pastor looked baffled until the group corrected him on his pronunciation.

Embarrassed, he promised not to repeat that blunder at the ceremony the next day.

Then the pastor came to the place in the rehearsal, for the exchanging of rings. As Raymond reached for an imaginary ring from his brother Elmer, Lorne Albertson (who sat in the pew behind them) placed a green plastic chicken leg ring in Raymond's hand. Again, the group broke into laughter. It took time for everyone to calm down and actually complete the rehearsal.

After the practice run, Reverend Pauls returned home where he told his family about the problem with that difficult English word. His daughters, Edna and Mary, practiced with him to help him say it correctly. They emphasized the unfamiliar 'th' sound over and over. The German language didn't have that sound, so he really had to work at it. He would be all right, he thought.

The morning of September 2nd 1954 dawned sunny and dry and the weather was beautiful. Unfortunately, it was also a dry and sunny day for harvesting so many relatives did not arrive at the church. There were fewer in the pews than the family had expected.

The groom and best man walked down the aisle following the Minister. Then Christine entered wearing a lovely yellow bridesmaid dress.

Tena was radiant in her white gown, carrying a bouquet of roses as she took slow measured steps toward Ray, to the tune of "Largo".

The bridal party sat down on their decorated chairs at the front of the church and the audience was seated. Jake walked up to the platform and sang, "The Lord's Prayer".

Reverend Pauls read Proverbs chapter 3, verses 5 and 6, “Trust in the Lord with all thine heart, and lean not on thine own understanding. In all thy ways acknowledge Him and He shall direct thy paths.” After preaching a message based on this verse, it was time for the ceremony.

Clearing his throat nervously, the pastor began and was soon at the phrase which had been the undoing of the rehearsal. What *was* the pronunciation of that word again?

“Tena Friesen, do you take this man to be your betrotted husband?” he asked.

Struggling for composure, Tena answered, “Yes,” and then waited, holding her giggles while Raymond was asked the same question and answered, "Yes".

While the bride and groom signed the register, Jake walked up to the platform again and sang, "O Perfect Love".

Raymond and Tena were pronounced husband and wife and turned to walk out of the church as the pianist played piano.

Pictures were taken and everyone entered the basement for the wedding supper which Helena and her daughters had prepared.

Jacob and Helena were moved by the sight of their

beautiful daughter. It had been a wonderful but emotional day for them.

Tena and Raymond left for a short honeymoon and then returned to pack up for their move to Minneapolis, Minnesota in the United States.

Christine left to finish her last year of Bible School, but stayed only until Christmas. She was much too lonely with no other family members there. Besides, she was engaged to Lorne Albertson who lived in Saskatoon and it was hard to be separated. They planned to be married in August.

It was a busy time for family weddings and one day in February Helena and Jacob traveled to Saskatoon for her younger sister Eva's wedding to Gordon Damm.

Christine applied for a job and was hired at the Veterans hospital. Her friend, Mary Ens of Osler, also worked in the city so the girls found an apartment and roomed together. Both girls enjoyed their work and life in the city.

The rest of the spring and summer was very busy again at the Friesen farm as the family planned for Christine and Lorne's wedding. Tena and Raymond arrived from the United States at the beginning of August and for several days Helena and her daughters were busy baking buns and cakes. The day before the wedding, potatoes and eggs were boiled for potato salad. Jello salads were prepared. The food was kept covered and cold in the cooling house over night.

August 11th, 1955 dawned bright and beautiful. The small farm house was humming with activity from top to bottom as everyone prepared to get the food to the church and then get ready.

Christine and her bridesmaids, sister Helen(Lena) and friend Mary Ens came down the staircase at the farm and stood, ready to go to the cars. Jacob gazed at his daughter and his eyes filled with tears. She was beautiful in her white gown, holding flowers. This would be another emotional day for him.

At the Osler Church, Lorne Albertson walked in with Reverend Martens from the Mennonite Brethren Church in Saskatoon. He was followed by his best men, Telford Rutin and Bernard Mayerly.

As the pianist played Largo, the bridesmaid and maid of honor walked down the aisle to wait for Christine. Helen (Lena) wore a lovely yellow dress and Mary Ens wore pink.

Christine walked in slowly to the music and met Lorne at their chairs where they sat down until time for the ceremony.

Tena sang "O Perfect Love" and Reverend Martens began his sermon. It was based on the scripture, Ephesians 5:32, and 33, and encouraged Lorne to love his wife as he loved himself and for Christine to respect her husband.

When Rev. Martens got to the vows, he had no trouble with the difficult 'th' sound in the word betrothed – but then again, this was not his first English wedding ceremony.

Jake sang "The Lord's Prayer" while the newly married couple signed the marriage register.

After being introduced as husband and wife, Christine and Lorne walked out to the music of 'Pomp and Circumstance'.

They settled in the city of Saskatoon and several days after returning from their honeymoon, were baptized in the Saskatchewan River by Reverend Martens.

OFF TO JAPAN

CHAPTER 66

After much study and attending candidate school at The Evangelical Alliance Mission Headquarters, Jake was accepted as a missionary to Japan. This was what he felt God wanted him to do.

On September 18th, 1955 at the Osler church, Jake was commissioned as a missionary to Japan by Reverend S. G. Gunzel who based his message on the scripture of 2 Timothy 4, verses 1 to 5; "I charge thee therefore before God and the Lord Jesus Christ, who shall judge the quick and the dead at his appearing and his kingdom; Preach the word; be instant in season, out of season, reprove, rebuke, exhort with all longsuffering and doctrine. For the time will come when they will not endure sound doctrine; but after their own lusts shall they heap to themselves teachers, having itching ears. And they shall turn their ears from the truth, and shall be turned into fables. But watch thou in all things, endure afflictions, do the work of an evangelist, make full proof of thy ministry."

The friends and extended family present at the commissioning service wished Jake well, and said their goodbyes.

Jake packed his suitcases into the car the next day and the family took him to the railway station in Saskatoon. Gathered at the station were Julius, Helen, Anne, Christine, Lorne, Dan, Nettie and their parents. Other friends and relatives had planned to be there but decided to leave this parting for the immediate family instead.

It was a hard day for Helena and Jacob, knowing they wouldn't see Jake for at least five years. There were hugs, tears and goodbyes as Jake turned to obey the 'All Aboard!' call of the conductor. He walked up the steps and turned to wave as his family waved back.

Jake settled into his roomette on the train and looked out of the window. His family was leaving the platform and soon, as the train picked up speed, he saw the family car passing under the tracks of the 23rd Street under-pass. His father was at the wheel as usual and it was the last glimpse Jake would have of his dad.

Arriving back in Osler, Helena sighed as she thought of her oldest son going so far away to a completely foreign land to study their language and culture. Jacob was quiet and subdued as he changed his clothes and walked out of the house toward the barbed wire fence to call his cows for milking. They were in a far end of the small pasture but at Jacob's loud "MOOOO" they perked up their ears and turned toward home and the barn. There would be grain waiting in the feeding troughs.

Sitting on the low stools, Dan and Nettie milked the cows in silence except to scold the animals when they tried to kick the pail out from underneath them. Life would seem different without Jake coming home once in a while. The thought came to Nettie that he had taken his violin with him and she had just learned to play it.

As the family settled back into their routines, Jake traveled through the breathtaking beauty of the Rocky Mountains. He didn't feel particularly excited about this huge adventure he was embarking on. After all, from the time he felt God was calling him to be a missionary, everything had fallen into place at just the right time and now he was on his way. It was simply the way things should be.

He slept well on the train and went to the dining car where his table mate had already ordered his meal. Jake ordered and bowed his head in a silent prayer of thanks. As he raised his head, he looked into the beaming face of the man who reached across to shake Jake's hand saying, "You're a Christian!" He was also a believer and a business man traveling from Germany. In spite of the bottle of beer beside his plate, which Jake was not used to seeing on a Christian's table, the two had a great conversation.

Jake arrived in Seattle where his mission organization had put him in touch with a group called "King's Garden". This group helped Jake to pack his two 'barrels' of everything he would need for his life on a mission field. The barrels would not travel with him, but would be sent separately.

In Seattle, Jake boarded an American Freighter to sail directly to the port city of Yokohama, Japan. The ship had staterooms for eight persons; all treated as first class passengers. They ate their meals with the captain and head steward.

As the Seattle sky shoreline disappeared into the distance, the country boy from the prairies severed ties with the expanses of the Canadian Prairies and sailed toward Japan.

Jake had heard about motion sickness but thought it wouldn't happen to him. However, he quickly discovered that the constant motion of the rolling waves did affect him. One night he dreamed he was at home on the farm and was hungry. He went to the cupboard and found some cold farmer sausage. When he awoke, he didn't feel like eating! He decided to do his morning routine in stages; brush on the shaving foam – then lie down; shave – horizontal again; wash his face; and have another rest. When he finally got up to the deck, he took a deep breath of the clean sea wind and filled his farmer's lungs with healing. He enjoyed the trip after that.

It was typhoon season so the ship tried to skirt the brewing storms and sailed directly into the huge waves, riding up and down. Jake found the breaking colours of the waves beautiful as he stood on the bridge with the captain. Jake was at sea for fourteen days and arrived healthy and safe and sound in Yokohama on October 22nd of 1955.

As soon as he could, he sent a letter home to let his family know that he had arrived and gave them a bit of a description of the trip. Helena and Jacob were filled with relief and gratitude to God for their son's safe passage to another country.

FIRST GRANDCHILD

CHAPTER 67

As December approached, the family turned their attention away from the cold and looked forward to Christmas. They also waited in anticipation for news from Tena and Ray who were expecting their first child - Helena and Jacob's first grandchild. Would it be a boy or a girl, they wondered.

That winter it seemed the snow would never stop. There were high snow drifts everywhere. At the back of the barn, the door was completely blocked and Dan couldn't take the manure out that way at all. Instead he had to take it out through the front door and pile it close to the west side of the barn. He didn't look forward to removing it from the yard in the spring.

In 1956, snow piled high along driveways and highways

The long driveway needed to be plowed often. Clear driveways were a necessity for the local dairy farmers because they needed the milk truck to pick up their milk and transport it to the city.

The Peters Brothers of the Osler district had their hands full as they were called on by many people to clear their roads. These young men built their own snow plow which was bigger, better and more effective than most plows

On the Friesen driveway, the snow was blown high on both sides of the road and the car seemed small in comparison.

Before going back to the house after milking, wood for the house stoves needed to be split. It was hard to do in the cold but the family always carried at least one arm load to the house whenever they finished chores. With three or four people carrying in the wood, the wood box was kept full most of the time. The coal pail was filled often from the coal bin behind the house.

Coal pail and scoop at the Hague Museum

The Christmas season's concerts and celebrations came and went. Julius, Anne, Helen, and Christine and Lorne were home along with Danny and Nettie. On January 1st, of 1956, the family sat at the kitchen table, eating their traditional New Year's fritters when the phone rang. Jacob rose from the table and answered.

"Hello?" he said. After listening for a few minutes, his face lit up with a smile and when he hung up, he turned to the family beaming with pride.

"Tena and Ray had a baby!" he told them. The family looked at him questioningly - waiting.

"Well? What did they have?" they all asked, "Was it a boy or a girl?"

Jacob's smile faded and he looked perplexed, "I.... forgot what Ray said. I'm not sure." In his excitement, he couldn't remember what his son-in-law had told him. This required a quick long distance call to answer everyone's question.

Julius made the call and turned with a smile, "They have a boy and his name is Byron Stuart!" Cheers went up around the table. Everyone was thrilled with the news.

A letter from Japan a few days later made everything seem more complete for Helena. Somehow, it seemed the family was all 'home'.

A NEW CAREER FOR ANNE

CHAPTER 68

During the Christmas holidays, Anne expressed her desire for a better job.

"I feel like I'm not getting anywhere and often wish I had a career that would bring some satisfaction," she said.

"Why not take teacher's college courses? You're great with kids and would probably enjoy teaching. I know I do," Julius commented.

"I'm missing one of my grade twelve classes, so I probably wouldn't be accepted," she replied.

"There is a school in Winnipeg called Tuxedo Normal School. It accepts people who only have their grade eleven. Why not apply for that school? I can get you the information," Julius encouraged.

Becoming a teacher was something Anne knew she would love to do and she decided to apply. When she received the information, she discovered it was an eight week course; much like Julius' Normal School course had been and would begin in the month of May. She wasted no time in filling out the application and sent it off to Winnipeg. In a few weeks she received a reply and was accepted.

Jacob was pleased to know there would be another teacher in the family. He knew Anne would do well. Anne left for Winnipeg and sent a note to let everyone know she arrived safely.

In the spring and summer of 1956 Helena spent as much time as possible in the garden, leaving Nettie to learn to bake bread and do the rest of the cooking. Nettie enjoyed the challenge and still had time to spend with her many friends from Osler.

Anne (with classmate) at her graduation from Tuxedo Normal School in Winnipeg.

In July, Anne graduated from Tuxedo Normal School and was immediately accepted for a position at a little place called Camper, Manitoba. It was in bush country in the north central region of the province and very primitive. Helena and Jacob were happy their daughter found a position so soon after graduation. There were teacher shortages everywhere and communities welcomed new graduates to their schools.

As August rolled around, there was more excitement as the family waited for the birth of Christine and Lorne's first child. Dale Ardene was born August 5, 1956. Everyone was thrilled with this new addition. Another grandson for Helena and Jacob brought joy to their hearts and this one only lived 25 miles away!

Shortly after Dale's birth, Tena and Raymond arrived for a visit with seven month old Byron and the whole family enjoyed that busy little boy's smiles.

Since Dan missed finishing his high school because of his dad's illnesses, Anne and Julius felt it was time for him to catch up and offered to pitch in financially to send him to boarding school at Caronport for his grade eleven. He looked forward to going.

Anne left to teach in Camper, Manitoba. That first year of teaching was challenging for her. She wrote to tell her family how primitive it was.

"Camper is right in the bush. My teacherage is more of a cabin than a house and the school is not close in proximity. Every morning I have to get my stove going, have breakfast and then walk through the bush to the school and start a fire in that stove," she told her family.

"One evening after staying at school to grade some papers, I walked home with my flashlight and heard something near me. I shone the light on a pair of eyes staring at me. I don't know what it was, maybe a cougar. Anyway, I was very glad to get home safely," she continued.

Anne's parents were concerned and prayed for her safety, as did other members of the family. However, Anne adjusted to the surroundings and the people and learned to cope with the poor living and school facilities. It was a learning curve that would help her in later years of teaching.

GRADE ELEVEN FOR NETTIE

CHAPTER 69

Nettie was prepared to spend the winter at home. She had finished grade ten and there didn't seem to be any prospects of her going to boarding school.

Nettie at 17 years of age

Julius returned home for a weekend after teaching in Imperial, Saskatchewan, for two weeks. He asked his parents for permission to take Nettie with him to that town.

"If you will allow her to come with me, she can take her grade eleven and keep house for the two of us," he offered and added, "Just like the year Christine kept house for me in Guernsey for her grade eleven."

He turned toward Nettie, "How about it Netts, would you like to join me in Imperial for grade eleven? You'll have to be my cook and housekeeper though."

"I would love to!" she responded. "Mom and Dad – would it be all right if I went with him?"

Jacob and Helena discussed this and Nettie was thankful when they gave their consent. She packed up her things and left with her brother on Sunday afternoon.

"Goodbye Mom and Dad," Nettie said as she was hugged tightly by her parents.

"We'll be praying for you," Jacob said and he struggled with emotion. He and Helena watched as the old '37 Chevy carried their youngest child away to a strange town.

As Julius and Nettie drove to Imperial, Nettie was surprised at all the hills and lovely scenery. She had rarely been away from Osler and was used to flat prairie land. It was an enjoyable ride and she anticipated a good year of school and meeting new friends.

When they arrived at Imperial, Julius brought his sister to the local Pentecostal pastor and his wife to stay with them until he found an apartment for the two of them. He had been boarding with a family.

After Nettie was dropped off, the pastor's wife smiled and told her, "When your brother wanted to bring you here for school, he approached us to tell us that you are a Christian and he wondered if we would take you "under our wing". We are glad to have you." Julius did this to ease his parents' concern about their young daughter being away from home.

Julius found a trailer to move into and Nettie enjoyed setting up house there. It had a stove with an oven, so she did some baking on weekends.

Julius loved to hunt and fish so the two were not short on meat. One Saturday, Julius brought home a duck and wondered if Nettie knew how to prepare it. She plucked the feathers, then eviscerated it and put it in cold water until Sunday morning.

"So you think you can roast this bird?" Julius asked, "I thought I'd have to teach you how to fry an egg."

"Pfft, I'll show you!" Nettie replied as Julius laughed.

On Sunday morning, she added potatoes to the duck in the roaster and slid it into the oven before they left for church. Nettie had baked an apple pie the day before and looked forward to that meal. So did Julius. He was surprised at his kid sister's ability to cook.

After church they arrived at home and Julius realized he had left the door key locked inside the trailer.

"Well, that's no problem," he said, as he walked to the house of the owners on the same property. He knocked on the door and explained his predicament.

"I'm sorry, my husband has the ring of keys with him and he's out on the field at the farm," the lady said. She gave Julius directions to the farm and Julius and Nettie left to find it.

Finally, they located the farmer out on the field and Julius walked through the dust to ask for the key. By the time they returned to the trailer they were hungry and Julius was a bit disgruntled. Nettie worried at how overdone and dry the meal would be.

When Nettie pulled the roaster out of the oven, the duck was very brown and dry in some parts, They ate it anyway and Julius was still impressed that his little sister could make a meal like that.

Nettie enjoyed writing her parents about the incident, calling it her most memorable meal. Her mother would have a good laugh about it, she knew.

In winter, Julius took Nettie ice fishing. He cut two holes in the ice, quite some distance apart, and they put down their lines. Nettie hauled up fish after fish, while Julius caught nothing.

"Hey, let's change holes," he said. It was about time he caught a fish, he thought. Unfortunately, the school of fish moved from Nettie's first hole to where Julius had been fishing before and she still hauled up the fish. Julius still caught nothing. Disgustedly, he gathered up the gear and suggested going home. They had enough fish anyway.

It was interesting to have her brother for an English and History teacher. Julius added a lot of humor to the classes but one day, one of his students had him laughing at the answer he gave to a question in English class.

"In the story of the soldier on the front lines, why did the fellow say he wanted to die with his boots on?" Julius asked his class.

After a moment a boy raised his hand and said, "So he wouldn't stub his toe when he kicked the bucket?" The serious part of that story was lost as Julius and the whole class broke into laughter.

There were times when the students tried to see what Nettie's reaction would be if they made remarks about their teacher, Mr. Friesen. However, after she shrugged her shoulders and responded with, "Hey - he's my teacher too," they stopped and became good friends.

Nettie enjoyed her time at Imperial High School. Her classes went well and she passed all of them. It was a good year but she wondered - what about grade twelve?

One day Julius asked her, "Would you like to go to Caronport for your grade twelve?"

"I'd love to!" she replied.

"If you want to go, I'll pay for your last year of high school there," he said.

Nettie was overwhelmed with her brother's generosity. He had already give her a chance to take grade eleven and now offered her the opportunity to finish high school. She looked forward to the next year as she already knew friends from Imperial area and from Osler who would be attending, and most importantly, her brother Dan would be there as well.

EMPTY NEST REFILLED

CHAPTER 70

The following spring Jacob and Helena traveled to the village of Blumenheim to visit his brother Henry and his wife. The couples' older children did most of the field work, since Henry suffered with very poor eyesight.

"How is the seeding going for you this spring?" Jacob asked as they sat at the faspa table.

"The boys are doing well with that but if we get another good harvest, I'm going to need more grain bins. The boys have pointed out that some are in poor condition," Henry replied.

Jacob glanced around at the table full with children, some fairly grown up and some still small. He turned toward his brother.

"I can't work at a regular carpentry job, but I could certainly build granaries if your boys help," he offered.

After some discussion, Henry took Jacob up on his offer. It would be a relief to have the bins built in time for the fall. They decided to start as soon as school was out.

As the granaries went up, Jacob enjoyed his young nephews and nieces. One day he asked the children why they didn't ride their bicycles around the yard.

"We don't have any bicycles," the children told him. When he realized the children didn't have any and thought about Dan's and Nettie's standing idle at the farm, he decided those bicycles needed a new home where they would be used.

Jacob bought a small pail of aqua blue paint and one of black and painted the bikes. When he returned to Henry's farm, he lifted them out of the car-trailer to the delight of the children. His nephew David was given the boys bike and his niece Anne received the girls' bike. Of course, with many younger siblings, they would be shared often but the children appreciated their uncle, who obviously cared about them.

Julius and Nettie arrived home after the school year ended and told their Dad about Nettie going to Caronport the next fall. Jacob was moved with gratitude for his son's willingness to share with the family. Julius would not be teaching that year. Instead, he had a job with the Swift Current Sun news department. He would be an assistant editor and reporter and looked forward to the new job.

Helen (Lena) decided to work in Voluntary Service with the Mennonite Central Committee in Cuauhtemoc, Chihuahua, Mexico, and left Canada to join this mission group.

Christine and Lorne decided to move to Minneapolis and moved in with Jacob and Helena at the farm for four months until they left for the USA. The Albertsons arrived at the Friesen farm at the end of August. Lorne kept his job in the city but helped with chores and farm work in the evenings and on weekends.

Little Dale soon became his grandpa’s favourite distraction from farm work and illness. When Dale was lifted from the high chair after meals, he toddled over to grandpa's chair. Jacob grinned with delight and lifted the little one on to his knee for some dessert – little spoonfuls of jam which the toddler enjoyed.

Jacob worked at finishing the inside walls and window sills in the enclosed veranda. He used an old chair to put the wood he needed to saw on. Dale was intrigued with the sound of grandpa's hammer and saw and needed to be kept out of the way but he imitated his grandpa. As far as he was concerned he was working with grandpa!

As Dan and Nettie left for boarding school, Jacob and Helena were happy to have the "nest" filled, even if it was temporary, with Christine, Lorne and their little son. With their help, the old veranda was painted and bright. Jacob added more plant stands and Helena brought her flower pots from window sills to the new stands. It was a lovely cheery room where Helena loved to sit and crochet.

Christmas that year was bittersweet as the family gathered for their celebration; Helen(Lena) was far away and Chris and Lorne would soon be leaving. Jake was in Japan.

After a wonderful Christmas dinner with everyone, Christine and Lorne left for the United States. As they left, Lorne turned to his father-in-law and handed the keys to his 1941 Chev.

"Here, Dad – the car is yours," he said. Surprised and pleased, Jacob thanked him and accepted the car. It would serve him well and he soon sold the old car to a Mexican Mennonite who needed it. Within a week they received a letter from the Albertsons. They had arrived safely.

Now there were four family members living outside of Canada. It would be something Jacob and Helena had to get used to but for now, the 'nest' seemed very empty again.

THE LAST ONES GRADUATE

CHAPTER 71

Anne found a teaching position in the town of Waldheim after returning to Saskatchewan from the little town of Camper in Manitoba. Waldheim was more to her liking and was familiar territory.

Meanwhile, Dan and Nettie kept very busy with studying and with gratis work at Caronport. The school had its own dairy cattle and gardens. Dan and a few other young men had the job of pasteurizing and cooling the milk after it was brought from the barn. The milk was heated in a big vat in the School Kitchen, then cooled and poured into tall metal cans from taps at the side of the vat. After that, the milking machines, cans and strainers had to be cleaned.

Nettie's gratis work was cleaning pots and pans, as well as the huge cooking vats. The girls assigned to this gratis complained about it at times. Every night they put curlers in their hair, and went to breakfast the next morning looking great. But by the time they had washed those steaming porridge vats their hair looked straggly and greasy and they smelled like porridge.

Nettie's own opinion about it was, "Why can't the boys do that gratis? They grease their hair with Brylcream (*a hair product for men)* anyway so they can slick their hair back like Elvis!" However, both young people enjoyed boarding school and in the spring of 1958 they looked forward to graduation. Nettie also looked forward to being a bridesmaid in August.

Julius had been dating a lovely lady by the name of Genevieve Myrna Phyliss Lembeck for the past two years. She was taking Teacher Training in Saskatoon and they planned to be married. Genevieve bought Nettie's bridesmaid dress and mailed it to her at Caronport so she could wear it for graduation.

Nettie wasn't sure how the dress would go over with the strict dress code at the school. The bodice was low in back and in front. However her Dean of Women, who had always seemed so stern, merely shrugged and said, "That's what you have, that's what you wear!" So Nettie wore the lovely mauve dress with its matching stole for the banquet.

Julius was to be her banquet guest, but he hadn't arrived yet and Nettie had no corsage. She paced the hall for a while. Her Dean of Women waited with her in the dorm and found an artificial corsage in her dresser drawer that matched her dress, and then said, "Let's go to the banquet, I'll be your family."

Nettie smiled her thanks and sat at the banquet table with the Dean on one side, and when Julius arrived, he sat on the other. Dan sat nearby with his banquet guest, Jake Neudorf, a neighbour from Osler.

Dan and Nettie had written to their parents and asked if they could be at the graduation exercises a week later. They received a reply letting them know that their father was not well at all and could not travel but their mother would come.

Helena arrived the morning of the graduation after traveling all night on the bus. The hustle and bustle of the campus was overwhelming for her. One bright moment came when Dr. Hildebrandt, the school President, spotted her and spoke to her in German. Even though everything was interesting for Helena, she was so tired and so worried about leaving Jacob at home in his condition that it was hard to concentrate on anything else.

AT the ceremony later that evening, Dan and Nettie walked onto the chapel platform to receive their diplomas. Nettie glanced down at her mother and found that Helena had nodded off to sleep in the pew. Nettie was disappointed, but sympathetic to how her mother was feeling. She and Dan never told their mother what she had missed.

The two young people packed up their things and headed home for the summer. It was good to be done with school and back home again. They pitched right back in to help their parents on the farm.

ANOTHER WEDDING

CHAPTER 72

Back home, Dan again took over the major chores and Nettie looked for a job. She really wanted to return to Caronport for Bible School in the fall but while waiting for something to open up, she taught Vacation Bible School with two friends, Edna and Betty, in several nearby country schools.

Wedding plans were being made with Julius and Genevieve and excitement was in the air.

Gen had chosen four bridesmaids, Nettie, Anne, a cousin Marie and a friend of Genevieve's. Each wore a different colour of the same style dress. Julius' groomsmen were Dan, Gen's brother and two of Julius' friends.

Helena bought a new hat and dress for the wedding and Jacob chose to use his Sunday suit. He had lost so much weight that the suit hung on him but he still looked dressy.

The day finally came and the family drove to Saskatoon. Nettie and Anne were dropped off at Gen's apartment on the corner of Clarence Avenue and 12th street to get dressed with the other bridesmaids. Then it was off to the United Church for the ceremony.

August 16th 1958 was a beautiful day. The church was full with friends and relatives. Genevieve paced in the minister's study as she waited for Julius to arrive. Finally he rushed in and apologized. His friends had deliberately kept him up all night – a mean trick the family all thought. Everyone sighed with relief and the ceremony began.

Genevieve was beautiful in her gown and slowly followed her bridesmaids and flower girl down the aisle. Organ music filled the auditorium and the ceremony was lovely. After a short honeymoon, Mr. & Mrs. Julius Friesen settled in the city of Swift Current where Julius continued to work with the Newspaper Office and Genevieve had a position to teach at Oman School.

Julius and Genevieve with Jacob and Helena.

Gen was welcomed as a member of the family and then on August 29th, another member was welcomed. Baby Ruth Anne Dell was born to Tena and Ray. Helena was thrilled and wished she could see her soon.

It was back to normal at the farm when all the excitement of the wedding died down, but Nettie still didn't have a job. She kept applying, hoping and praying she would be able to attend Bible school in the fall. However it was getting closer and closer to the opening of the school year. Still, she told her friends God would supply the funds. It seemed an impossible dream, but she continued to hope and pray.

Vacation Bible School was over and there was to be a VBS conference at the Mayfair Mennonite Church in the city on the 14th of September. Nettie and the two girls she taught with decided to go and found a ride with a lady from Osler.

It was an interesting evening where Nettie ended up playing piano for a quartet, and at the end of the service the handsome tenor from the group came to talk to them. Edna knew the fellow and introduced him as Joe Balzer.

"How are you girls getting back to Osler?" he asked.

"We've got a ride with a lady from Osler," they told him. However, when they looked for the lady who brought them, they found she had returned to Osler, leaving them stranded.

The girls approached the young man. "We need a ride after all," Edna told him.

"I'm sorry, I was going to get my brother to take you home, but he's left me stranded too," he said.

The girls checked their wallets and pooled their money. They had enough to take the evening train back home, if they hurried. Joe Balzer offered to walk them to the station, since it was not far from where he lived. As they hurried on their way, Edna pulled Betty ahead with her, leaving Nettie to walk with this stranger and said, "Come on, we're not wanted back here!"

Nettie was not impressed with her friend's actions, but remained civil with the fellow and they had a nice chat on the way. Joe walked on to the train with the girls and then took his leave.

When Nettie arrived home, she told her mother about this man she had just met. Over the next few days she had almost forgotten about the incident. Four days later, Nettie was down in the potato bin, getting it ready for new potatoes when she heard the sound of a truck on the yard.

Joseph Balzer

Curious, Nettie walked up the cellar stairs and looked out. There was this young man, talking with her dad and brother Dan. She hurried to tell her mother and then ran to the bathroom to get cleaned up and up the stairs to change clothes. She and Joe went for a ride to get acquainted.

Dan and her dad were concerned about Nettie's eagerness to go with this perfect stranger but Helena reassured them and told them she knew about him. Thus began another courtship in the family.

A PRAYER ANSWERED

CHAPTER 73

The school year was back in full swing at the beginning of September and Anne left for another year of teaching in Waldheim.

During the summer, Helena voiced her concern about the poor condition of the old chicken barn. It was falling apart and she wished they had a better place for the birds.

After settling back in Waldheim, Anne found out through conversations with friends, that someone near that town had a small red barn they wanted to sell and move off their property. She called home to speak with her dad about it.

"Dad," she said, after Jacob answered the phone. "There's a farmer here that wants to get rid of a little red barn and I'm wondering if you want it. We could have it moved to Osler."

"I'm definitely interested," he replied. "Find out how big it is and how expensive and let me know." So a deal was made and Helena looked forward to that barn.

Meanwhile the family was busy harvesting crops and gardens. After a busy day, Jacob relaxed at the kitchen table and decided to write to his daughter Lena in Mexico.

September 15, 1958 (*actual letter*)

Dear daughter,
Greetings in Jesus precious Name! Received your letter today, thanks very much, but we are surprised you didn't get our letter – that is – Mother, Dan and Nettie all wrote to you about 2 weeks ago. So I think we better have this one registered.

Right now mom is darning socks, Dan is reading the paper and Nettie is playing the piano. We have our oats threshed and the green feed stacked and most of our potatoes dug out. Also the tomatoes and plums are out – that's about all there was in the garden.

No, we haven't got the chicken house home yet. We sold two cows and if we can, we want to sell two more. We are trying to get ready for winter again. We have arranged for a boy of 16 to board with us and help with chores in return for it, while he goes to school in Osler.

September 16th: Yes, I feel better again, but have pain in the abdomen quite often, so might have to take another check up. Today we want to dig the rest of our spuds – the weather is nicer again today.

Good evening – September 18th. Yesterday was a very busy day. We got our chicken house home. The moving cost us $90.00. It sounds like a lot of money but there's a lot of work to it. And by the way, we got another little job done. We were losing chickens and didn't know who killed them, so Mother and Nettie urged me to set traps.

When we were ready for bed, I went and looked at my traps and there it was – a great big mink. So mom had to hold the flashlight while I killed it.

Today mom and Nettie finished the last few rows of potatoes and Dan hauled them home. I went to see Dr. Peterson. He wants me back to the hospital for another examination as soon as they have a bed available. Good night for now – I want to add a few lines tomorrow.

Can't wait 'till tomorrow - one adventure after another! Just before going to bed I went and had a look around the chicken house. In the same coop where I trapped the mink last night, there was a skunk. So I phoned George Hein and Jack came and shot it.

September 19th: Good morning – No new developments on the trapping grounds. Dan has gone for another load of bales. Nettie is also writing a letter. The sky is a bit overcast and the weather is cool. So we know that summer is no more here, although we've had no heavy frost yet. It's been a cool summer, but a good one. We hope to get somebody to bale our oat straw today.

I have to go and do some work, so I better say goodbye. May God bless you and all those that work with you - our prayers are with you everyday.
Love from Dad and Mom.

On September 20th Jacob was brought back to the hospital. He spent five days there but the doctors sent him home again, saying there was nothing wrong with him – he just had too little acid in his stomach. He did as much work as he could on the farm, but was in constant pain. How could there be nothing wrong with him? Helena wondered and worried.

At the end of the month, Nettie walked to Osler to get the mail and found a letter from Caronport addressed to her. She opened it and read that someone had sent $200.00 to the school for her to attend Bible School. Nettie was overwhelmed.

"Dad, Mom!" Nettie called as she walked into the house, "Listen to this! My prayers for Bible School have been answered!"

September 23, 1958(Actual letter)

"Dear Miss Friesen.

Christian greetings in our Saviour's Name!

Only a few more weeks remain until the beginning of Bible School here at Caronport. We trust that the Lord has been blessing and leading you to come back to take your first year of Bible School.

We would like to advise you that we have today received $200.00 which we were requested to put to your account for the coming school year. This will leave only $75.00 remaining for your fees and we trust that this will be an encouragement for you as you prepare to come to school.

Trusting that the Lord will open up the way for you to be found in the place of His appointment for you."

In His Service,
I Falkenberg
Secretary

Jacob's eyes filled with tears. "That is a wonderful answer to prayer," he said, then turned to Dan. "Well, if Nettie can go, then you should go too," he commented.

"How?" asked Dan, "I didn't earn any money this summer to pay for it."

"You worked hard here and you should be able to go. We'll work something out," Jacob said.

Dan glanced at his mother and then at his dad. Helena met his look and Dan saw the concern in her eyes. His dad was very unwell. Things were very uncertain. But Nettie was encouraged to prepare to leave for school in the next few weeks and the students were expected to be there by October 13th.

JACOB'S FINAL DAYS

CHAPTER 74

Nettie busily stitched name tags on all her clothing and then packed them and all of her books and necessities. She would be leaving the next day.

Jacob sat on a chair in the sun room off the kitchen with a worried look on his face. His feet were badly swollen. He was very concerned about not working for a living.

"I think I'll try to sell Watkins again," he said at one point. Both Helena and Nettie quickly turned toward him and spoke at the same time.

"But you can't! You're much too ill!" Helena exclaimed in German as Nettie responded in English at the same time.

Jacob was upset, "Every time I try to come up with a way to work, you all tell me I can't!"

Helena didn't comment but there was pain in her expression. Nettie didn't know what to say to comfort him. It was heartbreaking to see his condition and his concern for the future. She was reluctant to leave home.

In late afternoon Jacob sat in the rocking chair while Nettie played piano and sang his favourite hymns. "Tell me the

Story of Jesus", "He Leadeth Me", and "I love to Tell the Story".

As Nettie finished singing the last song, she turned and found he was not in the chair. Instead, as she looked through the open bedroom door off the living room, she saw her father sitting on the edge of the bed weeping. Nettie quickly went to him and sat down with her arm around him. He laid his head on her shoulder.

After a few minutes, he said, "Please tell your brothers and sisters how sick I really am."

Nettie promised, but she didn't know how sick he really was, after all, Dad would get better wouldn't he? The next morning, October 13th, she left for Caronport and her life was immediately filled with assignments, friends and gratis work. This time her gratis was correcting high school German, English and Math papers. It was pleasant work but the hours of each day seemed packed to the hilt and she kept reminding herself of those letters she needed to write. Soon, she thought.

Back home, Jacob began writing a letter to Christine and Lorne himself, but was unable to finish it. Helena added a few lines to let them know that Jacob's condition was much worse and on October 15th he was brought to the hospital again.

Before Jacob left for the hospital, he called Helena and Dan into the living room.

"Helena, will you forgive me for the times I failed you?" he asked.

"Of course I will, if you can also forgive my failings," she answered.

"I wish I could have managed things better, so you would be all right," he said.

"Don't worry about me. God will take care of me," she assured him.

Jacob prayed with them and in his prayer he said he might never return to their home again. He knew he would pass away soon.

As his brother Isbrand Friesen brought him to the hospital, Jacob still insisted Dan was to go to Bible School.

Dan arrived in Caronport on the next day. He met Nettie in the dining hall at supper and said, "We need to go for a walk." They left the hall and walked the 'mile' (*former airport runway when Caronport was a small airport*). Dan was very agitated and walked fast.

"I shouldn't be here! Dad is back in the hospital and there's only a young school boy doing chores. Mom can't handle things alone." Nettie listened and commented once in a while.

"Dad doesn't expect to return home again, but he insisted I go to school. So here I am, but I know I shouldn't be here!" Dan said, obviously very anxious. Nettie shared in his anxiety and understood how he felt.

Dan tried to settle into classes and concentrate, but five days later they received word their father had surgery. At 1 a.m. on October 21st, the night watchman knocked on Nettie's dorm room door. She went to the door and was told she had an urgent long distance call at the office.

Nettie hurried into some clothes and ran to the office. It was her brother Julius from Swift Current.

"Dad has cancer and is not expected to live. You and Dan should get ready early in the morning as I'll be picking you up to go home to Osler," he told her.

The next morning Nettie anxiously looked for her brother in the dining room and hurried to his table to tell him about their dad. After breakfast they quickly packed a few things and then waited for their brother from Swift Current to arrive.

It was a quiet, serious drive for the three of them with some conversation about what the future held for their mother and the farm. Julius told them he had called the other siblings and expected Anne to be home from Waldheim when they arrived. The Dells, Albertsons, and Helen would arrive as quickly as they could. Jake would not be able to come.

A few days later, a letter arrived from Jake in Japan (*sent before the news of his dad's condition*). Inside the letter was a picture of a beautiful Japanese woman he hoped to marry. Her name was Junko Okada. (*Pronounced June-ko*)

Helen arrived on the 27th, as well as Tena and Chris and their families. They all stopped at the hospital to see their father. In spite of his severe pain, Jacob's eyes lit up and he smiled at the sight of Dale and Byron, then the granddaughter he was meeting for the first time; baby Ruth Anne.

As the family sat around the farm kitchen table later that evening, the future of Dan's education and the farm was discussed. Lorne and Ray, brothers-in-law, offered to pay for Dan's first year of Bible School if he would remain at home again to run the farm. He agreed to that and drove to

Caronport to get his belongings. Ray and Lorne returned to Minneapolis to their jobs and planned to return when their father-in-law had passed away.

On October 29th, seven of Jacob's children stood near his bed. His suffering was hard to watch. Even when entering City Hospital, one could hear his cries of pain from down the corridor.

The siblings went out to the parking lot and crowded into Julius' car. There, each one prayed aloud for God to please take their father home to be with Him soon. After the children left the room, Jacob raised himself and said, "Please pray for me!" Helena assured him that the family was praying and when the children returned to his room he was more at peace.

The family returned to Osler, except for Anne and Nettie who stayed with their mother next to Jacob's bed. Reverend Pauls and Mr. Ben Buhler came to pray with him and stayed until Jacob fixed his eyes on something the family could not see and quietly went to sleep in the early hours of October 30th. His pain was over – he was with the Jesus he loved.

"I never want to enter that room again," Helena sighed as the family left the room to go home.

When they arrived at the farm, Helena went to her bedroom where she had suggested Christine and Dale should sleep, and told Christine that her Dad was gone. As Christine moved to get out of bed, Helena told her, "No – you stay here and sleep. I won't be able to sleep anyway."

She sat up in her rocking chair all night, thinking, praying, crying and sometimes dozing. Her thoughts were a jumble of grief, concern for the future, thankfulness that Jacob was not suffering any more and at the same time, disbelief that he was really gone. How would she manage?

The next day several neighbours and Reverend Pauls came over and sang a few hymns with the family. The hymns made everyone even more emotional. After a few minutes of sitting with the family and neighbours, Dan went outside and stood at the well near the barn. He began to haul up water. Pail after pail of water was pulled up and carried to the cooling trough. How could it be, he wondered, that normal every day chores still had to be done? Somehow it seemed disrespectful to go on with life as usual.

Julius came out of the house and joined Dan at the well. "Why did they have to sing? It's so hard for Mom. It was nice of them all to come. I know they care – but it makes it harder somehow."

Ray and Lorne, as well as Genevieve, returned in time for the funeral which was held on Sunday, November 2nd – a very difficult day for Helena who shook with grief and fatigue.

The next day, her children left and it was hard to see them leave. Only Dan was home with her again. The house was much too quiet with only the two of them and the young boarder, Dave Banman.

A HEAVY RESPONSIBILITY

Chapter 75

The loneliness and uncertainty of the future weighed heavily on Helena's mind. It was so quiet in the house and she keenly felt the absence of Jacob. Dan, and Dave Banman who helped with chores while attending the Osler School, were both quiet people. Some evenings the two went to town to watch the Osler Comets play hockey.

Helena's opinion of this activity was, "Doaut es domheit" (that is foolishness). She couldn't understand how grown men could get excited about chasing a little black disc around the ice rink, let alone waste their time watching while their feet got cold. But the greatest difficulty with this was being home alone those evenings. The ticking of the clock seemed to take over the silence. Often Helena took that opportunity to read the German paper, "Der Bote", and write in her diary.

Once again Dan was in charge of seemingly endless hauling of water. The windmill pump broke and he had never learned to use his dad's pump extractor to pull the pump rod out of the well. That meant he needed to haul water for the cattle as well as for the house.

Finances were very tight. Two of the cows had been sold for the needed cash to be able to make ends meet. Helena had only four cows left but a Mr. Hausman *(*not his real name*) was boarding six cows on the Friesen farm until spring when they would calve, so she continued to ship milk.

Helena wondered how she would buy feed for the farm animals. Fortunately, with all the years Jacob sold milk to the Dairy Pool, dividends had been building up and Helena received a welcome cheque in the amount of $1,504.20. It was enough to pay off debt and buy feed. She heaved a sigh of relief.

As the month of December approached, Helena decided to do her usual Christmas baking. It gave her something to focus on. Anne, Nettie, and Julius and Genevieve would be home and she could hardly wait to see them.

A few days before Christmas, the family came home. It felt strange to walk into the old farm house and not see their Dad sitting at the head of the table or in a chair in the living room. But soon there was the usual chatter and laughter around the table.

In the evenings Helena relaxed as she listened to her children gathered around the piano for a carol sing. Her new daughter-in-law Gen loved music too and had a lovely high soprano voice. The family enjoyed hearing her sing a beautiful descant to Silent Night as the family sang the carol. Having grown up with a German grandmother, Genevieve was familiar with some of the language so as the Friesens usually did, at least one or two verses of "Stille Nacht (*Silent Night)*" had to be sung as well.

The crackling fire in the potbellied stove, the sound of nut crackers breaking walnuts, hazel nuts and brazil nuts, the smell of peanuts and rich fruity Christmas cake, and family wit accompanied with lots of laughter – helped to ease the ache in Helena's heart a bit.

The ten days of holidays were over too soon though and once again, when Dan and Dave were doing chores, for Helena the silence was loud.

In January, the weather changed and blizzards made life difficult. Heavy snowfall blocked the highways and farm roads. It wasn't possible for the milk truck to make it to the farms. Huge drifts piled up around buildings. Besides hauling water, the milk would have to be hauled to the train station as well.

The tractor wouldn't start in such cold weather.

Groaning with disappointment, Dan decided to hitch the horses to the stone boat instead of the big sleigh. After all, he didn't need a big sleigh for the few cans of milk, he thought.

"Whoa!" Dan commanded as he positioned nervous Pat and slow Jim in front of the stone boat. The stone boat did not have a tongue to hitch the horses to - instead they were hitched to a chain. It was something Dan would regret.

He loaded the cans of milk on to the stone boat, stepped on to the little sleigh and sat down on the milk cans. The horses pulled forward and plodded through the heavy deep snow toward town. When he arrived in Osler, Dan was concerned as he saw the very icy streets. As he neared the railway station, he tried to slow the horses down, but the stone boat kept sliding into their hooves. This made them panic and start forward again. There was no brake on the boat. Finally Dan got them moving up hill toward the station and brought them to a slow stop. He unloaded the cans and walked back to the horses.

"Whew! Now what?" he wondered. Leaving the station was all downhill. He dreaded the idea, but managed to steer the animals toward snow drifts and gradually on to street level. Once out of town and back on the country trail, he was glad for the snow that slowed the progress of the stone boat. Reaching home, he sighed with relief, unhitched the horses and put them in their stalls with a pail of water and some feed. He was thankful to get into the house and next to the warm stove. Next time he would take the big sleigh! However, the roads were soon cleared and the milk truck was back each morning.

Five gallon and eight gallon milk cans owned by cousin Henry

MIRACLE CHICKENS

CHAPTER 76

As spring approached, the cows began to calve and soon there was more milk to ship. Mr. Hausman arrived one day to transport his cows, but Helena confronted him.

"I had to buy feed for your cows and have fed them all this past winter, even when they were no longer producing milk. So no – you're not taking your cows. I am keeping them through the summer so I can milk them," she told him boldly.

The man was surprised at her remark, but consented. "All right, I'll come back when summer is over," he said "But I'd like to take some milk home with me, if that's all right." Helena consented and Dan went with him to the cooling house. The man filled the milk bottle he brought and walked to his vehicle. Helena stood near the house, watching him leave. She had a satisfied look on her face. He could get his cows when she was done with them!

In April, the Caronport Chorale was scheduled to sing at the Third Avenue United Church in Saskatoon. Nettie was a soprano in this choir and looked forward to singing in home territory. The church was beautiful in architecture but also a beautiful place to sing. The acoustics were perfect and no microphones were needed. Dan and Helena came to the concert.

One hymn the choir sang was "There is a Balm in Gilead". The choir director had instructed the choir to use staggered breathing which meant the whole song would sound as if no breath was taken between lines. It was a lovely piece to sing with lots of expression.

After the performance, Helena approached Nettie and asked, "How could you possibly sing that whole song without taking a breath?!" Nettie smiled and explained, but she understood that her mother probably felt like taking a breath for the choir members while she listened.

On the 29th of April, there was another family wedding – one that Helena could not attend but wished she could. Her son Jake was married to his fiancée Junko Okada in Japan. A few weeks later, Helena received a lovely wedding picture of the couple. Junko was beautiful in her traditional Japanese wedding dress. Jake was handsome as usual.

Seeing the photo made Helena miss her family even more and she could hardly wait for Nettie to return home from Bible School.

A letter from Nettie brought the news that the Caronport Chorale would be travelling after school was over, so she would not be home as soon as expected. Also Christine wanted Nettie to go to Minneapolis, Minnesota to help her with little Dale after her second baby was born. Nettie planned to take the bus from Winnipeg to Minneapolis after their last performance in Manitoba.

Helena sighed with disappointment but looked forward to hearing the news of another grandchild. If only she could be free to go and help her daughter with the children.

Spring finally made its appearance and Helena's spirit was boosted by the melting snow, returning birds, new calves and budding trees. A call from Minneapolis brought a smile to her face. She had another granddaughter: Linda Jane Albertson was born on May 5, 1959.

Once the weather was a bit warmer, Dan worked on the red chicken barn. It needed some fixing after the move to the farm and chicken roosts and egg laying nests had to be built inside the barn. He worked hard on that and on working the land in preparation for seeding. When the soil was ready, he seeded wheat and oats and hoped for good crops.

As the weather continued to warm up, Helena ordered 200 baby chicks and a few weeks later Dan drove to Osler to pick them up at the train station. The weather was still too cold to have them outside over night so Helena put the box near the kitchen stove to keep the tiny yellow balls of fluff warm and well fed.

One warm afternoon she decided it was time to move them. The chicks had grown feathers and were jumping out of whatever barricades she put up, making messes on her clean kitchen floor. Helena spread fresh straw on the floor of the new barn and then put the birds in closed cardboard boxes to carry them to their new home and release them.

As the day progressed, Helena checked the little birds several times. The warm sunshine from the windows brought brightness and warmth and the chicks were busy chirping, running around and eating. When the sun began to go down, so did the temperature. Helena made a phone call to the Peter Janzens. "Peter, I wonder if we can borrow your brooder stove for our chicken barn. It's too cold for my chicks at night."

"Sure you can," answered Peter. "I'll have Reginald bring it over."

That evening Reginald came over, set up the stove and turned it on. He closed the draft completely. Helena thought it was supposed to stay that way all the time. But she realized the little birds were getting too cold as the stove was not heating properly.

That evening there was to be a prayer meeting at Helena's home. The first thing Peter did when he arrived was to go to the chicken barn. Reverend Pauls also went with him to see about the stove. They discovered the little stove was full of soot. The stove pipe was also plugged. Her brother-in-law shook the pipe and more soot filled the stove. They thought the fire was out, but suddenly the flame got air and exploded into the barn.

It was too much for the chickens. They began to die. By the time prayer meeting was over, Helena could tell how many she would have to throw out the next morning. Some mornings she threw out 10 chickens. She was in despair. She could not afford to lose them.

Late one evening Helena took the lantern, and again went into the barn. There were several more sick chickens. Helena knelt down on the barn floor.

"Dear Heavenly Father," she prayed, "I cannot afford to lose all these chicks. If it is possible would you please help me so they won't all die?"

She rose, looked around at them once more and turned to the house and to bed.

Early in the morning, she made a fire in her kitchen stove to prepare breakfast. Dan and Dave were soon downstairs and on their way to the barn to do the chores. Helena got the porridge cooking and set it on at the back of the stove to continue to simmer while she fed her chickens and geese.

As Helena walked outside, she was refreshed by the sweet sounds of the birds in the many trees in her garden. The eastern sky was aglow with pink and orange. She felt a sense of peace mixed with dread as she glanced toward that little red barn. What would she find today?

Helena opened the door to the barn, dreading more dead chickens, but discovered all of them healthy, lively, and waiting to be fed. Amazed, she sank down on her knees.

"Thank you dear God for your wonderful help and for answering so quickly!" she prayed.

She stepped away from the barn after closing the door and walked toward the house with a heart full of praise and a smile on her lips. What a miracle! Truly she worshipped a God who cared about every detail of her life!

THE PIED PIPER

Chapter 77

The middle of May brought Nettie back home again and Helena was relieved to have her back. Now there was more help in the house and Helena could concentrate on her garden.

There was more music in the home again as well and it lifted her spirits. She sat crocheting in the evenings while Nettie played the piano and sang.

With Dan and his sister doing chores, time seemed to go more quickly. Helena didn't need to milk the cows but worked with her chickens and geese, feeding them and collecting eggs. Helena was still lonely for Jacob but with the summer sun shining, the garden growing and two children at home, she felt like life was slowly getting better.

Nettie was able to get a job working for Ike and Betty Dyck at the local telephone switchboard and post office. Helena was relieved to know her daughter would be home for a while. It was only a 3/4 mile walk to and from work for her.

One evening the chores were done, the cows were back in the pasture and Dan was just finishing cleaning the gutters in the barn. Nettie had gone to the house to wash up and change. Helena walked to the garden to cover the strawberries so the robins wouldn't ruin them.

It was a beautiful evening. The birds were singing in the trees and butterflies and bees were still busy in the flower garden. The peaceful scene calmed Helena's heart. Soon she heard the sound of piano music floating out on the air through the open living room window. Nettie was enjoying playing some of her favourite piano pieces.

After walking through her garden, Helena checked the bird bath and found it empty, so she went to the well to haul up a pail of water to fill it. The sun was slightly lower in the sky and she decided to check on the chickens and geese. She found the chickens beginning to settle on their roosts in the barn but she couldn't see the geese anywhere.

White geese could easily be seen whenever they were in the pasture or on the barnyard, but this evening she couldn't find them. She walked out behind the barn to where the haystacks were to see if they had settled there for the night - but no geese.

"Dan, have you seen the geese?" she asked as he left the barn after finishing the chores.

"No, I haven't," he answered.

Puzzled, Helena walked toward the house and noticed that she had left the gate to the house and garden area open. She wondered if the geese were in the garden, but she hadn't seen them there earlier and they were not there now. She walked toward the west side of the house and there they were. All of the geese were crowded close to the open living room window, sitting quietly, listening to the piano music.

Helena went up to them, waved her arms and tried to shoo them away. The geese rose, honked, flapped their wings and sat back down. She began to chuckle as she took in the scene of a flock of geese listening to a piano concert. Turning around, she walked into the house and called Nettie.

"Get the accordion and come outside," she said.

"Why?" asked Nettie

"Just bring it out and start playing. The geese have been listening to you play piano and I can't chase them into their pen for the night."

Nettie grinned and picked up the accordion, slipped her arms through the straps and opened the snaps. She began to play as she stepped out of the door. The geese, honking loudly, waddled around the corner of the house. Nettie turned and walked through the gate and across the yard, glancing back every once in a while at the sight of the geese following in single file. Her mother was ahead of her and opened the gate to the pen.

Nettie walked through and made a circle around the pen until they were all inside. She slipped out of the gate quickly so her mother could close it.

"I didn't know geese were musical," Nettie laughed. They both stood for while watching as the geese crowded around the gate honking for more.

"No more for tonight," Helena told them. The concert was over.

Three of Helena's flock of 10 geese in the back barnyard of the Friesen farm.

FARM AUCTION SALE

CHAPTER 78

The weather was warm and dry in the summer months – just right for the haying season.

At supper one evening, Dan walked into the house after cutting hay as Nettie set the table for their meal. She looked at him as he removed his cap and glasses.

"You sure are full of dust!" she commented. He grunted an agreement and headed for the bathroom. After the sounds of running and splashing water, Dan emerged looking much different as he cleaned his glasses before sitting down.

"What's for supper?" he asked.

"The first new potatoes with cream gravy, lettuce salad and cold liver sausage," Helena answered. They bowed for a prayer of thanks and dug into the meal.

"Well, sis – I've got that field cut, so how about helping me rake that hay tomorrow?" Dan asked. "It's Saturday so you won't be at work. You can drive the tractor."

"Sure," Nettie replied.

The next morning Dan hitched the old rake to the tractor and Nettie drove to the southeast field, pulling the rake Dan sat on. As they moved over the rows of cut hay, he lowered the tines to pull the hay along. By mid afternoon, they were done and hauled the hayrack out to the field to bring a load or two of hay back to the feed lot.

Helena watched her children bring home the hay. For some time she had struggled with the idea of being on that farm another winter with little income to rely on. Anne and Julius wanted her to sell the farm but where would she live?

One day a phone call alerted her to the possibility of an available house in Osler. Mrs. Mary Guenther/Gossen wanted to sell her house. Helena told her children about the call.

"That sounds like a good idea, Mom," they told her. "When Mr. Hausman gets his cows, you won't have enough cows to ship milk anymore anyway. You need to seriously think about selling the place and move into Osler if you can."

Helena mulled the thought over and over in her mind. She prayed about what to do. It would be hard to give up the place where she had raised her family, but did she have any choice? Dan needed to get on with his education and couldn't be expected to remain home indefinitely.

"Why don't we call Mrs. Gossen and make arrangements to see the house?" Anne asked. After arrangements were made, Dan, Anne, Nettie and Helena drove to Osler to look at the house and property Mrs. Gossen wanted to sell. It had electricity and there were two cisterns in the basement.

"No more hauling water, Mom," was Dan's comment as he reflected on that endless task at the farm.

Helena walked through the house and saw the water pump beside the sink in the bathroom. She wouldn't even have to carry water up from the basement. There were two bedrooms upstairs, one downstairs and another in the basement. The living room was a bit smaller than the farm living room but the kitchen had more cupboards.

The property sat on three lots. There was a big established garden with lots of evergreen trees and hedges around it, as well as some fruit trees and lots of room for flowers. By the time they arrived back at the farm Helena was ready to agree to move to Osler, but Mrs. Gossen wanted $4500.00 for her place.

Julius and Genevieve loaned Helena the down payment of $1,000.00 and an offer was made and accepted. The deal was finalized on August 8, 1959.

As Nettie went to work the next Monday, she told her employers, Ike & Betty Dyck, about moving to Osler and hoping to sell the farm.

"That's interesting. My sister, Pearl Cunningham and her husband David are interested in moving to this area," Betty told her. "I'll tell them about your farm."

"That would be wonderful!" Nettie replied. She could hardly wait to tell her mother after work.

As she walked in the door at home, Nettie said, "Mom, Betty Dyck told me her sister and her family are interested in moving to this area. She's going to tell them about our farm and maybe they'll want to buy it!"

Helena turned with a surprised look as she turned farmer sausage over in the frying pan. "Oh that would be a so good!" she said.

The Cunninghams were interested and made an offer of $4000.00. It was much less than the family thought the farm was worth. After all – it was 80 acres and the three lots in town cost Helena $500.00 more than that. The family grappled with that idea but finally agreed to it. The price of farmland was not high in those days.

There was a lot of work to do in preparation before moving into town. The family decided to have a farm auction sale to sell everything Helena would not need in town. An Auctioneer was contacted and arrangements were made for the end of September.

Meanwhile, the regular farm work still needed to be done. Dan arranged to have the green oats baled and the wheat swathed, hoping to get it combined before the weather changed. Soon the oat field had a lot of bales sitting on it. Dan and Nettie hauled them to the feed lot.

The wheat crop was one of the best in years and now it lay in full heavy swaths on the field. Helena called neighbours in the area to see if anyone would have time to combine it, however, the answer was always the same – they didn't have time.

As the garden harvest was brought into the house and the leaves on the trees turned to beautiful fall colours, Helena tried again to find someone to combine those swaths of wheat before winter set in. She was moving into town, but it would be a shame to not be able to use or sell that crop. One farmer said, "I've cleaned up my combine and I'm not taking it out again, you'll have to get someone else." It seemed everyone she asked suggested she try someone else. After phoning many farmers, she gave up. It was getting embarrassing.

Helena began focusing on the auction sale instead. What should she sell? What should she keep? There was a lot of work ahead.

Auction Sale

(from original poster)

MRS. J.W. FRIESEN, OSLER,

will sell by Public Auction on her farm 21-39-4-W3rd
one mile east of Osler, on

SATURDAY, SEPT. 26th 1959
SALE STARTS AT TEN O'CLOCK D.S.T.

LIVESTOCK
1 GRADE HOLSTEIN, 4 YEARS

1 GRADE HOLSTEIN, 3 YEARS
1 BLACK MILK COW, 3 YEARS
1 JERSEY COW, 5 YEARS

1 GRADE HOLSTEIN HEIFER CALF
1 GRADE HOLSTEIN HEIFER, 2 YEARS
1 GRADE HOLSTEIN HEIFER, 1 YEAR
1 RED AND WHITE HEIFER, 1 YEAR
1 GRAY MARE, 12 YEARS
1 BAY GELDING, 10 YEARS
LIGHT SUSSEX CHICKENS

DAIRY EQUIPMENT

FIVE EIGHT GALLON MILK CANS
STRAINER, STIRRING ROD

MISCELLANEOUS
ONE CHICKEN BARN 26X18 (reserve bid)
120 BALES OF GREEN OATS
TWO-WHEEL CAR TRAILER
FENCE PICKETS
SCRAP LUMBER AND SCRAP METAL

MACHINERY
FORD TRACTOR WITH PLOUGH & CULTIVATOR
ONE-WAY
MOWER, HAY RAKE, HAY RACK
FIVE SECTION DIAMOND HARROW With BEAMS
2HP GAS MOTOR
SPEED PUMP, PUMP JACK
GARDEN CULTIVATOR AND HARROW
TWO WAGONS, BOB SLEIGH
CUTTER, STONEBOAT
WHEELBARROW, FORKS
SHOVELS, BARBED WIRE

HOUSEHOLD

ONE WOOD AND COAL HEATER
ONE SEWING MACHINE
KITCHEN CHAIRS AND TABLE
ONE WOOD AND COAL COOK STOVE
POWER WASHER
GALVANIZED BATH TUB
3 CLOTHES CLOSETS

MANY OTHER ARTICLES TOO NUMEROUSTO MENTION

TERMS: CASH
Mrs. J.W. Friesen,
OWNER

J.D. Reddekopp,
AUCTIONEER, PRO.LIC. NO 7428

As the time for the Auction Sale neared Mr. Hausman came to pick up his six cows. The few implements on the farm were cleaned up and lined up on the yard for the sale. Dan busily hauled everything out of corners in the barns and sheds to be sold. Inside the house, Helena, Anne and Nettie, organized and packed what was to be taken to town and what was to be sold.

September 26th was a warm beautiful day and people began arriving early in the morning to take a look at what was available.

Helena had mixed feelings as she watched people wander through *her* house, barn and yard, going through her belongings. She walked past the fence where her cows and horses were tied so people could see them and then to her chicken barn. She kept some chickens to put into her garage in Osler and some would be sold at auction. She had already bought a new damaged electric stove for the new place, in exchange for $100.00 and 100 chickens. There was a man from the village of Neuhorst that bought damaged furniture to re-sell it.

As the auctioneer called out for raised prices, Helena saw *her* things loaded on to other people's trucks and wagons and carted away. Dan watched as the horses were sold. He found it hard to see the animals become someone else's. How would they be treated? Would they have a good home?

When the day was done, Helena wandered through the empty barn and empty house, reminiscing. As she and Nettie walked through the garden past the plum and cherry trees, the rows of gooseberry, raspberry and currant bushes, she voiced one concern: "Who is going to look after my garden?"

"Maybe the people who move to the farm will enjoy gardening too. And you have a great looking garden at your new place in town, Mom," Nettie answered.

"I hope so," Helena replied.

Much of what she planned to keep and use had already been moved into the Osler house so after one more check of her farm, she sighed with the finality of it and got into the car as Dan drove her to her new home. What would life be like, Helena wondered?

MOVING TO OSLER

CHAPTER 79

As Helena walked into her house in Osler, she gasped in surprise. She had expected to buy a second hand kitchen table, but there in the dining room was a beautiful brand new big chrome table and another smaller matching one in the kitchen in a beige-pink marbled colour. There were eight matching padded chairs.

"Where did that come from?" she asked as she moved her hand over the smooth surface.

"It's from me," Anne answered, "You needed something new for this place."

"Danke schoen!" (thank you) Helena said as she looked at Anne with tears in her eyes. She moved toward where the new stove stood. Its damaged side was next to the cupboard so did not even show.

"Mom, I'll show you how to use it," Nettie told her as she followed instructions from the manual. After seeing the elements turned on, Helena shook her head and smiled.

"If anyone had ever told me when I was a child that someday I would have a stove that would heat up just by touching a button, I would not have believed it!"

The boxes were unpacked and things put in their proper places. Beds were set up and made. Helena primed the pump in the bathroom and filled a kettle with water to heat on the stove. She pushed the button for the right element and watched. She was still smiling.

Pump at Osler Historical Museum

The pump was connected to the first cistern in the basement which held soft water; the second cistern held drinking water. For this Helena did need to go downstairs to fill her kettle from the tap coming from the cistern. Mrs. Gossen had explained that in order to fill the cisterns when empty, she needed to call young John Dyck who hauled water for many people. The cost for 500 gallons at that time was less than $5.00.

Dan brought straw from the farm to put on the garage floor and then brought the chickens to Osler. However, as cold rainy weather descended in early October, the garage floor proved to be too cold for the birds, so Helena butchered some for canning and sold the rest.

On another trip to the farm, Dan brought their lonely dog, Jip, back with him. Poor old Jip was not used to being kept in a yard or in a porch for the night. He was frantic with worry, chewing door frames in an effort to get out.

As the month of October rolled around, Dan prepared to go back to Caronport for his first year of Bible School. Anne was back to teaching and Nettie remained at home, working at the Post Office. Helena applied for widow's allowance and waited for the farm deal to be finalized, but Nettie noticed that her mother was often very tired and sad looking.

"Mom, you look so tired every day. Are you all right?" she asked.

Helena replied, "Every night when I lie down to go to sleep, I see Dad's face in the room and he's always smiling at me. I just can't seem to get to sleep."

Her remark led to conversation in the evenings for several weeks while she poured out her life to her daughter. Helena started at her earliest memories; spoke of her difficult childhood with an alcoholic father and being sent out to work for others when she was just a child; her growing up years and the best and hardest places she worked; her admiration of her mother; her courtship and marriage to Jacob; the births and loss of babies. Finally there was the reminiscing of the past few years and losing Jacob.

As she poured out her stories, she began to relax and one morning said, "I can sleep now!" And Nettie realized her mother had just needed to grieve, to have a listening ear, to begin to let the past go and look forward to a new future.

One warm October day, Helena and Jip went "home" once more. As they walked in the direction of the farm the dog became wildly excited. He ran circles around Helena and then raced on ahead.

Helena walked through the gate to her garden. The bird bath had a little rain water in it. There was a bit of a breeze and she watched coloured leaves float down to the ground. The fruit trees and bushes were bare of leaves and the soil was black. Everything seemed to be waiting for winter. She stood looking at that huge garden patch that had fed her entire family for so many years.

As Jip came bounding up to her after circling and sniffing the yard, Helena turned toward the house and walked in. It was empty and eerily quiet. There was no stove with a crackling fire or soup simmering in the kitchen. The living room held no piano but she could almost hear her children singing. Would the walls remember those sounds?

At the bedroom door she paused. Seven of her eleven babies were born in that room - three babies waited for her in heaven. For almost a year now she had slept there alone. She moved away from the doorway and those painful thoughts and went to the veranda turned sun-room. Still bright, but now no flowers stood on plant stands.

She turned away and walked up that old wooden staircase and into those two bedrooms. In her mind she could see her children sleeping and thought of the many times she had gone up those stairs to tend to them when they were sick; the bowls of butta zupp she urged them to eat when ill, and the many quilts she made to cover them. Helena looked out of the window facing west and remembered the beautiful sunsets they had all enjoyed.

She went back downstairs again and lifted the cellar lid in the living room to walk down and see the empty potato bin, the empty shelves. So many memories crowded Helena's mind.

She walked back outside to the barn, opened its creaking doors, and stepped onto the cement floor between the gutters. No cattle now but the lingering smell of straw and manure was still strong. The horses' stalls and black smith shop across from it brought back the memory of the ringing sound of the hammer on the anvil and the stomping of horses' hooves.

Helena turned back to the cow barn and over to the ladder leading up to the loft. As she climbed up and peered into the loft she remembered the many times she checked on her missing children, only to find them up here with their laps full of kittens and straw in their hair.

She left the barn and opened the gate to the pasture and grain fields. The wheat still lay there, now wet from the rain. It would have to stay there for the winter and if it could be harvested in the spring, it would no longer be hers. It was a sad thought.

Helena looked eastward at the former airport hangar turned into a cattle barn, and the memories came back. They had been farming 160 acres before the Second World War but lost half of that to the Aerodrome that was built there.

"Eighty acres," she said out loud as she observed the fields and pasture now empty of cattle. "We raised eight children on these eighty acres." She walked back to the yard and stood for a moment gazing down that long driveway as sparrows chirped in the trees and gophers popped out of their holes squeaking warnings to their clan. She almost expected to see Jacob come walking down that road on his way home from work in the city.

Then she remembered the stress of Jacob's illness and his concern about how she would live after he was gone - and her reply to him: "Don't worry about me. God will take care of me." And it was true. God had taken care of her in ways she could not have imagined.

Finally, her heart full of peace about leaving the farm, Helena turned with a thankful heart to head back to Osler. A few late grasshoppers hopped out of her way as she made her way back toward town.

"Come Jip!" she called out, "let's go home." Jip looked at her with disappointment but followed reluctantly, his head down. Helena, on the other hand, walked back with purpose and anticipation of the future.

Helena walking across her Osler yard.

EPILOGUE

Helena never would have thought that many years after sharing her stories, told both in person and in handwritten form, that her life would be turned into books for her descendants and others to read.

The first book, "Helena – A Peek into the Past" contains the first 41 years of her life. "Raising Eight on 80", contains the next 21 years. Helena lived to be 102. How does one compress the last forty years of someone's life into an epilogue?

Helena embraced the next phase of her life with the same purpose and determination evident in years passed. She quickly became involved in the Osler Church ladies aide group, having the ladies into her home many times. She loved this new life and the interaction with other women.

Helena's quilts had always been pretty as well as practical. Now they became works of art as she found new patterns to work with. No one knows just how many quilts she made for the Mennonite Central Committee, as well as for each of her children and grandchildren as they graduated from high school.

Each week she baked and prepared for the possibility of guests who might arrive and they did, often. Helena especially looked forward to her children coming home and joyfully welcomed Jake and Junko who arrived on furlough in 1961 with their little son Kenji. It was new and precious to have a baby in the house again. They stayed with her off and on for several years.

She anticipated with excitement the weddings in her family. Nettie and Joe Balzer were married on September 17th, 1960; Helen and DeForrest Metcalf, May 22, 1961; Daniel and Ellen Bergstrom, July 26th, 1969.

Many hours were spent knitting mittens for Christmas for each of the growing number of grandchildren. She built a wooden table and chairs set, a cupboard and a stove for them from scrap lumber. One upstairs bedroom became the playroom the grandchildren still remember fondly.

The large garden (an entire lot) in which she spent hours, produced many fresh and canned vegetables and fruit to share with family and friends. Her pantry in the basement was a favourite gathering place for the teenage grandchildren who sampled her wares while visiting.

Helena's creativity seemed to know no bounds and one summer she decided to build a brick and clay oven like her parents had many years ago. She built this with her own hands and had the satisfaction of baking bread in it the old fashioned way!

In the spring of 1967, Helena created a three-tiered flower bed. Each tier was surrounded by a circle of stones and up through the center of the circle, she led a water hose to which she attached a sprinkler. Her flowers were lovely that summer. It was her Centennial Project.

The annual Banman reunions continued as they always had. Again – she worked for days, anticipating the joyful times they all shared. It was always hard to see everyone leave. Even though she led a busy life, she was often lonely and asked God to send someone to share her life with.

On November 26, 1967, Helena re-married. Mr. John M. Dyck became the answer to her prayer and she anticipated this life with some trepidation. It would be very different from living alone, however, she accepted his large family as her own and her life became even busier. Family Christmases now became a three day event; Christmas Day was usually spent with Anne; December 26th the big Dyck clan celebrated with her and John; December 27th was her own Friesen family celebration.

Helena and John did a lot of travelling and many of his relatives came for several days of visiting. One of John's relatives asked Helena this question at one visit: "Who combined your wheat crop at your farm when I didn't have time?" he asked.

"No one," Helena answered quietly. "No one had time. It was left on the field." The man looked shocked, then put his head down on his arms on the table and wept, wishing he had made time.

Helena had 15 years with John before he passed away on December 12, 1982.

Through the next years it became harder to look forward with purpose and anticipation as life became more difficult. After being involved in a car accident where she suffered a severe head injury, Anne noticed that Helena was often not well and seemed very tired. She thought it better to have Helena live with her in the city so she could take better care of her, rather than traveling back and forth to Osler so often.

August 15th, 1987, a rainy dreary day, most of Helena's belongings were sold on auction and her house put up for sale. This was not a move she looked forward to as she and her Banman sisters watched her things disappear from the house and yard. She felt her independence slipping from her grasp.

Once Helena was moved to Saskatoon, she fought the disappointment in leaving Osler but again tried to live with purpose. It was not easy, as both she and her daughter were very independent people.

The following year, Helena's determination to make the most out of life came crumbling down as she faced the grief of losing her son Julius to cancer on November 27th 1988 and then seven months later, on June 23, 1989 his wife Gen also passed away of cancer, leaving two dear grandchildren without parents. Helena suffered a mild stroke which left her unable to speak English or write in her diary.

She recovered somewhat over the next few years but when Anne was found to have cancer as well, the family met to consider finding another place for Helena to live. She expressed the desire to once again live on her own and was moved to a suite in Central Place on August 7th, 1991 where she could make her own meals, do her own laundry and do some baking.

Helena soon found friends in Central Place and enjoyed their company. She lived there for the next two years, but it became apparent that it was not safe for her to be on her own. She became unsteady on her feet, falling and cracking a vertebra in her back. While making cookies one day, she put the oven on broil and the burning cookies sent smoke through the building. Wanting to defrost the refrigerator, she lifted a pot of boiling water up to the small freezer and scalded her arm. When a room opened up in Central Haven Nursing Home, she was moved in on February 24th, 1993.

How was she to embrace this life? How could she find purpose in this? It was frightening and heartbreaking for Helena. She was facing the final chapters in her life and she dreaded it. She expressed her fears to Nettie.

"I could have been on my own longer. I would have been able to look after myself," she said as she twisted her napkin over and over in her hands. "I'm afraid I'll go crazy with nothing to do!"

This was the place people came to die. This was the place where your life was not your own – someone would be telling her what to do and when to do it. With tears and prayer, Helena poured out her heart to Jesus and after a while, found the courage to visit others in the Home that were in much worse condition than she was. There were several people she knew well - former neighbours and extended relatives and as long as she was able, Helena walked the halls and visited.

Gradually, as the years rolled by, she needed more and more assistance. Since she was unsteady while walking and fell several times, she was restrained in a chair to protect her from breaking fragile bones. Trapped like this caused her to panic and she was given drugs to calm her down. Some of the medication caused her to be unable to speak and after a few years of this, Helen(Lena) visited from Mexico and told the staff to take her off of one of them. Helena was then able to speak again.

Back row: Christine, Daniel, Tena, Jake, Nettie. Front, Lena, Helena and Anne

August 22, 1998 Helena turned 100 years old. A large celebration was held at Central Haven. She received congratulations from the Queen and Lieutenant Governor of Saskatchewan. The activity room at Central Haven was filled with family and friends. For some there was standing room only.

Nettie had translated Helena's life story and 22 years of diary entries in time for her birthday, (*from which these stories originate*) and had the books displayed for people to see and purchase.

Unfortunately, Helena was unaware of the occasion due to a sleeping medication she was given during the night. She awoke just as people were leaving the party.

THE FINAL MOVE

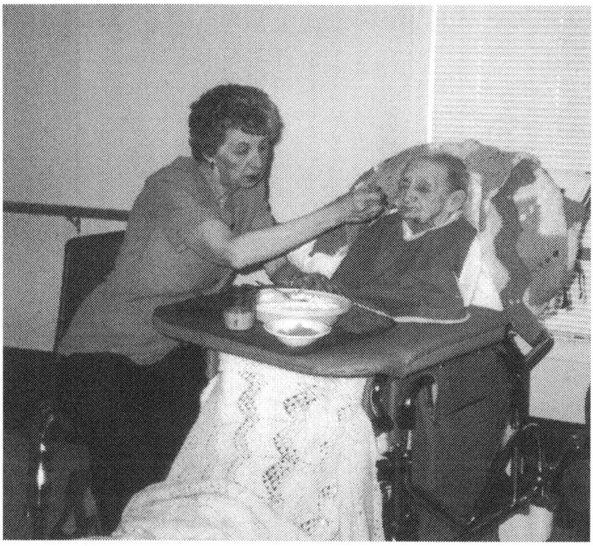

Nettie feeding 102 year old mother Helena

On January 5th, 2001, at 102 years of age, Helena moved for the last time. This time to be with the God she had loved and served for so many years. Anne, Helen(Lena) and cousin Maria Bartel, were with her as she left her frail body to join Jesus and family who had gone on before.

Her funeral was well attended by her children, grandchildren and great grandchildren, the Dyck extended family, Banman and Friesen families and the many community members who had been blessed by her hospitality and generosity.

The rest of the family gradually returned to their home cities and provinces, but Anne, who had watched over Helena in her final years, struggled with grief and with guilt thinking she should have done more for her mother. One night she had a dream where she again visited her mother at Central Haven. She dreaded walking into that place to see her mom in such a frail condition. She walked over to the wheel chair wanting somehow to comfort her mother. Suddenly Helena got out of the chair. She began to walk and then skipped with joy and she was no longer old, but young again.

Anne awoke, amazed at the dream. She knew God had given her that picture to reassure her. Helena was not old, Helena was not sick. Her mind, body and spirit were new again and she was rejoicing in the presence of God. Anne felt her heart fill with peace and thanksgiving!

Helena had been a woman of faith, strength and determination. The old German saying, "Daut jink aus daut gaunich jink, dan vaut daut nu ook gonnen" (it was possible when things seemed impossible, so things will be possible again) seemed to be her motto. She didn't give up; she persevered throughout her life and left a legacy for all of her descendents to follow.

Helena fits the profile of the "wife of noble character" in Proverbs 31; "She is worth far more than rubies. She gets up while it is still dark and provides food for her family; she considers a field and buys it; she sets about her work vigorously, her arms are strong for her tasks; she opens her arms to the poor and extends her hands to the needy; she is clothed with strength and dignity, she can laugh at the days to come; she speaks with wisdom and faithful instruction is on her tongue; she watches over the affairs of her household, and does not eat the bread of idleness.

"Her children arise and call her blessed. Many women do noble things, but you, *Helena,* surpass them all. Charm is deceptive and beauty is fleeting, but a woman who fears the Lord is worthy to be praised. Give her the reward she has earned and let her works praise her at the City Gate!"

FAMILY ALBUM

Helen (Lena)

Jacob (Jake)

Anne

Julius

Tena

Christine

Daniel

Nettie

Jake with Nettie

Lena, Nettie & Jake with horse and buggy

Annie & Aunt Justina Friesen

Julius

Favourite pastime

Julius & Jake

Jake & Danny

Crokinole – Julius & Tena

Nettie, Christine, Tena

Danny, the jolly farmer

Nettie with puppy

Jake's horses: Bud & Flash

Chris, Nettie, Dan & puppies

Julius, Lena, cousin Anne, Jake and Annie

SOURCES

World War 2 information:
www.historyplace.com/worldwar2/timeline/ww2time.htm

National Mobilization/conscription & Family Allowance Act:
www.thecanadianencyclopedia.ca

Aerodrome at Osler: Friesen family memories. Photo taken by a family member. Contractors: Perseski and Draboti (no record found of them, however they are names remembered by the Friesen Family)

"The Turner Co-operative Association Ltd".
Saskatchewan Gov't Archives file: ID-R-595,#1433
Government ministers, Harold E. Chapman and Alex Turner: served with the Canadian Cooperative Federation (now NDP).

1940's Prices:
TRAIN FARE – info; 1949 Canadian National Railway(Western Region) Conductor's Tariff No. C-185, effective Oct. 1/1949 – Courtesy of Western Development Museum Library, Saskatoon.

Gift Prices:
Osler Historical Museum Eatons and Simpsons Sears Catalogues 1935 to 1941

Young Co-operative Pages stories, written by Julius Friesen
Western Producer Archives, Saskatoon, Sask.

Osler School Meeting excerpts, teachers and information:
Osler School #1238 book published by the Osler Historical Museum in 1999.

Images: family photos and ink drawings by the author; labelled images used with permission.

Names Used in Book	Permission Given By
Banman, Dave	Dave Banman
Boldt, J.B. & Margaret	daughter-in-law Katherine
Buhler, Ben	son Jake
Buhler, Maria	son Ben
Cunninghams	sister Betty
Driedger, John	daughter Peggy
Dyck, John M.	daughter Mary
Ens, Ben	daughter Caroline
Ens, Mary	Mary Enns
Fehr, Dietrich	daughter Nettie & Mary Fehr
Friesen, Henry W.	sons John & Henry
Guenther/Gossen, Mary	son Elmer
Hein, George	son John(Jack)
Janz Quartet	Phyllis, daughter of Leo Janz
Janzen, David	daughter Elma
Janzen, Ike(Frank)	wife Gerry
Janzen, Peter & Reginald	sons Howard & Reginald
Kruger, Mrs. Justina	daughter Edna
Lobe, Al's Transport	daughter Donna
Loewen, John	daughter Brenda
Martens, Henry	son Harry
Neudorf, Abe & Jake	daughter/sister Ruth
Neudorf, Mrs. Maria	daughter Hella
Pauls, Reverend Jacob	daughters Edna & Mary
Peters, P.J.W. & Katherine	son Bill
Rempel, George	daughter Stella
Rostek, Bessie	daughter Barbara
Zacharias, Rev, Gerhard	daughter Linda

Manufactured by Amazon.ca
Bolton, ON

29398523R10223